MW00908408

THE
JUNGLE
WITHIN

Cover design by Genie Jar Digital
Williamsburg, Virginia

Brian Forrester
Visit my website at baforrester.com
Email: baforrester@gmail.com

Printed in the United States of America

First Printing: 2022
ISBN 978-0-578-36088-1

With all my love to
Jessica, McKenzie, Luke, Jake, Kate, and Sam

May God give you the wisdom to know what is right
and the courage to do it even when it's hard.

1

She was the kind of beauty that took my breath away.

Like the time in high school football when a blindside tackle knocked my wind out and I saw twinkling stars and a sparkly montage of bursting crystal thingees while trying to suck in my next desperate gulp of air.

Yeah, beautiful like that.

And better yet, she lay on a smoothed-out purple towel, glistening in all her glory under a warm North Carolina sun.

A day for the history books. All the ingredients were there: at the lake with my buddies and Miss America tanning twenty yards away, showing her curves to an appreciative humanity and reminding everyone that God, hallelujah, was a great Creator.

I'd never seen her before, which was odd, since I hung out at the lake every sunny afternoon playing ultimate frisbee. One of my friends, Stanley, apparently noticed my eyes googling out.

"Pace, you know what's next." He pointed to her. "It's page

one of the Guy Code. Gotta make your move. Show her you're the pot of bubbling manhood she's always dreamed of."

I shook my head. "Look at her, she's so out of my league. It's like Zeus sculpted her on Mount Olympus."

"I can't believe it." Stanley's face dropped in disappointment, making his double chin more pronounced. "You've lost your legendary swagger. Come on, where's the guy who once put the move on Lucy Skyler?"

"Lucy? That was in seventh grade. Her retainer fell out of her mouth. All I did was give it back to her."

"Yeah, with your lips." He gazed back toward the goddess on the towel. "This may be your only shot. Destiny hinges on this moment. What do you have to lose?"

A handful of other friends joined in, ragging me to "be a man" and to win one for the Gipper, and in their own dumb, rah-rah testosterone-filled cheers, reminding me how I'd be an embarrassment to the future of the male chromosome if I didn't at least try. Like whatever.

None of their immature taunts worked, and I could ignore those horndogs all day. That is, until Stanley rolled out the Secret Weapon, a singular force of mass destruction known to incite even the most yellow-bellied of cowards:

The Triple Dog Dare.

Where else do nineteen-year-old guys still use the Triple Dog

Dare (TDD)? We may have biologically grown out of puberty, but we were somehow frozen in perpetual middle-schooldom. Refusing a TDD was akin to saying your momma had curly hair on her back.

Stanley cocked his arms on his hips. “So there you have it. I Triple Dog Dare you to talk to her.”

I glanced across the field toward her again, and a strange braggadocio stirred from somewhere deep within. “Alright. I accept the challenge. But only if it will shut you morons up.”

Which began their sophomoric series of approving guttural growls and barking sounds; the universal signals of male stupidity.

I waved my arms and quieted them. “Need a game plan. I can’t just walk over to a suntanning girl and interrupt her. It’d kill the vibe. Not to mention it’s borderline creepy.”

Stanley nodded. “You’re right. We’ve got to make it look accidental.” He picked the frisbee off the ground. “Step One is accidentally throwing this frisbee in her direction, on purpose, enough to startle her. You go retrieve said frisbee, then boom! The love sparks start flying.”

“An *accidental* throw? That’s the oldest trick in the book.”

“But it’s proven. Just like the “fake-yawn-I’m-stretching-my-arms-to-hug-you” maneuver. Trust me, girls love this stuff.”

“And you’re the expert? You’ve never had a girlfriend. You play video games all day in your parent’s basement.”

“Excuse me.” Stanley feigned mock anger. “I’m saving myself

for the right woman, bro. And girls are turned on by my amazing hand-eye coordination. Only video games can perfect that."

I rolled my eyes. "So what do I say to her?"

"Don't overthink it. Let the words flow, be natural. But here's the trick: you need to carry a baby or a small child with you. Every woman loves something cute."

"Where are we supposed to get a baby? Out of thin air?"

"No, but calm down." Stanley rubbed his hands across his crew cut. "We do have a close second option: a cute, cuddly animal."

He pointed toward Mr. Roper, his lovable eighty-five pound sheepdog who always joined us at the lake. Mr. Roper epitomized the opposite of cute and cuddly; he was big and clumsy and smelly. And blind. He bounded everywhere, like a lumpy, happy-go-lucky potato sack, and he crashed into everything. Because he was blind.

"Let me get this straight. I'm taking your blind sheepdog with me?" I asked.

"Mr. Roper is a veteran. He's helped me dozens of times with the ladies. Kind of a good luck charm."

"Can't believe I'm actually gonna do this." I tussled my hair. "How do I look?"

Stanley gave me the once-over. "Let's see — the surfer blond hair. Chicks dig that. Nice tan, blue eyes, tight butt. Impressive biceps. If she says no, then I'm available."

“I’m gonna throw up in my mouth.” I whistled to Mr. Roper and he bounded over. “Alright guys, take some notes. One day you’re gonna tell your grandkids how I swept Miss Beautimus off her feet.”

My 100% fake bravado fooled no one.

“Wait…” Stanley handed me a small bag. “Mr. Roper does better if you carry along his doggie biscuits. If the conversation lags, just feed him. It’s adorable to watch.”

Too nervous to argue, I walked the first ten yards toward Sunbathing Beauty and convinced myself to act confident, even with snickering friends in the background.

Ignore them. Shoulders back, head up.

I had never actually “picked up” a girl before, but how hard could it be? A little small talk, make her laugh, compliment her looks, and then hopefully some chika-chika-wah-wah fireworks. Of course, that was just theory.

My skin flushed with a cold sweat, so I inhaled a deep breath and soaked in the surroundings, forcing myself to calm down.

Beside me, the Silver Lake lived up to its name. The early afternoon sun glimmered across the water and a cloudless blue sky reflected a magical sheen. Many couples and families sprawled around the acres of grass enjoying picnics and the twangy chords of country music.

Mr. Roper bounced faithfully by my side, trusting for guidance. Sometimes I’d forget about his doggie disability and he’d tumble into innocent bystanders, like a rolling fur ball.

Patting his head, I tried untangling his wet fur, but to no avail. He looked like one of those dirty mops in a janitor's closet.

Fifteen yards away and time to throw the frisbee. The success or failure of Operation Hot Woman came down to the toss. Throw it too short or too long and she wouldn't budge. It had to land really close, so she could hear it plop beside her, and by the time she raised her head, I'd run up with an apology, a smile, and a blind dog.

But before throwing it, I gazed once more at her beauty; her ebony skin, smooth as untouched butter, with dark hair twisted back and highlighting the delicate facial features of a golden-gilded seraph.

She wore white shorty-shorts and a string bikini on top, with a necklace sparkling under the sun in the crook of her neck, like a glowing starburst at the top of a constellation. The whole wondrous sight glowed perfectly in symmetrical line and form. Be still my beating heart.

I concentrated on a spot beside her hip, aiming the frisbee for close-but-not-too close. And I let it fly.

Showtime.

The disc zipped across the lawn with a perfect spin and felt good leaving my hand. It fluttered gently, bobbing along in the air, all the way to where she lay... hovering... as if it were preparing for the perfect landing… until it fell abruptly, like a trapdoor suddenly opened, dropping flat on her forehead with a loud *ker-blonk*.

Good God.

2

She sat up and raised her shades, confused, until she saw the frisbee lying beside her.

Rubbing her head, she turned and looked at me.

Since first impressions are critical, smart people always have a plan for those important moments. Here was mine:

Plan A: The plastic frisbee lands perfectly close to her. She turns and sees me, the wind gently blowing my hair, kind of like a slow-mo shampoo commercial. I smile sheepishly and offer a wink of apology for the nearby disc landing too close and rustling her from blissful slumber. Romantic conversation commences.

Plan A didn't work.

So now *Plan B*, which wasn't good because I hadn't thought of a Plan B. Caught off guard by the misfire, my facial expression was stuck somewhere between horror and *hello-nice-to-meet-you-I'm-the-dweeb-who-threw-the-frisbee*.

Bad first impression.

She stared, her cute manicured eyebrows crinkled in frustration, and her arms raised in a "What was that all about?" unspoken question.

I read somewhere that you have ten seconds to impress a new person, and if you fail, somehow the planet spins off its axle and the relationship takes a turn for the worst. Apparently an immutable law like gravity.

Ten seconds and the clock ticking.

I half-ran toward her, and before offering an apology, Mr. Roper got excited about the action and barreled away from me and straight on top of her with all eighty-five pounds of his good-natured but misguided love.

It was like watching someone fight a cloth carwash.

Mr. Roper flat-out tackled her, though in his defense he didn't see her, and upon his discovery of a new human person, he slobbered her face with his big pink tongue.

For a split second, I actually felt jealous.

"I'm so sorry!" My voice pitched high due to nervousness, like in seventh grade with retainer-challenged Lucy.

I pulled Mr. Roper off her, too much in shock to realize the catastrophe in the making.

Her charcoal eyes bore into me. "Is this how you say hello to all the ladies?"

"I'm so sorry. I didn't mean to hit you with the frisbee… and

Mr. Roper is blind."

"It's okay, no harm done." She rubbed Mr. Roper's wet fur. "He's cute. Though a little smelly. What's your name?"

"Pace. Pace Howell."

"Pace. Hmmm... that's different. And I thought my name was unique."

"What's yours?"

"Sage Collins."

"That *is* beautiful. Nice to meet you." My voice resembled a soloist in the Vienna Boys Choir.

"So were you trying to hit me with the frisbee or what?"

Busted. "*Wh*... What do you mean?"

She pointed toward my ever-supportive friends, standing in the distance and doubled over, laughing hilariously and enjoying the show. The moment they realized she saw them, they tried playing it off, unconvincingly.

I hung my head. "They dared me."

"Were you scared? Did you think I'd bite?"

And then my worst fear: clamming up. A complete loss of words, due to the triangulation of her stunning beauty, her razor wit, and my utter embarrassment.

The insides of my head resembled a dystopian wasteland of smoke and fire, like the naked desolation after a nuclear blast, and I had nothing to say, especially with her divine eyes piercing into me.

I do dumb things when nervous. Almost like I'm out of body. And the Dumb Thing happened that defied explanation, taking place in less than two seconds.

Noticing a bag of chips on her towel, no doubt her afternoon snack, brain waves must have sent a signal to my hand that said, "*Eat*!" or either my mouth sent a message to my brain saying, "*Help*!" since no syllables or words formed on my paralyzed lips.

So I lifted a hand, subconsciously, and crammed something in my mouth. A nervous, knee-jerk reaction in the face of crisis. And I took a bite.

It was a gritty, bland taste, like stale Melba toast, and a terrifying shudder instantaneously rose up my spine.

Mr. Roper's doggie biscuits.

She looked at the half-eaten biscuit in my hand, then gazed at me. And laughed. *Hard*.

"If you were that hungry, I could have shared some chips with you." She smiled, biting her lower lip, like trying to hold back another laugh.

There was no witty reply, no one-liner to save face, and if the earth had cracked opened and swallowed me whole at that exact moment, I would've died a happy man.

We're talking an epic fail of historic proportions, and in the long history of pick-ups-gone-bad, this would've won the Golden

Raspberry Award. Crash and burn. Five-alarm fire. The poster boy of losers everywhere.

All I managed to say was, “I got nervous because you’re so pretty.”

Such a doofus.

She stopped laughing and stared with a deep smile, one that didn’t part her lips. A beat of silence. “That was sweet.”

She rubbed her forehead. “I guess it was worth the bruise you gave me.”

Packing her towel and belongings, she slung a bag over her shoulders. “I need to go, Pace. But let me give you something.”

She pulled a small card from her bag. “Maybe we’ll bump into each other again. But without a wet dog.”

With a wave, she walked away into the golden sunshine, a silhouette fading into the distance like a melting dream. And looking at her card, I never expected the words I read:

Defender Church
Sundays 9AM & 11AM
A Band That Rocks
Come As You Are
Practical Messages
www.defenderchurch.org

In the days afterward, my friends gave me a hard time about the Silver Lake disaster, well deserved, especially after almost killing a girl with a freight train mutt and going all Fear Factor on her with a Milk-Bone.

The guys joked me like a pack of wild animals on red meat:

I hear doggie biscuits help clean teeth and freshen breath.

You're messing with one of God's girls!

You two should get married and become missionaries.

Yeah, there's a missionary position you need to learn about.

Get together and practice tongues!

Be careful about the laying on of hands.

And on and on it went. But respect was earned since I took a chance and had something to show for it. Her church invite card felt like winning a Willy Wonka Golden Ticket.

So after checking out Sage's Insta page — full of more stunning pictures and zero evidence of a boyfriend — and then the church website, I tried talking Stanley into going with me the next Sunday.

"Tell me I'm not crazy for doing this."

He didn't blink. "Oh, you're definitely crazy. But that's what it takes, man. The eye of the tiger."

"So it's not creepy to show up at her church?"

"A little bit, yeah. But obviously her faith is important to her. So maybe this is some type of test. You get more into Jesus and she'll get more into you."

"Will you tag along?" I tapped his chest. "You know, be my wingman?"

"The term *wingman* wasn't designed for usage in the hallowed halls of worship."

"Since when did you get a conscience? You've hit on girls at funerals."

Stanley thought for a moment. "Point taken. But no way — NO WAY — will I be caught dead in a church. I don't vibe with those holy rollers. Ain't gonna happen."

"I bet other hot girls are there."

And that did the trick. Defender Church, here we come.

3

Driving into the Defender Church parking lot felt like a Disney World experience, minus the mouse ears.

Caffeinated workers in bright yellow “I ♡ My Church” t-shirts waved huge foam fingers and directed us to a parking spot near the front. I half expected “It’s A Small World” to be playing somewhere.

The church building resembled a massive brick movie theater, a multilevel structure with lots of glass and no steeple. Not your grandmama’s church.

Near the entry door, a white tent welcomed guests with coffee and a “New Guest” present, a gift bag containing a branded travel mug and a flyer promoting the Spotify playlist of the church music team.

A friendly older gentleman opened the door and pointed us toward the main atrium, a buzzing area reminiscent of a Turkish bazaar. Colorful signs draped the walls: Guest Information, Cafe, Kids Check-In area. Dozens of large, flat-screen TV’s dotted the walls and flashed an urgent "Worship Experience" countdown clock. Seven minutes until lift-off.

Carrying that New Guest bag tattooed us as visitors, and everyone went out of their way with waves and hellos. But no sign of Sage. We attended the eleven o'clock service, a calculated risk, since I figured everyone our age wanted to sleep in as late as possible. Hopefully, she didn't attend the early service.

Stepping into the massive auditorium, an usher led us to our cushioned seats about midway back, and music thumped from the speaker clusters as par cans flooded the stage with theatrical light. Jesus had gone Hollywood.

It had been years since I last visited a church, for a cousin's baptism, a small country church that smelled like moth balls and had uncomfortable pews and orange carpet and an old lady playing organ. How times had changed.

Defender Church resembled a Millennial flash mob, a hipster-fest with a sea of rimmed glasses, pierces and plugs, and mismatched attire that basically screamed, "I didn't try too hard this morning!" and "We're Christians and can still be cool, really!" A lot of the guys wore scarves and some of the beards must have taken longer to comb than their head hair.

So any fear of being underdressed quickly vanished. No one wore anything resembling a suit, fine with me, since I had opted for a pair of comfortable jeans and a teal t-shirt. Another thing...

almost everyone there was Wonder Bread white, odd since we lived in a diverse community. At least Sage would stick out.

The jumbo screen flashed four minutes until Showtime, and a wild assortment of wandering beatniks and Bohemian artist types filed into the surrounding seats. It looked like a spiritual Woodstock.

Stanley leaned over. "Alright, you got me here. Congratulations. But it's a one-shot deal. If the amazing Sage doesn't show up, you're on your own. I'm not coming back."

"You never know. Maybe you'll walk the aisle today and get saved."

"Now *that* would take an act of God. Like one of these hipsters shaving off their Fu Manchu mustaches. Not gonna happen."

Stanley and I had never really talked about God and faith, but now seemed a good time. I asked, "Do you believe in the Man Upstairs?"

He paused. "You've heard of circumcision, right?"

My eyebrows raised. "Excuse me?"

"Circumcision. The removal of foreskin."

"Uh, yeah?"

"Why would God make guys with foreskins then tell them to cut it off? It's like God saying, 'My bad, fellas. But do you mind taking a sharp knife and fixing my mistake?'"

"You don't believe in God because of circumcision?"

"That's not the only reason." Stanley flipped through a church bulletin. "It's also the other stuff. The poverty, natural disasters, evil. Why hot dogs come in packs of ten but buns in packs of eight. You know, the deep mysteries of the universe."

"So you're an atheist?"

"I don't like pigeonholing myself. But to use a floating term, I'd call myself a logicist."

"I'm guessing that has something to do with logic."

He nodded. "And math. All the conundrums of the universe can be solved by mathematical computations. No tomfoolery with superstitions about God. If an earthquake happens in India, it probably goes back to some geometric algorithm."

I waited for him to smile, but he looked serious. Not a surprise. Stanley thought logically about everything and could have been the founding member of the Spock fan club. He must have inherited it from his dad, a straight-laced engineer who always had cool tech toys lying around the house.

"So what about you?" he asked.

"Well, uh..."

I had every intention of answering, until the sanctuary doors parted and my frontal lobe jolted into a breakdance.

Sage walked in.

And for a brief moment, the world stopped spinning and my heart skipped a beat and angelic choruses filled this orbital ball we call the Earth.

She entered with a group of friends, smiling and radiant, a queen with her entourage. And if possible, she looked more stunning than at the lake. Floating along in a breezy tank and a summer skirt, she wore her hair out, all natural and big and beautiful, like it was asking my fingers to run through it. An aura of celestial light surrounded her.

Sage didn't see me, not that she was looking. She'd probably forgotten about the invite or at least didn't think I was crazy enough to take her up on it. She sat near the front, at the perfect angle for me to stare at the side of her face, so smooth and caramel.

"I do believe in God," I whispered to Stanley. "Since he created something as beautiful as her."

A moment later, the countdown clock struck 0:00 and the lights faded and an electric guitar started screaming. Eleven o'clock at Defender Church.

For the next ten minutes, the crowd stood in participation, immersed in a multimedia mishmash of sight and sound, singing under the direction of a spiked-haired singer with holes in his pants and an assortment of head-bobbing musicians rocking and rolling with hillbilly sensibility in honor of the holy J.C., blessed be He.

Stanley and I actually enjoyed the show, but since we didn't know the songs, we simply took in the sights, in my case, Sage, who clapped and punched the air with a passion that made me want to yell *Sweet Jesus*.

With a flourish, the band wailed on a final, dramatic note before the music guy told us to have a seat. A cool-looking, twenty-something pastor stood and welcomed everyone with a few announcements and a lame attempt at PG-rated church humor, followed by another song by the band — this one slow and introspective and sang on a stool — and then a short video introducing the sermon of the day.

And that's when we met Vin, a middle-aged-still-valiantly-trying-to-hold-onto-youth Lead Pastor. He sported a too-tight jersey T-shirt and a dark pair of skinny jeans. He wasn't fat, but he hadn't ran any marathons lately, either.

The more passionate he became, the more heavily he breathed, and all I could think of was that poor button on the front of his aforementioned skinny jeans, holding on for dear life, pushing back against the girth of his Gospel passion. If that little guy lost the fight than someone in Defender Church would lose an eye.

"Too many chicken potluck dinners," Stanley said, way too loud.

But Vin turned out to be a likable guy, and a good speaker, and holding my attention was no small task. He spoke about how "God has a purpose for your life" with the main point being, "Are you in step with His purpose for you?"

It was a question I'd never thought about. If God did exist

somewhere up there, with some heavenly plan, than I must be really sucking at it. It had been a tough first semester away at college, and my parents brought me home at Christmas because of grades, or my lack thereof. It's not that the work was too hard. I just didn't go to class. Too many parties. I screwed up.

My plan was to study animal biology, a lifelong passion, but the rigid university structure and boring lectures squeezed the life out of me. So my parents forced me to move back home and get a job, earning back the privilege of higher education by commuting to a nearby community college. Couldn't blame their reasoning.

Over the past spring semester, I acknowledged my immaturity and worked to get back on track. My job at Luigi's Italian Restaurante paid the bills, but being a career busboy wasn't on the bucket list. Plus, I hated meatballs. My life needed a jolt, a challenge, an electric zimzum.

So God's purpose? *Hmmm*. Vin waxed eloquent about a Bible guy named Abraham who left his home and embarked on an adventure, shaking his life from the routine. Then he closed the sermon by highlighting Defender Church's "missions" team.

I didn't have a fat clue about a missions team. Was that like a church special forces unit? A religious SWAT team?

He explained how a volunteer team was heading to the Amazon and helping sick folks living on the banks of the river. Vin mentioned last-minute team openings and how an informational meeting was taking place after the service.

Sounded interesting, but I didn't give it much thought. That is, until he asked for team members to stand and be recognized, and Sage rose with a handful of others.

Hello, my beautiful Amazon woman.

And right then and there, a missions meeting was in my immediate future.

4

The service ended and the crowd hurried out.

Across the auditorium, Sage stood by her seat, talking and laughing with her friends.

"You're going to the Amazon meeting, aren't you?" Stanley's question snapped me out of a gaze.

I grinned sheepishly. "You know me well. Do you mind?"

"Go for it, but I'm catching a ride home with someone else." He reached for his phone and started texting.

"Thanks, wingman." I pat his shoulder. "The moral support meant a lot."

"If a miracle happens and you two somehow get together, you owe me big time."

"Deal. But one more favor. Walk with me over there to say hi to her. It'll be less awkward. But just don't mention the circumcision thing."

Stanley placed a hand over his heart. "I'll be a good boy."

Approaching her, the cold sweats started again. What would I say? At the lake, I'd already proven my talent for being a complete imbecile. Time for redemption. The options flittered across my mind:

Bonjour belle Sage. Je suis le muffin étalon de vos rêves qui est arrivé pour vous faire perdre pied.

Translation: Hello, beautiful Sage. I'm your dream stud muffin who's arrived to sweep you off your feet.

My only French after two long years of classes. I'd memorized the phrase and could insert anyone's name into it, though I never had the guts to try it.

Or, maybe I could play the evangelical Christian card:

Well, hey there, sister. Hallelujah! Wasn't that a great worship service? I was so blessed.

No, that would land like a lead balloon. Turns out, I didn't have a chance to formulate a witticism because Sage turned around and made eye contact.

Her face froze for a second, then she broke out in a big smile.

I may have peed my pants.

She ran over and gave a warm hug, her enveloping fragrance making me think of the term *Island Gardenia*, since that's how I imagined the smell of a tender flower blossoming in the sun.

Stepping back, she pointed playfully. "Pace, right?"

"Yeah. You've got a great memory."

"Hard forgetting a name like yours." She glanced at Stanley. "Thanks for coming, guys."

"This is Stanley." I wrapped an arm around his shoulder. "He's the owner of the big dog you met."

Right after saying it, I wanted to kick myself. *Don't remind her of your most embarrassing moment, idiot.*

"Hey, Stanley." She shook his hand. "I remember your face. You were one of the guys laughing at Pace."

His face fell a little. "Uh, yeah. Sorry about that. We were laughing with him, not at him."

Her head tilted. "You're not supposed to lie in church."

"Okay, we were laughing *at* him." Stanley turned toward me. "Man, she's good."

Time to change the subject. "That Amazon trip sounds amazing. Is it okay if I check out the meeting?"

Forget the French, I must have hit all sevens on the slot machine.

Sage's expression lit up. "Absolutely! I've been on the trip several years. Changed my life. The children there are so precious. And we could really use a few more team members. Come on, follow me."

Leading us to the atrium, where Stanley said a farewell, she guided me toward a side meeting room while stopping and talking to people along the way. She knew everyone.

At that's when I first met James, God help me.

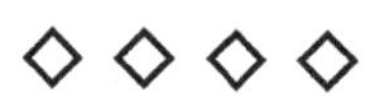

James looked like he had stepped from the glossy pages of a preppy magazine with his black hair, thick eyebrows, and alpha male vibe. The quintessential jock.

A head taller than most other guys and with a lean, athletic build, the dude must have attracted ladies like a Death Star tractor beam.

Which reminded me of a theory I developed years ago. There are two types of good-looking guys: (1) Those who are attractive and don't know it; and (2) Those who are attractive and definitely know it, and they want you to know they know it.

James was a solid number two. Pun intended.

When he noticed Sage, he nonchalantly lifted his head in a silent motion that communicated, *Hey girl, walk on over here and step into in my pulsating aura of coolness.*

He held two coffee cups from the church cafe and offered her one. "Got a white mocha for you." His voice smooth as butter.

"Thanks, James." She smiled and touched his shoulder affectionately. "You always remember my favorite."

And then he glowered at me, from my hair down to my sperrys, trying to compute the new unknown alien in the galaxy he ruled. But since I'm tall, he didn't tower over me like he did the others.

"Oh, this is Pace." Sage pointed to me. "And Pace, this is James. He's on the missions team, too."

We shook hands, the grip tight and aggressive, and for a moment we stood there in awkward silence, like an elementary school stare-off.

Sage mercifully broke the tension and motioned toward the meeting room. "I guess we should grab some seats. Pace, come sit with me."

A confused look washed over James's face, like her words bore the equivalent of a smart slap across his chiseled cheekbones. Game on.

Sage led me to a seat at one of the classroom tables while James found a place behind us and walked past with the hint of a bruised ego.

And then the Tasmanian Devil entered the room, all one hundred and fifty miles per hour of her, a petite lady weighing no more than a buck five, who exploded into the doorway with the gentleness of a backfiring exhaust pipe, bouncing, more than walking, to the front of the class.

"Who Da Mom?" she asked in a loud, high voice.

The dozen or so missions team members answered in unity, "You Da Mom!"

I turned to Sage, bewildered. She leaned over. "That's Lola, the team leader. Considers herself everyone's mom."

I didn't know what to expect for our Amazon team leader — maybe a retired Marine sergeant or a weathered, tough-as-nails missionary — but I sure didn't imagine hyper-Lola.

She looked the complete opposite of the Defender Church demographic: in her early sixties with oversized glasses that made her eyes resemble an anime character.

"We're only two weeks away from wheels up, everybody." She glanced at me. "And we've still got a couple of airplane tickets to fill. Once we get them finalized, I'll feel a hell of a lot better."

Lola covered her mouth, embarrassed.

Sage whispered, "She cusses a lot, but she loves God. And don't let her fool you, she's a beast on the missions field."

A cussing missions team leader? Are you kidding? I'd follow this woman to the moon. She opened a laptop and gave a twenty-minute PowerPoint on what to expect in the Amazon.

I jotted a few notes:

- This was her 13th time to the Amazon
- The trip focuses on medical missions, but anyone can serve
- When we meet people's physical needs, it opens them up to their deeper spiritual needs
- We arrive in Leticia (where Colombia, Brazil, and Peru come

together), board a boat, and travel to different villages along the Amazon River

- The trip lasts nine days
- Lodging is primitive; Showers happen when it rains
- We will work long hours serving people
- We will witness firsthand the wonders of the Amazon rainforest

Pictures flashed on the screen of the numerous people the teams had served on past trips, highlighting Amazonian children hugging sunburned volunteers. I'm all about cute kids and helping people, but my heart did a yippee-ki-yay when Lola showed pictures of the amazing animals.

From anacondas and sloths to macaws and howler monkeys, I geeked out, remembering all the books and documentaries I had studied about the Amazon, the most biodiverse tropical rainforest in the world.

For anyone with a love of animal biology, it stood as a lush amusement park, an ecosystem teeming with thousands of species of mammals and birds and fish. Who needed a college professor? I'd let the Amazon teach me.

Lola's eyes narrowed, as much as they could, and she clicked on a final slide. The picture, grayish and granular, showed the Amazon River with a mysterious black hump in the middle of it.

"And this is the only known picture of the mythical Hipupiara." She turned toward the screen, placing her finger on the image. "It's a reptilian-like creature believed to live within the Amazon River, blamed for many suspicious deaths each year. No one has ever seen it up close, or either they didn't live to tell about it. So who knows? Maybe we'll catch a glimpse."

Everyone laughed. The Sea Monster story was a bit much, but Lola needed to spice up the presentation somehow.

Either way, the trip was exactly what I needed: an adventure exploring another corner of the world, investigating my biology passion, and if lucky, cozying up with Miss Sage.

And yes, of course, helping people.

But then came the price tag: $2,100. Ugh. Talk about sticker shock. I could possibly scrounge half, but not all of it in such a short time. So in a split second, I fell from a mountaintop of euphoria to the valley of defeat.

Finishing her presentation, Lola moved side to side across the room like a pent-up pinball machine. "You have the opportunity to change a lot of lives, but it's not easy. You're gonna face a lot of sh*t."

She placed her hand reflexively over her mouth. "Sorry… got a little excited." She cleared her throat. "But if you're going, I need the full payment in forty-eight hours."

Lola closed the laptop, tilted her head back and bellowed,

"Who Da Mom?"

"You Da Mom!" the team shouted back.

But I just sat there, silent and dejected, thinking about the 2,100 reasons I wouldn't be able to go.

5

When the meeting dismissed, Sage must have read the disappointment written across my face.

"You alright?" She placed her hand on my arm.

"The trip sounds awesome," I said. "But there's no way to find that kind of cash in two days."

She didn't immediately reply, so I turned toward her. And that's when I noticed two charming quirks about Sage that made my insides do somersaults.

First, whenever she was thinking, she'd bite her lower lip ever so gently, and something about it looked so inviting and primal that I wanted to nibble on it.

Secondly, was the way she played with her hair, twirling and twisting those long curls in her fingers and tucking the loose strands behind her ears.

Her. Just perfect.

She stopped biting her lip. "If God wants you to go, have faith the money will come."

"My faith is a bit weak right now."

"It happens to everyone. That's why you need to pray."

"That needs some help, too."

"Give me your hand." She stretched hers out toward mine. "I want to show you something."

Sage cupped my hand in hers, and with her free hand, she slowly spread out my fingers, sending a *hi-ya* electric jolt as her red nails rubbed my palm.

"Prayer is really simple." She looked up, into my eyes. "Just remember each of your fingers is an element of prayer."

She touched my thumb:

"This one reminds you to worship — keep God first."

My index finger:

"And this one means to confess things, asking for a clean heart."

My middle finger:

"Tell God how thankful you are for the beautiful things in life, stuff you take for granted."

My ring finger:

"Then bring your request. Tell him exactly what you need."

My pinkie:

"Finally, pray for someone else. Don't pray only selfish prayers."

She touched my palm:

"And this is where faith comes in. Prayer and faith work together."

She closed my fingers into a fist:

"Faith conquers the biggest obstacles."

And that's when James stepped to our table, ruining the magic. He had obviously been listening to the conversation, and as Sage held my hand his breathing sounded like a hyperventilating Darth Vader.

"Yeah, good luck with raising the funds." His voice sounded completely insincere, and the wise guy smirk on his face didn't help.

"Thanks," I mumbled, ticked that he broke one of the most important Guy Rules: *Don't interrupt another dude when he's talking to a hottie.*

Sage checked the time on her phone, then gathered her belongings. "Gotta go. But keep me posted about the money." She gave me her number. "Text me."

"Okay." I tried sounding cool with the fireworks exploding in my chest cavity. "And thanks for the prayer advice."

She glanced up. "Thanks for the coffee, James."

And just like that, with a wave, Sage glided out of the room and left her fragrance lingering in the air, a carnival of happy smells, like cotton candy and roses and the summer breeze all jumbled together.

James waited until she left the room, then turned to me with a side glance. “I know what you’re doing. You’re only here because of her. No one’s fooled, bro.”

It took a second to process the Large Insecurity Mass standing beside me. “I’m not trying to fool anyone.” I shifted. “And so what? Why is it a problem for you?”

He stepped closer, a few inches away. “Because you’re not Sage’s type.”

“And you are?”

“I believe *she* thinks so.”

How could this clown stake claim to someone who wasn’t even his girlfriend? What a jerk. “Do I threaten you, James?”

He snorted under his breath. “Dude, hardly. I’m saving you from heartache. We both know how this is going to end.”

“Really? The way I look at it, we’re fishing from the same pier. May the best man win.”

He seemed shocked that someone dared challenge him. Perhaps his size and good looks intimidated others, but not me. I had the brawn and he knew it.

James lifted his chin, and his face flushed. “Unlike you, I have the money to go on this trip. And when Sage is far from home, all vulnerable and lonely, I’ll be there for her. So don’t worry, I’ll make sure she’s comforted. I hear the moon over the Amazon is very romantic."

I imagined my fist crunching his perfect nose, caving in that pretty boy face, and leaving a couple of black eyes for a lovely raccoon look.

But I released my clenched hand and took a deep breath. "Absence makes the heart grow fonder," I said, meeting his gaze. "Sage is a smart girl. She'll make the right choice."

James inched closer, his mouth barely containing a snarl. He didn't say a word, only stared, and with a condescending huff he finally lumbered out of the room, shaking his head.

After letting the hallway clear for a few minutes, I headed to the parking lot, still hot from butthead James. Was this how so-called Christians acted? I wanted to cram a thick Bible up his wazoo.

Walking out the exit doors, I passed an outdoor playground where a young boy dangled from monkey bars. And almost on cue, something terrible happened.

The child fell… *hard.*

The crunching sound made me wince, and for a moment, the little guy lay on his back, not moving or making a sound.

I ran the ten yards to him, and kneeling by his side, surveyed the damage.

He suddenly rolled around frantically and held his arm while wailing loudly. Most likely a broken bone. With his face contorted, the boy thrashed and struggled to breathe. His eyes widened, unable to communicate through his pain, desperate for help and reaching for me with his uninjured arm.

"You're gonna be alright, buddy." I wiped the tears from his face. "Hold on, I'm here to help you."

A man exited a nearby door.

"This boy needs help!" I yelled. "Do you know his parents?"

The man understood and nodded, running back inside.

And while waiting, I did something I hadn't done in a long time, possibly even years.

I prayed.

The words rolled out, though not very pretty or theological, and surprisingly, brought a peaceful calm.

The word, "Amen" barely left my lips as a frantic mom busted open the door and ran toward us, screaming hysterically. After consoling her child, she asked me to call 911.

Fifteen minutes later, paramedics lifted the boy into an ambulance and sped away, leaving me standing alone on the playground mulch beside an abandoned swing set.

I didn't even learn the kid's name.

A memorable Sunday morning, to say the least. It was upsetting to witness an innocent child experience such pain, but little did I know a dump truck of heartbreak was coming my way next, ready to wreck everything I held dear.

6

Two days later, we had a family meal at Spaghettiville.

Ten minutes away from our house, the restaurant hosted all the major milestones: beginning-of-the-school-year talks (curfew times, homework expectations), post-game celebrations (lots of soccer growing up), occasional birthdays (mostly Dad's), and Father's Day (again, Dad).

He adored the place but the rest of us merely put up with it. Because he paid. Whenever it was a Spaghettiville night, Dad asked, "Anybody want some Eye-talian?" and we'd murmur and climb into the car and spend the next couple of hours sitting at a checkered tablecloth booth with my parents on one side and me and my younger sister, Cameron, on the other.

It certainly wasn't fancy. It smelled like a mixture of Prego's sauce and strong bathroom cleaner but it somehow grew into a family tradition, kind of like wearing your most comfortable underwear. We even ate there following grandma's funeral because it felt so familiar and safe.

So if you were looking for authentic Italian cuisine, this wasn't the place. But it came cheap and you got big servings, especially unlimited breadsticks. We kept eating there even after I started working at the "competition" — Luigi's — because (1) I didn't get a discount and (2) I knew way too much about the Luigi kitchen.

One thing I did like, however, no matter how crazy life got, I could count on the same familiar rituals during our visits. It served as a reset button when everything else went off the hinges.

My parents always ordered a tropical drink called the *Copacabana*. Colorful and exotic, it arrived in a container shaped like an hourglass with a purple umbrella and cherry on top. They loved sipping from the same straw.

And then there was Wally. He hung on the wood-paneled wall, a bass fish that wiggled and sang. Wally the Fish danced and performed for guests every thirty minutes, whether you liked him or not, his repertoire limited to two country songs.

Half-past the hour he'd sing:

Hey, good lookin'

What ya got cookin'?

Howza 'bout cookin' somethin' up for me?

Then on every hour, he'd belt out a classic Patsy Cline number. That fake fish had to be older than me.

But undoubtedly, the Spaghettiville highlight was Peggy, our longtime waitress who seemed like one of the family. Even in her eighties, she skittered around like someone half her age and sported brown-colored hair and called everyone “Honey,” “Baby,” or my personal favorite, “Sugar Lumpkins.”

Best of all, she told the worst corny jokes in the world and repeated the punch lines several times, like she thought saying it again made it funnier.

She arrived at our table and placed the menus down. “Hey, ya’ll. How’s my favorite family doing?”

After some small talk, here came the joke. “OK... so why didn’t the toilet paper cross the road?”

We shook our heads, and her eyes lit up. “Because it got stuck in a crack!”

She owned the greatest laugh, a booming *bwah-ha-ha* that made you chuckle even if the joke didn’t. And true to form, she laughed harder than we did.

“It got stuck in a crack!” She slapped the table.

After recovering from her own joke, she pointed to me and Cameron. “Let me guess — sodas for you two and one Copacabana for the mister and missus.”

Mom raised her hand and gave an embarrassed grin. “Actually, Peggy, tonight we’ll just have two waters.”

Stop the presses. In the countless hours spent at Spaghettiville, my parents never bypassed “their drink.” And two waters? They never drank plain water.

We sat silent for a few moments, munching on breadsticks. I cleared my throat. “Went to church this morning.”

“Yeah?” Mom’s eyebrows raised. “How’d that go?”

“Quite the experience. Definitely no hymns or organs.”

Dad wiped his mouth with a napkin. “I miss those good ol’ hymns. Your grandmother loved ‘How Great Thou Art.’”

“It’s all guitars and jumbo screens now.” I fiddled with my napkin-wrapped silverware. “The songs sounded like something on the radio.”

Dad shook his head. “Everything goes commercial. It’s a shame.”

“Actually, the service was pretty good.” I leaned my elbows on the table. “And the church helps people, especially in the Amazon.”

“In the Amazon?” Cameron stopped chewing and turned to me. “What’s in the Amazon?”

She asked for it, so for ten minutes I gave a rundown of the entire missions trip, from the medical needs to the spectacular Amazon rainforest.

By the look on their faces, my passion about a church trip surprised them. I half-expected Mom to feel my forehead for a fever, but the explanation really must have moved her since her eyes filled with mommy tears.

“How much does it cost?” she asked, almost a whisper.

"$2,100. I can't afford it."

"Right now you need to invest your money in education." Dad pointed his half-eaten breadstick at me. "Not in some wild sight-seeing trip."

Mom looked perturbed and gave him a cold stare. "This could be part of his education. He's always loved studying that area of the world. Might be his only opportunity."

Dad shrugged his shoulders. "Sounds like a luxury trip to me. I'm fifty-one years old and I've never been to the Amazon. Never been out of the country."

"That's your own fault." Mom leaned slightly away from him. "But don't rain on someone else's parade."

Dad shot her an irritated glare and the table grew silent again, just as Peggy served our dinner.

"Plates are hot." She lowered the dinner in front of us. "Be careful."

Cameron and I dug into the meal, but Mom and Dad seemed preoccupied and hardly ate a thing, pushing their food around their plates.

"What's wrong?" I pointed to their dishes. "Does it taste bad?"

My parents glanced at each other with silent agreement, and then Dad piped up. "We've got to talk about something really important."

Uh-oh. By now, Dad should have been slurping on his

noodles in his loud and obnoxious way. We officially had a situation in Spaghettiville.

"I'll just come out and say it." He played with his napkin, then laid it down. "Your mom and I are separating."

In that moment, the earth's spin slowed and the sound of a heartbeat filled my eardrums and I wanted to upchuck penne pasta. It was like someone screwed with the video game settings and we'd entered the abandoned train station in the Matrix.

Brain neurons misfired and my eyes bounced side to side, desperately trying to make sense of the nuclear bomb that obliterated our fake Italian dinner. Mom's tears flowed freely and Dad couldn't look us in the face and Cameron sat frozen and bug-eyed.

"We're so sorry, kids." Mom dabbed her nose with a tissue. "We never imagined this. Not in a million years."

"Wh... What happened?" I asked.

"It's hard to pin down any one thing." She looked down at the table, but not at us. "It's been gradual. We've drifted apart."

She broke into more tears. "Sometimes good things come to an end."

No. How can it happen? At one point, though it's gross thinking about, Dad probably felt the same hot attraction toward Mom that I felt toward Sage. So how could these two drift apart?

For years, I'd joked them about touching each other way too

much, hugging and kissing to the point of embarrassment, especially when my friends visited. They enjoyed getting handsy and loved watching our sickened reactions.

But now that was over? It couldn't be, not this couple who sat hip-to-hip but seemed a galaxy removed from each other.

Cameron refused to speak, her eyeballs glossed over in a death stare. As an introvert she followed this pattern, needing time to process, then at a future indeterminate date, she'd snap and unleash a hellish emotional torment.

But my feelings gushed like a sidewalk fire hydrant. I wanted to rip the plastic lining off the tables and heave breadsticks across the room and be slapped across the face and awakened from the nightmare.

I was finally getting my life back together and there they went blowing it all to hell again. And how could they do it in Spaghettiville? With one fell swoop, they forever ruined the place. I could never come back again and look at this poor unfortunate table, the ground zero for my family's annihilation.

And I wept. So much that other patrons must have noticed, but I didn't give a flying flip.

Mom cried alongside me, while Dad cupped his face in his hands and Cameron crossed her arms and stared into the wild blue yonder. The rest of the conversation was white noise:

They would switch to separate bedrooms…

Dad would move to an apartment soon…

They loved us and would never talk bad about each other…

We would get through this and become stronger…

Blah blah blah. And then Peggy walked up, oblivious to our open wounds.

“Looks like ya’ll been suckin’ on some lemons.” She chomped on a huge wad of gum. “What did the grape say when the elephant sat on it?”

Our table, occupied by four zombies, was not in the mood for corny jokes. But out of respect for our friend, we shook our heads and braced for the punchline.

“Nothing!” She slapped her knee. “The grape didn’t say nothing. It just gave out a little whine!”

She raised a gut-busting, rafter-shaking guffaw. “Get it? It gave a little whine! *Wine*!”

And from the back of the restaurant, over Peggy’s laughter, Wally the Fish twisted and sang:

I love you honey

I love your money

But most of all I love your automobile

7

The next afternoon I met Stanley at Silver Lake, hoping it would take my mind off the family drama.

He had borrowed his dad's drone and wanted to show off the *Aries 609+ NanoNova's* flying skills. The quadcopter, that's what Stanley called it, resembled something from a science fiction movie.

He whisked it high into the sky and operated the controls like Alicia Keys on a grand piano. It broadcasted a high-definition picture to the controller screen and gave breathtaking views of the surrounding area. Silver Lake looked fantastic. The drone buzzed around remarkably quiet, barely above a whisper even a few feet off the ground.

"People know this quadcopter as the Aries." He rubbed his hand across the tail. "But I call it the FBI model."

"Why's that?"

"Stands for Female Body Inspector. This fancy machine helps

you appreciate creation, if you know what I mean."

Two attractive women sat thirty yards away, and Stanley gnawed on his tongue as his fingers operated the levers, leading the Aries close to them before lowering it in for a perfect voyeuristic view.

But he flew the drone too close, and the girls noticed. They studied the hovering object then turned their gaze toward us, the only two guys standing and looking at them, with one of those guys holding a controller in his hands.

Busted.

The blonde smiled at the camera and then defiantly lifted a one-finger salute, yelling a few choice R-rated words.

Stanley took the hint and guided the drone back to us.

"You win some, you lose some." He flashed a sly smile. "They lost, we won."

For the next half-hour we relaxed in the shade of a majestic Oak tree, and that's when I told him about the bombshell my parents dropped the night before. It felt good to talk about it and get the weight off my chest.

At first Stanley sat in stunned silence, picking at glass blades. The news hit him hard. My parents had always treated him like one of their own; God knows, he certainly ate enough meals at our house to qualify as family.

"Man, I'm sorry. Love is a strange brew." Stanley rubbed his chin stubble. "I've actually developed a mathematical formula for relationships."

"Why am I not surprised?"

"It's a complex equation, but the layman's version is this: Love = Intentionality + Chance." He dug into his pocket and pulled out a quarter. "Take this coin for example. Did I ever tell you how my parents met?"

I shook my head and leaned against the tree trunk, bracing myself for another of his fantastical stories.

"When my dad was single," Stanley said, "he worked a deadbeat job in Texas. He wanted a change, so he decided to move. Problem was, he had no idea where to go. So he drove to the north Texas border and decided to flip a coin. If it landed heads, he'd turn his 1988 Chevrolet Impala toward Carolina. If tails, he'd go to California. The quarter landed heads, so he drove to Carolina, eventually met Mom, and *voila*! Here I am talking with you. But think for a moment. What if that coin had landed tails?"

I lifted my hands toward him, in worshipful admiration. "The world would have been robbed of the brilliance known as Stanley Jennings."

"Yes." His hands mimicked his head exploding. "Love = Intentionality + Chance."

"So the Love Equation is supposed to make me feel better?"

He stared. "There are forces at work beyond your control,

Pace. No matter what you do, you can't change the Love Equation. So don't blame yourself. Things will work out the way they're supposed to."

He glanced away, upward, and did a double take. "Whoa. We've got to check that out."

I looked up. "What?"

He ignored the question and powered on the drone, lifting it fifteen feet above our heads beside an extended tree branch. On it sat a nest, and a mama bird flew away as the drone neared.

Stanley nudged the controls. "Let's see if any eggs are in there."

The drone moved closer, and the controller screen displayed four light blue eggs.

"Robin eggs." I stared at the screen. "Did you know robins usually only lay four eggs and then stop? One egg a day. They stop laying them when the clutch of eggs has the proper feel underneath their bodies."

"Where did you get all your useless animal knowledge? You had it even back in elementary school. I remember we visited the zoo once and you said elephants live forty years longer in the wild than in captivity."

I shrugged. "Lots and lots of reading."

"Nerd alert!" He lowered the drone back to the ground, and we sat again, watching the bustling crowds around the lake.

"Did you realize nature operates with the Love Equation, too?" He motioned toward the tree branches. "Think about it. The mama bird intentionally made that nest. But it's pure chance it was built here in North Carolina, in this old Oak tree, right above our heads."

"Deep thoughts. You're hurting my brain."

"So what about the Love Equation for your life?" Stanley raised and lowered his brows several times.

"Huh?"

"You know. Sage?"

"It would take Stephen Hawking to figure that one out."

"You never know. She could be *The One*."

"So how do you know if a girl is The One?"

"She has to meet the criteria on my Top 5 list."

I couldn't help but laugh. "You have a list?"

"You don't?"

So for the next fifteen minutes, we debated the highly unscientific criteria for our dream woman.

Stanley's Top 5 List:

1) Hot

2) Her mom is still attractive

3) Great kisser

4) Good birthing hips

5) Likes listening to Neil Young music

His list was sexist, chauvinistic, and completely Stanley.

My Top 5 List:

1) Hot
2) Smart
3) Confident
4) Compassionate
5) Faith

Stanley tilted his head in a thoughtful pose. “It sounds like you’re perfectly describing Sage.”

“Maybe you’re right.”

“So what are you waiting for? You need to be intentional and chase her. Then rely on the chance side of the equation. Too bad the Amazon trip is too expensive. That would have been the perfect opportunity.”

I couldn’t hold the good news any longer. “Remember how Sage told me to pray about getting the money?”

“Yeah. Did you?”

“For the first time in a long time.” I pulled a folded check from my pocket and waved it. “And something happened.”

Stanley’s eyes widened. “Whoa! Where did that come from?”

“Mom, earlier today. She insisted. It covers the trip, and a little extra.”

He smiled. “Cupid is throwing you a lifeline. You gotta go for it.”

I stared at Silver Lake, lost in thought. Mom’s check felt like guilt money, and I didn’t want to waste it chasing after a girl. Maybe Dad was right about investing in college.

But... this offered an opportunity to make my parents proud by serving other people and getting my life back on track. Plus, it forced me out of the house for a couple of weeks. I didn’t want to be there anyway, when Dad left for his apartment. Watching the moving trucks would send me over the deep end.

And then I pictured the robin’s nest again; the simple beauty of those tiny and fragile eggs, symbolizing a fresh start, a new birth. *I had to go.*

I borrowed Stanley’s quarter. “Heads Amazon, and tails I use the cash for college.”

He rubbed his hands with anticipation. “I love high stakes.”

Flipping the coin high into the air, it landed on the grass by my feet.

Heads. The Amazon.

The destiny path stretched out before me, under an old gnarled tree beside Silver Lake, with the help of a drone and Stanley’s crazy Love Equation.

I needed to contact Lola regarding the airline tickets, then text Sage. She’d love hearing about the answered prayer. If everything went as planned, I'd be three thousand miles away in a few days and chasing the adventure of a lifetime.

But as I was about to learn, that adventure would end up chasing me.

8

ONE DAY BEFORE DEPARTURE

After sleeping until noon the next day, I finally rolled my lazy derriere out of bed.

With my parents at work and Cameron at school, I had the house to myself. And the laundry and packing to myself, too. Mom always helped with our clothes, but she deserved a break with all the marriage stuff happening.

I needed nine days of clean clothes, so that meant the joy of washing. Sticking a fire poker in my eye sounded more fun. Doing laundry seemed like a preview of hell, with eternal perdition somehow involving Satan and dirty underwear.

Located at the end of the house, our laundry room was in a narrow hallway leading to a guest bathroom, and above the dryer hung a rectangular plaque: *"Laundry Today… Or Naked Tomorrow."* A mishmashed pile of dirty clothes overflowed from the hamper and lay at my feet, taunting like a landfill waiting to be climbed.

My plan involved packing tons of t-shirts and boxers but only a few shorts, since they could be reworn. Some travelers recommended bringing long sleeves and pants to deter the swarming bugs, but I couldn't imagine covering up in that Amazonian furnace. If I became a bug buffet, so be it; hopefully the repellent would do the job.

I hunted for the detergent scooper, but instead found laundry "pods." Hoping for the best, I dropped one inside the washer and chose the heavy load option. Round One had begun. If only the Howell family could be washed in the super-scrub cycle and come out smelling like Spring Meadow.

Pulling out my phone, I sat on the floor against the closet door, unable to get Lola's Sea Monster story out of my head. Strike it up to my love of fantasy and all things strange.

I searched YouTube about the creature, but, as always, fell into the deep rabbit hole of other bizarre and titillating videos, like the Top 10 Scariest Movie Creatures; People Using An Escalator For The First Time; and The Farting Preacher, followed by the Best of Farting Preacher.

I finally searched for "Amazon Sea Monster," surprised at the dozens of hits with timeframes covering the past two decades. A 2014 news story caught my eye about the mysterious sinking of an Amazon riverboat.

Titled "The Hipupiara Strikes Again?" the video showed a

Spanish-speaking news anchor detailing the tragedy, with a grainy graphic over his shoulder of the supposed creature, the same picture Lola used in her PowerPoint.

As he spoke, the English caption scrolled at the bottom of the screen:

"Hundreds are missing and believed dead in a tragic riverboat accident that has many pointing to yet another attack by the legendary Hipupiara.

According to reports, the boat — named the Pizarro — undertook a vicious hit before taking in water. The Pizarro quickly capsized, sending its passengers into one of the most dangerous areas of the Amazon River.

Witnesses report an enormous, reptilian creature seen among the wreckage, attacking the screaming and helpless passengers and pulling them underwater. Out of five hundred passengers, more than four hundred are missing and feared dead.

Though authorities have never verified the existence of the Hipupiara, this is another in a series of shocking events, perhaps pointing to a mysterious and violent creature strong enough to overturn a modern steel vessel.

The search for bodies continues, which is proving difficult, due to murky water and the swarming schools of piranha. Meanwhile, authorities have doubled efforts for hunting and killing this feared creature, warning everyone to proceed with extreme caution when traveling the River, especially in the Tres Fronteras area."

The video faded black, and my breath hitched. The Tres Fronteras area. That's exactly where we were going. Leticia, on the left bank of the Amazon river, located at the point where Colombia, Brazil, and Peru meet together. *Tres Fronteras.*

A door handle jiggled and the front door squeaked open.

Cameron was home from school, and by the way she threw her book bag on the kitchen counter, she didn't seem happy. Walking around the corner, she saw me sitting on the laundry room floor.

I jerked my chin up. "How was school?"

"You really want to know?" She pointed at her shirt. "Look at this. See the chocolate stain? We had a Key Club party after school and somehow the ice cream missed my mouth and landed on my new shirt."

A sophomore, Cameron had grown into a pretty young woman. Guys had started taking notice with their sly side glances and not-so-subtle head turns.

She opened the fridge, staring, and her shoulders drooped. "There's nothing to eat. All we have is mayonnaise and five varieties of sauces. How do you live on sauces? What's wrong with this place?"

I grunted rising from the floor, my butt numb from sitting too long on the linoleum. "The grocery store hasn't been on Mom's priority list. She has a lot on her mind."

'Maybe I do, too." She slammed the fridge door and stormed into the living room, collapsing on the worn leather couch.

"So, bad day?" I followed and sat on a side chair.

"Bad life." She folded her arms and stared out a nearby window.

"Look on the bright side." I stretched my words out slowly. "We've still got each other."

Her eyes darted to me without her head moving. "When the crap hits the fan around here, you'll be on a plane thousands of miles away. Must be nice. Wish someone would give me money to fly away and escape."

She kicked a picture frame from the coffee table and sent it flying across the room.

Here we go. I'd been waiting for her bottled-up emotions to come roaring out. Walking over, I found the glass shattered on our 5x7 family photo. But instead of getting mad at her, I knew Cameron needed to work the anger out of her system. Maybe kicking a picture frame or two would help. When parents fight, life sucks.

She scowled, her face reddening. "You always leave when things get tough."

"What?" My empathy was short-lived. "That's stupid. This trip wasn't planned around their separation. How was I supposed to know?"

"You don't have to go, but you're choosing to. Selfish, if you ask me. Maybe that's why your life's at a dead end right now. Everything's always about you."

Heat flushed through my body. "That's ridiculous."

"Really? Blowing Mom and Dad's money at school. Partying it away. Sleeping through half your classes at community college. Not doing anything around the house. Leaving your dishes in the sink. When's the last time you mowed the yard for Dad?

"He loves the exercise. And Mom has a special way of loading the dishwasher."

"You forgot her birthday party last month. And you know why? Because Stanley invited you over to watch *Space Pirates*. A dumb movie that you've seen like fifty times. You didn't even have the decency to answer the phone when we called from the restaurant."

"A simple scheduling mistake. And hello? It's common courtesy to mute your phone during a movie, thank you very much."

"Your head's in the sand, Pace. You're not engaging with the people around you. Life is passing you by and you're missing it."

She knew the exact buttons to press. "Where do you come up with this crap?" My voice raised. "You're crazy."

"Crazy? Tell me one thing about my life right now. Go ahead."

I looked at her stained shirt. "You're in the Key Club. And you like chocolate ice cream."

She stared, unsatisfied.

"Oh, you want more?" I racked my brain. "You're dating... what's his name? Steve."

"It's Scott, and we haven't dated in six months. Have you noticed he hasn't been around?"

"Figured he was a busy guy. You know, working at Food Town."

"He works at a yogurt shop."

"Technically that's food, isn't it?"

"See what I mean? If it's not about you, then you tune out."

I clenched my jaw. "So I'm not perfect like you. Sue me. Sorry that I don't live up to your glorious standards. What do you want me to do? Cancel my trip? I can't help it that Mom and Dad have their problems. And I certainly can't feel responsible for staying here and babysitting you."

Her lips quivered like they always did before a full-out cry. "You're such a jerk!"

"Really? For helping people in the Amazon?"

"What about helping people in North Carolina, like your family?" She placed her hands over her face and hid a flood of tears.

I sat there for a few minutes, stubborn, listening to her weep. Pure torture. There were two humans in the world I couldn't watch cry — Mom and Cameron. Maybe they didn't realize how their tears tore my heart out, but when the water works flowed, game over.

I had to do something, so I scooted beside her on the couch. "Sorry." After wrapping an arm around her, she nestled her face into my shoulder blade. Another long cry ensued.

Cameron finally lifted her splotched face. "I'm sorry for saying those things. That wasn't fair." She blew the hair away from her eyes and sniffled. "I think the trip will do you good."

I blinked a few times. "But you just said I was selfish for going."

"It was my emotions talking. Don't guys ever understand?"

"Women are complicated."

"Men are too dumb to figure us out." She faced me. "So do you promise?"

"Promise what?"

"Promise to let this trip change your life. Let's face it, all you do is bus tables and watch movies. Helping people can help you."

Her description oversimplified things, but I didn't want to argue and cause more tears. "I guess so."

"Not good enough. Raise your hand and promise."

"Really? Raise my hand?"

"Yes."

I rolled my eyes and lifted my right hand. "I cross my heart and solemnly swear, Girl Scout honor, stick a needle in my eye, with God as my witness, that a lot of Amazonians will be helped.

And maybe me, too."

Her head tilted with a knowing gaze. "Yeah, yeah. Humanitarian work. But you also have to win the girl."

"What? *Girl*?" My pretend shock wasn't very convincing.

"I'm not an idiot. Why else would you go to church the other day? You went for a girl." She stuck a finger in my chest. "You, Pace Howell, love the chase."

She knew her brother. I paused, staring at the carpet, and my empathy returned. "Sorry you have to be here when Dad moves out."

Her voice softened. "Sometimes you gotta suck it up and deal with things."

"We're going to make it through this."

"Yeah," she whispered.

"Will a sauce sandwich make you feel better?"

"We're out of bread. I may just have to lick my chocolate stain."

"Then how about a hamburger? My treat."

"If you insist." Cameron stood from the couch. "My tears always work, don't they?"

Oh, how I loved her but sometimes wanted to smack her. In a sweet, brotherly way.

Tomorrow was departure day, and ready or not, clean clothes or not, in twenty-four hours I'd stand in another part of the world.

But not before we paid a visit to Good Burger, affectionately known as Turdburger, and enjoyed an artery-clogging Fatty Melt and fries since I'd be eating God-knows-what for the next two weeks.

With an excited shudder, I wondered what awaited in the Amazon.

But then a more harrowing question crept up from within: what awaited me upon my return home?

9

DEPARTURE DAY

A simple plan:

The airport was an hour drive away…

10:30 am flight at Raleigh-Durham International (RDU)…

Lola suggested arriving at the airport by 8:30 am, which meant waking at 7 am and in the car by 7:30 am…

And then… my alarm didn't go off. Or maybe it did, I can't remember. With my parents at work and Cameron at school, it was REM Stage Four deep sleep.

Eventually, in a haze, I rolled over and checked my phone.

Eight thirty.

WHAT?! I should have already arrived at the airport.

A wordy durd left my mouth and I kicked the sheets away, a possessed man fumbling for clothes and a toothbrush. I texted Lola about my lateness, and at eight forty dove into the car, hit the gas, and prayed for no cops. I'd ask forgiveness later.

The razor-thin margin of making the flight made me so uptight I had to nervous pee. With every red light, school bus, and slow-driving grandma conspiring against me, I pounded the steering wheel. How embarrassing would it be to miss the flight? Another colossal failure for my growing exhibit in the Hall of Shame.

While stuck in the rush hour traffic jam, I opened the note Mom had left by my bedside.

Pace,

I am so proud of you. Keep following your dreams! Don't worry about me and Dad. Things will work out, I promise. Can't wait to see your face again and hear all about the trip. I'll be thinking of you every day. Looking forward to hugging my sweet little Pacey-Poo!

I love you,

Mom

Dad sent a voicemail saying much the same things, minus the lovey-dovey talk, mentioning his thankfulness for a son willing to try new things. He encouraged me to take lots of pictures, so we could look at them over a future meal. Probably at Spaghettiville.

I had to make this flight. What idiot oversleeps on such an important day? I'll tell you who… *Pacey-Poo.*

The dashboard clock ticked away not only the minutes, but my dream. I thought about grabbing my skateboard out of the trunk and riding it to the airport; it'd be faster than sitting on constipated I-85.

And then, like a ray of sunlight piercing a dark sky, the traffic moved again. I floored the Subaru.

An hour later, at nine forty-five, the RDU sign appeared. After parking, I ran toward Departures like someone being chased. Check-in and security lines awaited.

One of my suitcase wheels was damaged, so I half-rolled, half-dragged it, envious of the other travelers with their perfect rolling luggage. And of course, a lady in the metal detector line wore every imaginable piece of jewelry, like a living breathing Tiffany store.

At ten twenty, I full-out sprinted the airport corridor with my heart beating through my chest, knowing every second counted. But as I neared the gate and ran past a last-opportunity coffee shop, a customer wheeled into my path and in a blur of motion, with no chance to react, we crashed into each other.

Coffee splashed onto both of our shorts.

A split-second later my brain registered the unfathomable: the customer was a man. With a familiar face. A man with a familiar face named James.

Yes, that James.

"What the hell?" He stared at his stained shorts, then me, with the expression on his face looking like he'd been shot.

"Oh man, so sorry. Didn't see you." I picked his spilled cup off the ground. "I'll buy you another one."

"Another coffee?" His voice raised. "How about new shorts?"

I could only say sorry so many times, and in a way, I was glad my shorts got stained, too. At least misery had company. And on the bright side, we both smelled like chocolate chip frappuccino.

James didn't see the bright side. Fire flashed in his pupils, and with an exaggerated huff, he stormed to the bathroom. The bad blood between us got bloodier. The good news, however: at least he wasn't taking off in an airplane, which meant I hadn't missed the flight.

When I entered the gate area, Lola waved and excitedly clapped her hands like a middle school cheerleader. "Pace, you're here! We were all so worried."

I tried making light of the situation. "It's fun living on the edge."

She put her hands on her hips. "Well you almost fell off that edge." Then she opened her arms and hugged me tightly.

When James walked up a few moments later, several team members pointed and giggled at our stained shorts. We must have looked ridiculous. Standing beside each other, we resembled two halves of a spotted cow.

Lola gathered everyone and stood on a chair, like a general

addressing her army. She spoke at her hyperactive best, a bit annoying that early in the morning.

"We're so happy Pace made it," she said. "Luckily, our flight got delayed. Otherwise, he would've been waving goodbye to us."

For the first time, I relaxed and scanned the team's faces. Oddly, Sage wasn't there. Maybe she went to the restroom or grabbed some breakfast. There had to be a logical answer.

A second later, Lola gave it. "Some of you have asked about Sage. I've been holding off until the last minute, hoping her situation would change. But I guess it won't. I got a text from her late last night, saying she broke her arm in a sand soccer tournament yesterday. She was at the emergency room in the early morning hours. Looks like she won't be able to make the trip."

The group groaned in disappointment, and my mouth dropped open. What? Sage wasn't going? The breath left my lungs and my brain couldn't process the information. It felt like someone had spun me around, leaving a swirling room and a knot in my stomach.

"Say a prayer for her." Lola spoke softer. "I know it's upsetting losing a team member, especially one experienced as Sage."

She paused for dramatic effect, then got louder. "But now look at me. Everyone of you look me in the eyes. We're still gonna have a great trip. Guys, we have important work to do. This will be awwwwesome!"

Not exactly an Abraham Lincoln speech, and our sleepy head

nods proved it.

Lola's eyeballs grew bigger and more impassioned. "Obviously, ya'll need some motivation. You know what it's time for? Lola's Word of the Day."

A few group members mumbled.

"Today's word is *Telesthesia*." She adjusted her glasses and scanned our faces. "It means a sensation received at a distance without the normal operation of the senses. When we step off the plane in Leticia, you'll experience sensations you've never dreamed of! Telesthesia!"

The airline gate announcer called forward the Platinum Five-Star Exclusive Gold Members. They passed by with an air of smugness while the rest of us peasants congregated in a winding line, shifting and shuffling for position. The caste system alive and well. Even with the modern technology of flying people in a silver cigar at alarming speeds above the ground, humanity still resembled a cattle herd when trying to board.

After finally calling our zone, we found our seats. I sat at the back of the plane away from the rest of the group, near the bathrooms. Because of purchasing the ticket late, my reward would be the constant flush of the airplane suction toilets. Great. But thankfully, the aisle seat allowed for stretching my long legs.

I gripped the armrest. It was really happening, leaving North Carolina and heading toward the great unknown. With my recent family upheaval, home felt more unknown than the Amazon. Mom and Dad and Cameron… maybe something unexpected could transpire and my parents would get back together. Miracles still happened.

Action stirred at the front of the plane. The attendants stood at the door and motioned someone to come in quickly.

And inside stepped Sage.

Her face glowed and her smile gleamed and when the team saw her, they burst into claps and cheers. I wanted to do the salsa.

She wore a pink cast on her left forearm, but it didn't detract from her glorious entrance. In a strange way it actually enhanced it. Even if she wore a full body cast, my eyes couldn't peel off her; somehow her presence made anything and everything instantly enchanted.

James lifted his hand, and she sat beside him in the empty seat. I'm sure any minute she'd ask about his stained shorts, and then she'd get an earful about me.

Sure enough, a moment later Sage turned around and gazed toward the back of the plane. Our eyes met and she waved. It was only a friendly gesture, but because she actually looked for me, it sent an exhilarating quiver through my liver.

A word came to mind: *Telesthesia*.

Minutes later the plane taxied the runway, then picked up speed, and with a jarring weightlessness the ground faded away.

10

A couple hours later, we landed in Miami for a three-hour layover before our next leg to Bogota, Columbia.

Stepping into the immense concourse, my stomach grumbled since I hadn't eaten any breakfast. Airplane pretzels only go so far.

The Miami terminal bustled with activity and the roar of conversation. It hummed like an eclectic festival of sights and sounds, with throngs of people aglow with sunshine from the vaulted ceilings. Toto, we're not in Kansas anymore.

Larger-than-life wall murals showcased a few of the state's magnificent animals: the West Indian manatee, a humpback whale, the double-crested cormorant, a loggerhead sea turtle. At least the airport wasn't all Donald Duck.

Despite the commercialization of Florida, it offered a limitless playground of wildlife bounty for those who preferred natural adventure over Space Mountain, like an appetizer before the Amazon main meal.

Lola gathered the team in front of the concession area, which was a circular space with walls stretching a hundred feet high. The air wafted a tempting combination of Cinnabon, grilled chicken, and Starbucks.

"There's lots of grub to choose from." She pointed toward the food court. "So eat something and let's meet back here in forty-five minutes." Bouncing back and forth, she barely contained her excitement. "But hurry back. We've got some team-building to do."

The group dispersed and headed in a dozen different directions with Sage closely shadowed by James, a hormonic scud missile ready to intercept any enemy attack. Sad, really.

She waved me over with an invitation to walk with them, but I declined politely, opting to keep a safe distance from Mr. Full-Of-Himself.

Sage had to be flattered that two guys gave her so much attention, but I'm sure she disliked being constantly drooled over. So I dialed it down a notch. The next nine days would offer more opportunities for interaction, and the group would probably soon start fighting like siblings on a station wagon road trip.

I bought pizza and sat at a table by myself, watching the passing humanity parade. You can learn a lot about Homo sapiens over lunch in an international airport. There are the country bumpkin types carrying enough luggage for a Mt. Everest expedition; the high-powered business zoot suits on their phones, finalizing that Hong Kong deal; or the folks who dress for air travel like people visiting Walmart at midnight, wearing flip flops and too-short pajama pants.

But most curious of all were the parents leading their kids on leashes, as if these otherwise normal grown-ups were saying, “I give up. Where's the nearest margarita?” Only in America do people carry their dogs and walk their children. A sure sign of the apocalypse.

An airport security guy on a Segway zipped back and forth, patrolling the area like a Secret Service agent wannabe, and judging from his I’ve-got-acid-reflux facial expression, he majored in food court protection. *Eat your egg rolls in peace, people*. All he needed were rainbow tassels hanging from his handlebars and a pair of bronze nunchucks. I wondered how many jokes he heard about Paul Blart the mall cop, and then marveled at how evolution developed us from hunter-gatherers to pot-bellied men riding motorized dollies.

After crushing three huge pizza slices, I met the group back at our waiting area with a Mango Tango Chiller smoothie in hand. And after swallowing a gulp, a jackhammer drilled inside my head.

Brain freeze.

Stanley once taught me the scientific term for brain freeze: “*Sphenopalatine Ganglioneuralgia*.” He made me repeat it a hundred times before I finally memorized it, and he loved saying how the brain operates twenty-four hours a day but only stops for two things: brain freeze and falling in love.

I glanced at Sage, radiant in her white high-waisted shorts and a green tank top, leaning back in the pleather chair with her arms wrapped around her knees. Her perfectly toned legs were guarded by the imposing arm cast that offered a subtle warning for anyone stupid enough to mess with her. Talk about a hot roller-derby chick.

More brain freeze. My head continued tingling, as if someone tickled the inside of my skull with a feather duster. Stanley said the only way to get rid of brain freeze was by warming the roof of the mouth with your tongue. It didn't work.

An open seat beckoned beside Sage, and when I sat beside her, she straightened and smiled.

I pointed to her cast. "Sorry about your arm."

"Yeah, kind of a bummer. Broke it playing soccer."

"I've never broken a bone. A few stitches, but that's all."

"It's my third broken bone. All playing sports."

"Maybe you should consider tiddlywinks or cross stitching."

She shrugged. "No guts, no glory. At least I scored. And played the rest of the game."

"So you broke a bone and still scored?

"Competitive to a fault."

"I once went swimming with my goggles full of water."

"I love guys who take risks."

"Yeah, besides my annual running with the bulls and scuba diving with sharks, I also juggle chainsaws."

She gave me a cute *whatever* look.

I smiled. "My actual hobby is weightlifting."

Sage glanced at my biceps. "Yeah, I can tell. Nice."

I changed the subject. "Lola didn't think you'd make the trip because of your injury."

"She knows me better than that. I wouldn't miss this for the world. Broken arm or not."

"So what made you want to come back to the Amazon?"

"Oh, that's easy — the kids." Her eyes flickered. "They'll grab your heartstrings. Wish I could bring them all back home with me."

"So they could play some of your bone-breaking contact sports? Maybe tackle football?"

"No, rugby." She lifted her cast. "Who needs pads?"

Not only was she hot, but funny, too. "By the way, I love your pink cast. A bold fashion choice."

She playfully touched my knee, and her hand lingered for a moment. "It's Armani. A girl's gotta look good." She flashed her deep brown eyes. "You need to sign it."

Digging into her backpack, she pulled out a permanent marker. "It's like getting a temporary tattoo."

"Then I better not screw it up." I thought for a moment before writing:

A BROKEN ARM NEVER LOOKED SO GOOD. *Pace*

She read it and covered her face in mock embarrassment. "I love it."

And then a pair of big feet invaded the space in front of my chair: James's feet.

"Bro, hate telling you this." His voice sounded gruff and unfriendly. "But you're in my seat."

I straightened in the chair.

Oh no he didn't.

11

I'd had it with James. With plenty of other open chairs, he was seriously cramping my style.

"Did you reserve this chair?" I felt my face redden. "Are we still in kindergarten?"

He seemed taken aback. "I went to grab a drink." Then he pointed under the seat. "That's my stuff."

Sure enough, his carry-on duffel bag sat underneath. A million ugly thoughts ran through my brain, but I took the high road.

"Fine." I rose from the chair. "Since I still feel bad about the coffee."

During our exchange, Sage had quietly slipped away and sat beside another girl. When James noticed, his face showed clear disappointment.

I motioned to his lonely chair with a tinge of justice. "It's all yours, enjoy."

I found a new seat a few feet away, and Lola stood in the middle of everyone — eight of us, all college students — and made us say our names and a few things about ourselves. I'm terrible at remembering names but much better at inventing nicknames.

These were the initial impressions of our group, using my best Sherlock Holmes deduction skills:

Lola Carlson ("Da Mom")
Our fearless, ADHD team leader stuck in a time warp circa 1995; a mother hen with an affinity toward fanny packs and strawberry hard candy; her lack of a mouth filter offered both refreshing and incredibly awkward conversations.

Steve Adams ("Banks")
His face resembled the George Banks character in the Mary Poppins movie; small and wiry and built like a licorice stick; good-looking, but if you put a walrus mustache on him and a stove pipe hat, he'd resemble a suspicious character in a murder mystery who might sprinkle arsenic in your drink; contemplative and intelligent.

John Hester ("Big Country")
Huge, grizzly bear of a guy, but sweet and tender; looked more at home on a tractor than in an airport; easy to imagine he came from a town with a Sweet Potato Festival every October; I swore he smelled faintly of smoked barbecue; he

laughed at everyone's jokes; a guy you wanted to hug.

Sarah Peterson ("Red Goth")
She wore black outfits with bright red low-cut Converse sneakers; her hair shined fire engine red, a pyrotechnic show erupting on top of her head; an unusual beauty; a poet and photographer and introvert; her brooding, artistic vibe seemed more Greenwich Village than North Carolina.

James DeWitt ("Jerk")
My pain in the arse.

Crystal Lowell ("C-Lo")
Loud and boisterous and funny; some naughtiness in her sense of humor; she enjoyed making people a little uncomfortable for her own personal amusement; small in height and with a flair for fashion; a take-charge, over-the-top personality, like a firecracker going off in a room.

Sage Collins ("Sage" is beautiful without a nickname)
If I stood alone in the middle of a golden barley field, she'd be my cool country breeze.

I felt like an outsider, brand-new with this church missions stuff and fearful of becoming the flat tire of the group. How would our hodgepodge gang gel together? If we were a band, they'd call us Lola and the Traveling Misfits.

"It's time to play Would You Rather." Lola rubbed her hands together. "I'll ask you a question and you choose an answer. But make sure to give some reasoning."

She started with C-Lo. "Would you rather get a tattoo on the side of your face or go topless on live TV for five minutes?"

C-Lo answered like she had addressed the question a hundred times before. "I'm not against tattoos, and if someone wants one on their face, fine, it's their body. But my face is a business card, and since I plan to be a lawyer one day, the judges wouldn't take too highly to a tatted-up forehead. So I'd choose the topless TV. And though I'm not for the sexploitation of women, it's just boobs, people. Guys go topless, why can't the ladies? Free the tatas. Five minutes and it's over, but a tattoo is permanent."

"But with the internet, your exposed boobs would be permanent, too," Banks said. "And would a judge think too highly of a porno lawyer?"

C-Lo cocked her head. "For a few judges, it might be in my favor. They're not angels, you know. I bet some of those old geezers go commando under their robes."

"Alright, alright," Lola interrupted and faced Banks. "Would you rather have the squirts for six months or projectile vomit?"

He looked insulted by the question. “Having diarrhea requires close proximity to a toilet. There’s not always one nearby, so the risk of an embarrassing incident is high. But with projectile vomit, a bathroom isn’t necessarily needed. You could be inside or outside — throw up in a trashcan or bush, for instance — and because it’s projectile, the odds decrease for ruining your clothes or smelling like a sewer system.”

Everyone nodded at his logical explanation. Perhaps he and C-Lo could open their own law firm.

Lola turned to Red Goth. “Would you rather know it all or have it all?”

For the longest time, she didn’t answer, her eyes staring upward in deep thought, like in a coma. A few awkward seconds went by before she spoke.

“Most people would probably answer ‘know it all,’ but that would be dangerous. Could the human brain truly contain knowledge of all things? Would the collective weight of intellectual and moral cognition bring happiness or a curse to a person? But ‘having it all’ could be easily shared and enjoyed, meeting the practical needs of people and bringing the world together as a unified village. No one likes a know-it-all but everyone loves a generous giver.”

“But if you know it all,” James said, “you could cure cancer and stop wars. Material things aren’t as powerful as possessing knowledge, even if your head exploded in the process."

"*Auribus teneo lupum.*" Red Goth blinked. "It means, 'Holding a wolf by the ears.' It's a situation where doing nothing and doing something to solve it are equally risky. Problems are best solved communally instead of individually."

"Hmmm... deep thoughts." Lola shook her head. "This year's team waxes philosophical. So, James, would you rather fart popcorn or have your breath smell like burnt flesh for the rest of your life?"

He straightened. "I think it's possible to hide the popcorn in your pants, depending on the amount of gas. But bad breath ends all hopes of a social life. Plus, I could get rich and famous making popcorn out of my butt."

The group laughed, and it marked the first time I witnessed James's sense of humor.

Lola looked at Sage. "Would you rather find true love or get ten million dollars?"

"True love," she answered quickly. "Love is infinitely more powerful than all the money in the world. You can't take money with you when you die, but you can take love."

That's my girl. I lost myself gazing at her, swept into the kaleidoscopic swirl of her hypnotic spell and wondering how heaven sculpted such a perfect creature.

"Pace? Hello, Pace?"

"Huh?" I answered, snapped from fantasyland by Lola's voice.

"Pace, would you rather save ten thousand people — but nobody would know — or save ten thousand people, die in the process, but become a legendary hero?"

I said the first thing that popped in my head, which is usually the most honest answer. "I'm not really interested in being a hero. If I perform a great deed, people don't need to know about it, with the exception of my parents. After disappointing them a lot lately, I'd like to make them proud."

"Well bless your heart, that's so sweet." Lola walked to Big Country and placed a hand on his round shoulder. "Last question. Would you rather fight a shark or fight a lion?"

He scooted toward the edge of his chair. "Definitely fight a shark. Contrary to popular thought, punching a shark in the nose doesn't work. It's better punching at the eyes and gills, they're the most sensitive. But lions are killing machines. They've earned the name, 'King of the Jungle' for a reason. I'd go for Jaws over Mufasa any day."

After meandering tangents of conversation, the time quickly slipped away and our connecting flight started boarding. Lola wanted a group photo using her phone, so she gathered everyone behind her for what she called a "Facie." We tried telling her the correct term was "Selfie," but she didn't seem to care.

The three-and-a-half hour flight to Bogota was pleasant and

uneventful, and after a brief layover in Colombia, we boarded our last flight to Leticia, Amazonas.

Almost there.

12

Finally, Leticia.

The capital of the Colombian port of Amazonas and neighbor to the Brazilian city of Tabatinga. Leticia and Tabatinga are really just one big city with an international border running through the middle. Believe me, geography becomes more interesting when you travel.

We took a bumpy bus ride to our hotel. The bus was cheapest for a group our size, but it was fun watching the small mototaxis — covered three-wheeled tricycle-type vehicles — whirl around us looking for other needy tourists.

I pressed my nose on the glass, excited about being in a new country, but the darkness made it hard to see except for the blur of trees and nondescript buildings. Not very exciting. The rain had stopped, but pockets of muddy water littered the dirt roads causing gigantic sloshes and splatters every time the tires hit a divot.

Around midnight we unloaded at our little hotel, which resembled more of a bed and breakfast. Perfect for a one night stay. Well-maintained and lighted, and only three blocks from the river docks, it shined with bright yellow exterior walls and a host of small gardens. It would make a great postcard for South America.

Though just eight of us, we brought enough baggage for at least twenty since we hauled extra boxes and suitcases of donated pharmaceutical and medical supplies.

It wasn't as hot as expected during the unloading, in part because of the recent rain, but Lola told us the temperature would rise to nearly ninety degrees during the day. Something about equatorial humidity.

She also warned of the potential of missing luggage and confiscations by customs, but remarkably, everything made it. Except for James's stuff. His suitcase never showed up at baggage claim, but the airline promised they would find and deliver it to the hotel by early morning. He could manage one night without too much difficulty.

Ironic that we carried thousands of sanitized latex gloves while he had to wear funky underwear. I loved it.

As we entered the small lobby, a Colombian couple probably in their fifties, stood behind the front desk dancing and lip-synching to a radio. They sang an old Michael Jackson song without a care in the world, and we watched for a moment, laughing.

Then Lola let out a happy scream and bounced toward them with her legendary energy. The three hugged in joy.

She turned to us. “These are my dear friends, Carlos and Lorena. They own this hotel and have hosted our teams for years. They’ve graciously agreed to cook us a late dinner. So go freshen up in your rooms and meet back here in twenty minutes.”

Dinner at twelve thirty in the morning? Worked for me. Though physically exhausted from the long travel, everyone caught a second wind.

And why not? We were in Leticia, the southernmost city of Colombia and a major port on the Amazon River, the springboard to the legendary jungle all around us.

I dropped my luggage in a room shared with Big Country.

The space was minimalistic but comfortable, with white ceramic tiles covering the walls. No chocolates on the pillows, but no worries. On the wall behind the beds hung decorative multicolored poles with hooks on the end, spread in a fan-like shape.

Big Country noticed me staring at them. “The best fishing in the world right here. I’d love to catch some piranha, just for bragging rights.”

Oh, yes, the piranha. We weren't at Silver Lake anymore. I couldn't wait to catch a glimpse of those small predators, so legendary for their vicious feeding habits.

"I wonder what they taste like?"

His eyes grew big. "I hear fried piranha is delicious."

I ran my hand across one of the pole handles. "I've read they're not too hard to catch, but definitely intimidating. When they're taken out of the water their eyes turn red and they growl."

"Sounds like the last girl I dated." He fake-punched my arm.

The room felt stuffy so we opened a large window. The hotel had no air-conditioning, but the ceiling fan and night breeze cooled it down.

Sitting on the bed, I checked my phone, surprised that the hotel offered free wifi. The speed was painstakingly slow, so I gave up. Good riddance, if you ask me.

After slipping into a pair of clean shorts, I walked with Big Country back to the lobby and into an outdoor garden area radiating under the Colombian night sky. Several round tables awaited, each with a flickering candle, and surrounding us in the trees rose the chatter of friendly birds. Sounded like parakeets. Already, I dug the Amazon vibe.

A hotel employee cooked in an adjoining kitchen, accompanied by the fizzle and pop of a skillet. It didn't take long to smell meat grilling.

The rest of the team slowly made their way to the tables, most everyone tapping on their phones, desperately trying to text family or post pics. But one by one, they discarded the phones out of frustration. A bunch of twenty-somethings without the internet for twelve days. It could turn into *Lord of the Flies.*

I sat between Red Goth and Big Country and marveled at how they couldn't be more polar opposites, both in style and personality. Our team definitely had diverse characters.

Then C-Lo, sitting at another table, spoke loud enough for everyone to hear. "How cool were those mototaxi thingees? I want to ride in one before we leave."

"You might not believe this — " Lola's breath got fast. "But I've often dreamed of quitting real estate and moving here. Driving a mototaxi as a job."

"Your dream job is driving a rickshaw?" Banks asked.

"Why not?" she blurted, defensive. "A dream job doesn't have to make a lot of money. It's simply a means to an end. Then on my days off I'd endlessly explore the villages along the Amazon."

Then Lola's eyes grew big, in the way only hers could. "Hey, that's a great question: what is *your* dream job everyone?"

Banks head snapped up. "I'm studying to be an accountant. But I dream of being a pro poker player. Sleep all day and work at night. If you're good, you can make some serious cashola. And I like the energy of a casino."

Lola made a face. “You don’t strike me as the Ocean’s Eleven type.”

“Yeah, more like the 403(b) type,” C-Lo snorted.

Banks shrugged. “Hey, it’s sexy when financials reconcile.”

“Professional golfing for me.” James spoke matter-of-factly. “I’m all about jet-setting to tropical locales and wearing cool clothes. With golf, you can play for years, much longer than contact sports. And when you get old, just join the senior league.”

C-Lo wrinkled her nose. “You, wearing a pair of plaid golf knickers?”

“Hopefully ones without a coffee stain,” Lola said.

Everyone laughed, and James gave an annoyed smile. Without his luggage, he still wore stained shorts.

Red Goth spoke barely above a whisper, fiddling with her fork the entire time. “I don’t care about money or fame, but I do care about our planet. I’d like to work for a conservation group that protects millions of acres of ecologically important land in Australia. It’s like PETA, except you defend the earth.”

James stretched his neck closer, showing interest. “Why Australia?”

“Lots of reasons.” She stared upward, in thought. “Amazing cities and beautiful beaches. The Outback.”

“I love Outback.” Big Country spoke with his drawl. “Their Bloomin' Onion is amazing. Ever tried dipping it in honey butter?”

C-Lo jumped back into the conversation, not that she ever stayed quiet for long. “I say don’t focus on a dream job, but focus on the dream guy. Hopefully someone rich. Then you won’t have to work.”

James’s forehead crinkled. “So basically your dream job is to be a gold digger?”

She tossed her ponytail. “Honey, if I don’t dig, somebody else will.”

“What happened to you being a lawyer?” Lola asked.

“I’d rather be eye candy for some rich guy.” C-Lo’s expression didn’t change. “That way, I could spend my days in a spa rather than in a boring court room.”

Banks threw his hands up. “At least the girl has goals.”

“My heart is for kids.” Sage spoke gently, in a calming way. “I hope to be a physical therapist for disabled children. The right treatment could change their lives forever.”

“Wow. Your job makes ours look pathetic,” James said.

She grinned. “It’s all I’ve ever wanted to do.”

“You should be anointed for sainthood.” C-Lo leaned forward on the table, face resting in her hands. “Sister Sage has a nice ring to it.”

“I didn’t mean it that way.” Sage shook her head and blushed a little, which looked entirely sexy, in a saintly type of way.

“My dream job is to continue the family roofing business,” said

Big Country, adjusting his faded baseball cap. “I’ve been laying roof ever since I could climb a ladder. A close second would be a professional bass fisherman, for much the same reasons as James with golf, but without the knickers.”

I didn’t get a chance to answer — even though I would’ve said either animal biologist or tour manager for Sonic Lobotomy, my favorite band — because at that moment Carlos and Lorena walked to the front of our tables, looking excited to tell us something.

13

Carlos commanded a room without even trying.

A stout man with a barrel chest and bushy eyebrows, his jovial face looked ready to tell a thousand stories. In America he would've resembled a smooth car salesman with his slicked back graying hair, but in Colombia he appeared dignified and patriarchal.

Beside him, Lorena stood tall and skinny; a woman created for sundresses. She wore a flower in her hair and a constant smile on her face, exuding an air of unruffled hospitality. More understated than Carlos, she seemed like the sturdy compass to his wild spontaneity. They touched each other constantly, affectionately, like newlyweds.

"A toast to the team." Carlos held a glass and spoke with smooth English. "We welcome you to Leticia and to the wonder of the Amazon."

He raised the glass to his mouth, and we lifted the water bottles from our tables. Lorena drank from Carlos's cup while we followed with gulps from our own.

“We’d like to sing a song for you.” Lorena’s speaking voice contained a soothing melody to it. “It’s an old tune with lyrics as deep as the jungle. The words are on your table if you want to follow along.”

They harmonized in a beautiful, almost haunting, Spanish duet:

Sing to me, my bambuco
Of open eternal Colombia
Aperladitas and delicacies
Mountains rising like breaths
Proud to be born in my country

Speak to me, bandoneon
With pewter inhaling the harvest skies
Liana hearts and emerald plateaus
Ancient souls like brandys
Proud to die in my country

Carlos sang with his arm around Lorena’s waist, and when they finished, he kissed her. We all applauded.

“Now for tonight’s meal.” Carlos clapped his hands twice, and on cue, the cook carried plates to our tables containing crepe-like pancakes.

"This is Casabe, a yuca tortilla." He pointed to the dish. "It's a popular street food which many eat for breakfast. Perfect for this time of night. Light but filling. Enjoy!"

Lola prayed over the meal, and then I dug in, a little disappointed that the first bite tasted leathery and flavorless. Maybe it was an acquired palette. But after some chewing it got gradually better, and by the end, I thoroughly enjoyed it.

After dinner, Lola stood from her chair and checked her watch. "It's late and everyone needs rest. We're scheduled to be on the boat at ten in the morning, so meet back here at nine thirty. And I recommend taking a long shower since it will be your last one for a few days. Believe me, this group is gonna take stink to a whole 'nother level."

Banks swirled his cup, clanking the ice. "Where exactly are we going tomorrow?"

"A long way down the river," she answered. "Pastor Jose selected a few villages that really need our help. We'll join up with him and some other teams on the boat. Probably about thirty of us all together. A merry, floating band of missionaries."

"Are the villages dangerous?" C-Lo asked.

"Girl, this whole trip is dangerous." Lola angled her head. "And that's why you need to abide by my three non-negotiable rules: Rule one: Do exactly what Jose says. Rule Two: Never, ever, go anywhere alone. And Rule Three: If in doubt, repeat Rules One and

Two. Ignore those rules and the Amazon may swallow you whole."

She placed her hands on her hips. "Now let's make like sheep and get the flock out of here!"

My body ached with fatigue, but I couldn't sleep.

As a child, my family vacationed in Myrtle Beach and often arrived at night when the ocean couldn't be seen. I remembered struggling to fall asleep knowing the big blue Atlantic waited outside the hotel walls, concealed by darkness yet breathing its rhythmic roar.

Some things never changed. After a full day traveling inside a cramped, pressurized airline cabin, I felt like that little boy again. Especially with the great Amazon River snaking somewhere beyond my door, whispering in its ancient language and motioning me closer. Since childhood, the river had captured my imagination; all I needed was a quick look, fifteen or twenty minutes max.

At one thirty in the morning, I decided to explore. Big Country wouldn't know. His snores shook the walls like the combination of a lumberjack felling a redwood and two horny alpacas fighting to the death. I grabbed the binoculars. Though dark outside, they might come in handy.

Minutes later, I walked out the front lobby door and into the hazy, sleeping streets of Leticia. The city offered perfect terrain for exploring by foot, with empty parks and quiet roadways. An adventurer's dream.

Everything was closed, but in a few hours the streets would bustle with hawkers, backpackers, and money exchangers. Leticia wasn't the cleanest place, though; the roads overflowed with discarded trash, and broken concrete lay in piles beside small homes and businesses.

Nearing the docks, it felt like entering a bizarre upside down world, a final outpost of civilization. I took a deep breath. A damp smell hovered around and through me, as if the rainforest crouched with its underbelly over my head, a primeval jungle cat toying with its prey.

Then I saw it, glimmering as oil, under a dark sky and bright moon: this river called the Amazon.

Its water lapped against the moored boats, seductively licking the river taxis and dugout canoes, reminding sailors that she was the one in control, not them. Though it flowed docile, I knew the river later turned treacherous, transforming into monster rapids and cataracts, its banks stretching across South America like the world's largest roller coaster.

Everything I ever read about the Amazon River came back in a dizzying stream of consciousness: four thousand miles long, containing more water than any other river, and flowing through the world's largest tropical rain forest; a width of one-and-a-half to six miles, with an average depth of forty feet and descending in some areas to three hundred; scientists estimated it at a hundred and forty million years old.

My body shivered as I knelt and placed a hand in the water with a mixture of fear and wanderlust, almost worshipful, showing reverence in the presence of such untamed power. What dangers lurked beneath the water's surface?

It's a strange feeling being alone in a foreign country, covered by the dark of night and standing near something so terrible. Perhaps I should have been more careful.

All around me was an ecosystem of tarantulas and bats and snakes and piranha, sloths and toucans and crocs, the soundtrack of birdsongs, the resilient histories of indigenous peoples, ghost town villages, maze-like deltas, and canyons and badlands. And all of it sustained by the mystical hand of a copper-colored waterway more dangerous than any man or beast, representing nature in its wildest state.

The place kicked some serious butt.

A man sat on the dock shore, a good distance away, illuminated under the moonlight. A fisherman. A closer look through the binoculars revealed he was mending a net, pulling and tying nylon fibers to stitch the various rips and holes.

On the river, a two-story container ship lugged forward, close to the shore. The vessel seemed empty of crew except for one man standing on the port side of the bottom level, hands on his hips.

His boat drifted in front of my view, its masthead light glowing a dull orange. The light-skinned man had a square jaw and prominent cheekbones, and he wore a white panama fedora hat. He stared at me with peculiar interest, in a threatened way, like I shouldn't be there.

Instinctively, I swiveled the binoculars back toward the fisherman, but he was gone. Something felt wrong. Time to get moving.

And then angry Spanish filled my ears.

I turned with a jolt. The fisherman stood close and in a combative stance. He looked native to the area with his brown skin and short salt and pepper hair, his skin weathered due to years on the water.

A string of sharp words fell from his mouth, and I heard the word *gringo*.

Over his shoulder and down the shore three men rushed forward, appearing out of the shadows.

The fisherman had friends.

Oh crap.

14

I considered running, but that would make me look guilty.

So I decided to explain myself and hope someone understood English. If that plan didn't work, the only remaining option was to fight. Though outnumbered, I was bigger. But what if they carried weapons?

Lifting my hands, I showed my innocence. "I don't speak Spanish. No Espanol. I'm just a tourist."

No response. The fisherman got aggressive, inched closer, and pushed my shoulders. He smacked at the binoculars hanging from my neck, then brandished a knife in his hand.

He lifted the blade to my face with a sadistic smile as the other men approached and cornered me, a hungry pack of lions ready to attack.

Code Red. I had a feeling things weren't going to end well.

And then, from behind, a loud horn sounded several times. A rickshaw squealed to a stop beside the dock, and Lola jumped out wearing her pajamas. Carlos followed from the driver's seat.

Spanish erupted from Lola's mouth with machine gun speed, and the men stepped back, startled by her verbal stampede.

Carlos yelled something, too, and I heard the word *policia.*

Shouting went back and forth for a few moments, but the four men finally backed away. Whatever Lola and Carlos said apparently worked.

The fisherman pointed at me with a snarled lip, then spit on the ground by my feet. He spoke to the other men, and they grumbled while retreating into the darkness.

Meanwhile, beside us on the river, the boat chugged away. The man wearing the white fedora had disappeared and the vessel looked completely empty, a ghost ship fading into a black hole.

"Let's move." Carlos hurried to the mototaxi. "Now."

We hustled into the vehicle and sped away, as fast as possible in a three-wheeler. Carlos drove and Lola and I sat side-by-side on the back seat.

"I'm so sorry." My voice trembled from the adrenaline. "I only wanted to see the river."

"The river dock isn't the place to be at night." Carlos made a sharp right turn. "You're very lucky."

Lola grabbed my hand. "We have rules for a reason. Never, ever go anywhere alone. Do it again and I'll personally give you a beat down."

"Yes, ma'am." I turned toward her with guilty eyes. "But I don't understand what happened. What did I do to bother them?"

"You encroached on their territory." Carlos turned left into a narrow street, and the vehicle made a straining sound. "Wrong place and wrong time."

I stared out the window, the night breeze hitting my face. "Were they doing something illegal?"

"A big percentage of Tabatinga is involved in drug trafficking," he said. "Tons of cocaine get moved through these parts annually. Arms trafficking, too."

"I'd bet my butt there was something fishy on the boat that passed us." Lola pointed a finger in my face. "And it had nothing to do with fishing."

"There *was* a creepy guy on that boat." I pictured the white fedora and cold stare. "He gave me the heebie jeebies. And he didn't look local."

Carlos nodded. "Russian criminals operate here. Geographically, this is the perfect place. They're closer to the drugs and arms dealers. And from Brazil, it's easier moving their shipments to Europe and eventually into Russia."

"What would they have done to me?" I didn't really want to know the answer.

Lola pat my knee. "You have a pretty face. But after they were through, it wouldn't have been so pretty."

It took a moment for their words to settle in. A Russian

criminal syndicate. I was almost a byline on a police report. NCIS: Leticia.

"Crime syndicates oversee the smuggling schemes." Carlos glanced at us through the rear view mirror. "They use both the skies and our water. There's a lot of security in the area, but they're outnumbered by the bad guys. The checkpoints are laughable. The city borders are virtually non-existent, and criminals easily move from one country to another."

He pulled beside the hotel and shut the engine off. "More groups mean more violence. And it's about protecting their territory. So they seek out poor, desperate families — locals, like those fishermen — and pay them to run interference."

"Those guys were lookouts?" I'd never considered it.

"Yeah, and you looked odd to them," Carlos turned and faced me. "A young man, all by himself, watching with binoculars. They got nervous. And when they get nervous they do dangerous things."

"Promise me you'll never walk off like that again." Lola lowered her chin, eyes peering up. "Next time, they won't scare so easily."

"What did you say to them?" I asked.

Carlos laughed. "Lola has a way with words. Colorful words. No matter the language."

"Crazy women scare men." A look of pride washed over her

face. "Works with all nationalities."

"I recognized a couple of those men." Carlos shook his head. "Bad apples. And believe me, I've seen all types of things when I've been on my boat at night."

"You have a boat?" The guy had a hotel, a rickshaw, and a boat. Did he have a bat cave somewhere?

"Most everyone here has one. I've grown up on this river and know every twist and turn. Boating is my favorite hobby."

We stepped from the vehicle and walked into the hotel lobby. Empty, since it was so late.

"That's enough adventure for me tonight." Carlos rubbed his eyes. "This old man needs some rest. Sleep safe, my friends." Then he looked at me. "And that means stay in your bed!"

"Yes, sir."

With a wave, he disappeared behind a lobby door, leaving me and Lola standing by ourselves.

"I didn't know you could speak Spanish," I said.

"There's a lot of things you don't know about me. For instance, I have a third degree black belt."

My mouth dropped open. "You have a black belt in karate?"

"Taekwondo. And don't sound so surprised."

"I mean, you're just not the typical-looking..." I could feel myself digging a hole. "...you know, martial arts person."

She stared with Bruce Lee eyes. "Looks are deceiving. I could kill you right now with just two fingers. And I'm tempted, believe me."

I believed her.

"So why did you walk out there by yourself?" Lola put her hands on her hips. "What were you thinking?"

"I wasn't thinking. Just got caught up in the excitement of being here. No one else has ever done this?"

"None that came back alive."

I hoped she was joking. "Sorry," I mumbled.

Her expression softened. "Pace, I care about your safety and the safety of this team. Remember, we're not in North Carolina anymore."

North Carolina. My parents. Cameron. School. Something got triggered on the inside. "It seems whether I'm in Carolina or the Amazon, I always find a way to screw things up."

Lola stepped closer and grabbed my arm. "Listen to me, young man. You're not a screw up. You understand?"

I nodded.

"But you are hardheaded."

I half-smiled. "It's not the first time someone's described me that way."

"Learn from me. Hardheaded is not the way to live, but it sure is a good way to die." Her face didn't show anger, but rather a deep disappointment. Guilt filled my chest. I'd rather make someone angry than disappoint them.

I fiddled with the binoculars. "How did you know to come for me?"

"After talking late with Carlos and Lorena, I got back to the room and took one last look out of the window. That's when I saw you walking away. By the time I found my shoes, you had a big head start. Carlos was kind enough to help find you. And in the nick of time."

"I'm still wondering what you said to those fishermen."

Her eyes flashed fire. "Let's just say I warned them about *telesthesia*. If they didn't back off from you, they would experience sensations they had never dreamed of!"

I bent down and hugged her. "Thank you."

"No, thank God you're not hurt. And get ready for the rest of this trip. You haven't seen nothing yet."

15

"Today's word of the day is *diapause*."

Lola stood in the outside atrium with our gathered team at nine thirty in the morning. "It means dormancy between periods of activity."

She cast a quick glance toward me. "Last night was supposed to be a dormant period before activity kicks off."

I rubbed my heavy eyes. No one else knew about last night's events, and I planned on keeping it that way. When I had finally slid into bed, my brain raced and it took forever to fall asleep. At least another five hours of sleep would have been nice.

The rest of the team appeared weary but excited. Everyone was present except James, who left earlier with Lorena to buy clothes since his suitcase never arrived. We all felt sorry for him, except me. He could be a real jerk, so suffering through dirty Fruit of the Looms seemed like karma.

But enough about James. My eyes focused on Sage.

After all the travel, she still looked fresh as the Brazilian morning dew, and with the backdrop of green foliage surrounding her, she glowed iridescent, wearing a metallic top, black denim shorts, and leather sandals. Amazon goddess perfection.

After a prayer, Lola led us on a walk toward the docks to meet our leader, Jose, and the other teams.

Leticia looked completely different in the daytime. The roads choked with a gluttony of motorbikes and scooters, growling with revved motors and blowing horns, all zipping past the markets which were stocked with fish and fruits and live chickens. The heart of the city bustled like a miniature Times Square.

The signage of countless souvenir shops crowded the sightline in bright reds, greens, and blues. Marketplace stores snuggled close together, an outdoor mall with endless rows of rolled-up metal doors and gnarled painted wood. And so many restaurants. Looking around, I realized one could enjoy breakfast in Colombia, lunch in Peru, and dinner in Brazil. The wonders of Tres Fronteras.

Drawing closer to the water, a mishmashed line of thatched bungalows nestled beside the shoreline. Scattered in the river were boats of different colors and sizes, with men loading fishing vessels and families bobbing in bamboo rafts.

The jungle canopy surrounded the river like fur lining and tantalized explorers to go deeper, ever deeper, so the rainforest could swallow travelers with its insatiable appetite. Just another day in the mouth of the mighty Amazon.

"It's so hot my butt's sweating," C-Lo said, walking beside me.

I didn't skip a beat. "Then I'll start calling you hot ass."

She paused for a step, seeming shocked that someone dared go head-to-head with her borderline humor. Then she laughed. "That's pretty good. I officially like you, Pace."

"You officially have good taste." I smiled and stared ahead at the river. "Look at this place. It's amazing. I get goosebumps thinking about the history of this water."

"All I want to do is jump in that water." She wiped the sweat from her forehead. "Want to join me for a quick skinny dip?"

I called her bluff. "Rather not embarrass the locals with my incredible physique. How about when we get downriver?"

She narrowed her eyes. "I'll hold you to it."

"If the indigenous tribes walk around buck naked, why can't we?"

"Two words: mosquito bites." Then she pointed ahead. "Look, I think that might be Jose on our boat."

Twenty-five yards away awaited a white three-story riverboat, like something out of a Mark Twain novel. The name, "Conquista," painted bright red, sat above a brown hull.

Dozens of people milled along the higher decks, and yellow lifesavers dangled from the upper white railings. Jose stood alone at the lower helm waving toward Lola and our group, with something dark hanging around his neck.

Navigating through the crowds, we walked up the boat ramp and met him at the top. Then I saw it clearly. A large boa constrictor wrapped around his shoulders and neck, but he handled it with ease, completely comfortable, while the snake provided the perfect ice breaker as our team stepped aboard.

"This is Squiggles." Jose adjusted the reptile. "She's a ten foot long momma who recently gave birth to a bouncing baby boa."

He paused. "Get it?"

Bouncing baby boa. It took everyone a second to catch the joke because he didn't smile. A cringe-worthy pun. Which somehow made it funnier.

"We welcome you aboard the Conquista." He spread his arms in a sweeping gesture. "Or as I like calling it, Cirrhosis of the River."

Again, a few groans from the group.

Jose looked to be in his early fifties, only because of his thinning black hair, and he had the build of a Navy Seal, strong and lithe and wiry. Someone you wouldn't want to fight in a back alley.

And despite his winsome personality, the snake slithering around his neck gave him a don't-screw-with-me presence. All I could think of was *Cobra Commander.* His nickname fell into my head like a gift from heaven.

"Jose is the foremost expert on the river and its villages." Lola clasped her hands under her chin. "So listen carefully to what he says."

She pointed to the boat's large steering wheel, where a fake shrunken head sat as a decoration, alluding to the grim history of local headhunters. "Unless you want to end up like that."

The team gathered around Jose — and Squiggles — as he gave the rundown. "Welcome to Leticia. I've already briefed the other teams. We have lots of returnees so the details should go smoothly. And Lola could run the trip by herself."

She backed away. "Just keep that devil worm off my neck."

"You know Squiggles is harmless." Jose rubbed his scaly pet. "Unless he's hungry."

Footsteps clambered up the aluminum ramp and James appeared, out of breath and wearing a bright yellow shirt that read in big blue letters, PROPERTY OF AN AMAZON GIRL. Still wearing his stained shorts, he looked like a walking Colombian flag.

I didn't know whether to laugh or salute him.

Jose continued. "Where we're going, there's no access to technology, showers, electricity, or western toilets. Kind of like parts of North Carolina."

Lola pointed. "Hey, watch it."

"Just checking if you're listening." He smiled. "The villages we'll visit are generally Spanish speaking. But fortunately, we have translators with us, including Lola.

"And remember the river means everything to the villagers.

It's their restroom, bathtub, water supply, and washing machine. Everything they eat is either fished from the river or harvested from the land. But do not eat their food, even if they offer it. Not unless you prefer a nasty stomach bug, or worse, hepatitis. Wouldn't make for a nice postcard home."

Lola interrupted. "We're here to help *them* medically, so you must stay healthy this week. On an earlier trip, I once made the mistake of eating a village meal. Bad decision. I got the back door trots, if you know what I mean. Thunder down under."

I shook my head. TMI, Lola.

"They have no doctors, so you'll see advanced diseases and injuries." Jose clenched his jaw. "Prepare yourself. Also lots of dehydration issues because of the heat and high humidity.

"We've come to change their lives and the lives of their children. We'll offer medical clinics in three different villages. A couple we've been to before, but one we've never visited. Expect some distrust at first. At night, I'll preach to the people and hopefully we'll see good responses. Then maybe we'll celebrate with fireworks and a keg party."

He paused. "Just checking if you're listening."

Lola pointed to Squiggles. "Jose, make sure you warn them about the creatures."

"Oh, yes." His tone turned serious. "Never, ever, venture off by yourself into the surrounding jungle. Unless you want to become a snack. Last year, a local man got drunk, wandered into the jungle, and fell asleep against a tree. When they found him the next morning, it was too late. A large anaconda had wrapped its mouth around him and already swallowed half his body."

Jose patted his reptilian friend. "Of course, Ms. Squiggles would never do that to anyone. Right, Squiggles?"

The snake didn't answer.

"The bottom line is this." He spoke slowly, purposefully. "Fear inaction more than failure. Our actions, though imperfect, can help many people. We must do something. Living with mission means taking someone else's problems as your own. So get some rest. We'll unload this evening when we arrive at the first village and set-up for a full day tomorrow. Prepare to serve hundreds of people."

Lola interjected. "Did you hear what he said, people? Rest! *Diapause*! Enjoy dormancy between periods of activity."

The group dispersed to the upper decks, but I stood staring over the rails. *Fear inaction more than failure*. Jose's words echoed in my ears. For far too many years, I'd lived the opposite way.

For a passing moment, fear washed over me and I longed for home. At least busing tables at Luigi's was safe and predictable whereas the wild and woolly Amazon offered dangers at every turn.

The boat ride would prove to be just the beginning.

16

The riverboat's diesel engine grumbled to life, and we chugged downriver as Carlos and Lorena waved from the docks.

Goodbye, Leticia.

The trip of a lifetime awaited, with the Amazon River serving as our great highway into the unknown. If someone had told me a month earlier that I'd be traveling down the world's most mysterious waterway, it would've been as ridiculous as me joining Cirque du Soleil.

Leticia's boating traffic zigzagged around us: smaller boats growling with their loud outboard engines; larger ships lugging lumber; people rowing in canoes. On the shore, rows of weathered stilt houses stood like silent sentinels and watched over the proceedings as they had for centuries.

But the farther we traveled, the activity faded away, followed by the slow monotony of forest-lined shores.

Up ahead, the thick foliage of the rainforest awaited. My body shuddered as the river sucked us away from civilization. I recalled the scary sensation as a kid when riding my first roller coaster — Satan's Sphincter — with the slow uphill climb causing more anxiety than the stomach-turning mega hill. The riverboat trip felt strangely the same.

Soon, the jungle surrounded us. At times, the giant trees blocked the sun and covered our entire boat in shade for long stretches. The bugs drove me crazy, so I sprayed my arms and legs until they felt sticky. At least the breeze brought relief. With each passing minute, the air smelled more like a vast greenhouse, the fragrance of rich soil and moist vegetation.

I thought about the video on YouTube: the Sea Creature and the upturned boat. The *Conquista* looked eerily similar, and I imagined the sheer terror of a capsized riverboat of this size, especially with a dangerous monster somewhere in the water. Back home, the Sea Creature story sounded absurd, but in the Amazon it seemed all too real, and entirely possible. Too late to turn back. I was strapped in, and the roller coaster hill awaited.

Walking to the upper levels, I discovered an assortment of hanging hammocks, perfect for a breezy nap. Many were already occupied by members of the other teams, some from California and others from Tennessee. I introduced myself to several and found them to be hardcore volunteers. If they were nervous or afraid, they sure didn't show it.

They were older than our team members, middle-aged and

primarily doctors, nurses, and dentists. No surprise, since they carried themselves with purpose, and being in their midst motivated me to do more with my life.

But I hoped they didn't ask about my occupation. *Luigi busboy* didn't carry the same panache as an orthodontist or a family practitioner. So I decided on a new way to describe my job: sanitary waste engineer in the catering industry. But no one asked.

Eyes burning with lack of sleep, I found an open hammock on the third level and lay down for a quick rest. The engine hummed a lulling soundtrack, inviting a peaceful slumber.

I woke two and a half hours later. Rolling off the hammock, I noticed the sun had inched further across the sky. Mid-afternoon. But the scenery seemed unchanged with more dense trees and empty shorelines. I hoped to see monkeys swinging from the limbs or pygmy tribes brandishing spears, but none could be found. Just miles and miles of more greenery.

I ate a peanut butter and jelly sandwich then walked down to the second level. And there stood Sage, by herself, leaning against the rail. Finally, something interesting to look at.

Since James napped on the third level, it was an ideal time to talk with her. Plus, she had nowhere else to go. A captive audience, as they say.

When she saw me, her eyes sparkled. "Glad you're finally awake. I walked by your hammock and you were snoring."

I turned my head, doubtful. “Come on. Really?”

“I couldn’t tell which was louder. Your snoring or the boat’s engine.”

I laughed. “Sometimes I dream I’m Lightning McQueen driving in the Piston Cup Championship.”

“Your pistons were definitely firing.”

“I’m sure you snore sometimes.”

“Ladies don’t snore. We purr.”

I studied the slowly passing trees. “This view makes me want to sing ‘Welcome To The Jungle.’”

“Guns and Roses.”

I turned toward her, surprised. “Slash’s guitar solo in ‘Sweet Child of Mine’ is my favorite of all time.”

Sage nodded. “Van Halen’s ‘Eruption’ is a close second.”

She was already the perfect human specimen, but her knowledge of eighties tunes launched her into revered status. “What about Jimi Hendrix?” I poked a little further.

“Technically, he’s the sixties.”

Man, she was good. “Do you have a favorite eighties love song?” I asked.

“That's easy. ‘Will You Still Love Me?’ By Chicago.”

I nodded. “A classic.”

“How about you?”

“I’d say ‘Honestly’ by Stryper.”

She smiled. “Definitely in my top five.”

“Okay, you passed the test.” I gave a teasing look. “My dad taught me all those old songs. He called the eighties the golden age.”

“My dad, too. Whenever he was around.”

“Did he travel a lot?”

“Yeah, to other bedrooms.”

Her abruptness startled me, and she mentioned it matter of factly, like she had made peace with it. “After the last affair,” she said, “he came home and announced he was leaving. That was several years ago. Haven’t seen him much since.”

I imagined what it must have felt like growing up without a dad. And what kind of father could ignore Sage, such an intelligent and beautiful creation?

She looked to the side, over my shoulder. “We moved to Carolina three years ago, to be near family. Now it’s just me and mom. My older brother is married. But we’re still cleaning up the family mess.”

“That sucks.” I turned and leaned back on the rails, my foot propped on the lower rung. “My parents announced their separation right before this trip. The moving trucks are probably at my house as we speak. So being a few thousand miles away is kinda nice.”

“As long as you don’t get killed on the Amazon docks at night.”

I paused. "How do you know about that?"

"I shared a room with Lola last night. Couldn't fall asleep so I watched her come and go. She told me all the details when she got back. Keeping secrets is not her strength."

"Yeah, I was stupid. It could've been bad."

Sage rested her pink cast on top of my hand before moving it away. "But thankfully you didn't get hurt. That would've ruined your trip, real fast." She looked away for a moment, then turned back. "By the way, I'm glad we met at Silver Lake. I still laugh about it."

"Not my smoothest moment."

"But it was so endearing." She bit her lip. "And just think, if we hadn't met, you wouldn't be on this boat."

"Your church invite was exactly what I needed."

Sage gave a mischievous smile. "After the incident with the frisbee and dog, I figured you needed a little help."

"It was really that bad, huh?"

"Bad, but in a good way." As the wind blew her hair, she pushed the curly strands away and her brown eyes met mine.

My voice raised slightly. "It's a gift I have, making a fool of myself. Especially when it comes to girls."

She turned away, facing the trees. "Since we're talking about this, and please don't take it the wrong way, I'm not looking for a relationship right now. I want this trip to be focused on serving people. No distractions. So just friends. Okay?"

Surprisingly, I agreed with her. Truthfully, it wasn't the best time for me to be in a relationship. I needed to become a better *me* before I could ever make an *us*. So I was okay with the Friend Zone. But hopefully not forever. And while her lips were still maddeningly kissable, there was so much more to learn about Sage; her past, her present, her likes and dislikes. She was an endless bowl of ice cream and I couldn't get enough.

"Completely understand." I gripped the boat railing, leaning back. "I'm trying to put some pieces in my life back together."

She seemed relieved and turned toward me again. "So what's going on with you and James? I sense some tension."

"It's that obvious? We got off to a bad start, but things will get better."

"It's terrible about his clothes being lost." Her forehead crinkled. "He and Lorena could only find T-shirts. None of the Leticia stores had any shorts that fit him."

"Yeah, I feel bad about that," I said unconvincingly, wondering if his shorts still smelled like Starbucks.

Her head tilted. "In case you're wondering, I gave him the friend speech, too."

I shrugged, my hands raised. "I'm good with being friends. And I think we should make a pact, signified by a special handshake."

"A handshake?"

"You know, the crazy kind you see athletes do after a great play?"

She hesitated. "Okay…"

So I taught her a handshake stolen partly from the movie *The Parent Trap*, the scene with Lindsay Lohan and her driver. One of my sister's favorite movies. Because she watched it hundreds of times, I remembered it clearly:

…Shake hands once

…Followed by a round of patty cake

…Followed by slapping the back of each other's hand

…Followed by a hip bump on each side

…Followed by facing each other, hands underneath chin and wiggling fingers, followed by shaking hands again

We practiced until perfect. It was a great excuse to touch her, and I wanted to hold her hand forever since it felt so smooth and so right. A custom fit, like it was specially molded for my palm.

While still holding her hand, I bowed my head in royal fashion. "Always friends."

She bent her knees in a curtsey. "Always friends."

But no matter what she said, I swore there was something more in her eyes.

Then Sage waved over my shoulder, and I turned around.

Red Goth stood a few yards away, pointing a camera at us. Well, actually, not at us. She focused on something behind us, and when I saw it, my heart skipped a beat.

An oropendola.

17

"What kind of bird is it?" Sage leaned in. "He's so cute."

"An oropendola." I stepped closer, noticing a twig in its beak. "Legend says these birds have magical powers. And they make long, hanging nests for protection from snakes. Their homes dangle from branches and resemble woven baskets."

"They're basket weavers?" Red Goth focused her camera lens. "How cool. I love sculptural basketry."

Sage pointed to the bird. "His yellow beak and feathers remind me of a fancy suit with a top hat and tails."

I laughed. "He looks like a Vegas lounge lizard. But they're great singers. Their voices sound like flutes or panpipes."

Red Goth snapped more shots until the bird flitted away and disappeared into the jungle's lush foliage.

Sage pointed to the camera. "Gotten any good pictures today?"

"Yeah." Red Goth stared blankly from underneath her wool

bowler hat. “A few surprising ones.”

“Make sure to post them,” she said. “We loved the ones you took last year.”

“Sure.” Red Goth nodded and walked away, before hesitating and turning around, like she wanted to say something. But she must have thought twice, because she bit her lip before turning away again.

“I’ve tried getting close to her,” Sage whispered to me. “She’s sweet, but a bit of a loner. I’m gonna go talk to her.”

Sage waved and walked away, and a warmth ran through me, like sitting in the golden sunshine on a perfect fall day. I caught myself smiling. We had enjoyed our best conversation yet, and some of her mysterious layers were gradually falling away.

For most of the next two hours I sat by the rails, my hair blowing in the wind while gazing at the coffee-colored water and unchanging jungle scenery. With every passing minute we descended deeper into the ancient rainforest. What adventures awaited us? Would we eat monkey brains and discover uncontacted tribes and maybe shower under majestic waterfalls?

We floated along in the middle of nowhere. If something happened to us way out in the Amazon boonies, we’d never be found. My body shivered. Not a pleasant thought, disappearing into the deep bowels of a silent jungle.

But after an endless blur of trees, I saw something in the

distance.

Finally, a village.

Thatch shacks and stilted hovels nestled into the plateau, while dugout canoes floated beside the shoreline. Underneath the towering palms and liana vines, the hamlet formed a palette of rich greens and browns, the latter caused by dirt trails crawling throughout the village. It looked like a National Geographic documentary.

The entire area smelled strongly of wood burning, so heavy I almost choked. The air also reeked of mold, as if someone had placed a damp blanket in a gigantic ziploc bag and opened it upon our arrival.

To my surprise, our boat driver switched on the third deck speakers and Spanish dance music came to life, with the bass thumping and echoing among the trees. Soon a large crowd of villagers gathered by the shore and waved as we approached. It looked as if the entire village had congregated.

As we docked, however, things grew clearer. And my heart dropped.

Many in the crowd had serious injuries or infections: bloodied cloths around heads and arms; dislocated limbs; rashes and scabs and sores. It resembled a lepers colony. Nothing prepared me for the great needs standing before me, a broken mass of humanity anxious for our help, with arms stretched toward us in desperation.

After we stepped off the boat, the excited villagers surrounded our team, especially seeking out Jose and Lola. It was like a reunion of old friends.

As the rest of us unloaded boxes of supplies, a village boy clung to me, wanting to help carry things. Skinny as a rail and probably no older than eleven, his face shined with a big grin and bright eyes. His pitch black hair sported a cowlick in the crown.

I don't know why the little fella followed me around, but he smiled and worked by my side the entire time. He was a great helper.

After hauling several items, I leaned over to him and pointed at my chest. "Pace."

We didn't speak each other's language, but we could at least learn each other's names. With understanding, he pointed to himself. "Yeisson."

I shook his hand. "Nice meeting you, Yeisson."

I noticed James down by the riverboat, struggling with a heavy container too big for one person. Running over, I grabbed an end, with Yeisson following and grabbing the middle. Despite the issues between me and James, I knew we had to operate as Amazon teammates.

He seemed surprised. "Thanks for the hand." We grunted with the heavy load several more steps before lowering it.

James wiped sweat from his forehead with the bottom of his

shirt. "I know you're dying to joke this t-shirt. So go ahead and get it over with."

"I wasn't going to say a thing."

He looked at the shirt and shook his head. It said, CHECK OUT MY AMAZON TANLINES.

"I know it's ridiculous," he said. "But we couldn't find any stores that sold shirts my size without cheesy sayings. And none of the shorts fit. Unless I went retro with old school booty shorts."

"You could've started a new trend."

"No way," he said. "With my butt hanging out, they'd change the name from Daisy Dukes to Daisy Pukes."

His answer caught me off guard, and I laughed. Our first personable exchange. Maybe he wasn't such a turd licker after all.

We walked back toward the boat for more packages, with Yeisson still at my hip, and I decided to engage James in more conversation.

"What are you studying in college?"

"Nursing."

"*Nursing*? Really? I imagined something more sports-related."

"Jocks can also be nurses, you know," he said. "Actually, male nurses are a growing trend. And I'm following in my mom's footsteps."

"Your mom's a nurse?"

"Yep. So I'm making her proud by becoming a murse."

"A murse?"

"Male nurse."

I busted out laughing. "And I'm assuming that's why you like medical missions?"

"Yeah, I also came last year. It's a one-week crash course in injuries and bacterial diseases."

"I'm not a fan of bacteria."

"Did you know your belly button contains over two thousand types of bacteria?"

I smirked. "So maybe I should hold off on that belly button piercing?"

"Hey, it's a good place to hang an air freshener."

We lifted another large box and carried it up a hill. Every time James and I grunted under the weight, Yeisson did, too — though he barely touched it.

I looked around the village at all the hurting people. "I've never done anything like this before. All the sickness makes me nervous."

James gave a pat on my shoulder. "You'll do fine."

He paused. "Hey man, I know I've been a jerk to you. Sorry about that. We got off to a bad start."

The apology shocked me. "I haven't been the Apostle Paul, either."

"It's weird how a girl can make two good guys become rivals," he said.

"Well, I'm not much of a rival. Sage put me in the Friend Zone."

"Me, too, but that's okay. Think about all the downsides of having a girlfriend."

We lowered the box and stretched our backs, with Yeisson imitating.

"First of all, girls are expensive." James emphasized dollars by rubbing his thumb and fingers together. "You're always broke. And they force you to go shopping."

"Also the emotions," I added. "They want to talk feelings all the time."

James nodded. "And the pressures of finding them the right gift on birthdays and holidays."

"All they want is potpourri and scented candles, anyway. And they change the way we dress."

"Yeah," he said. "They want us to wear polos instead of sports jerseys."

"And soon, we're whipped with a capital W."

We grabbed another big carton, thankfully the last one. "But to be fair," James's tone changed, "there are advantages to having a girlfriend. Like, the right woman can make you a better human being."

"True. They civilize us."

"And they're great decorators."

"They can fold fitted sheets."

"And they find stuff in closets that's invisible to males," he said.

"Their hands are soft to hold."

"And their lips…"

"Always a date for Valentine's," I said.

"Massages."

"Smooth legs."

When we laughed, Yeisson did, too. "Hey, want to help me with medical stuff for the kids this week?" James asked. "I'm an assistant to the doctors, and there's a ton to do."

"I don't know anything about medicine, but I can be a glorified gopher."

"Then consider yourself an assistant to the nursing student assistant, the one with the cheesy shirts and coffee-stained shorts."

I felt bad all over again. "I'm gonna loan you some shorts. We're roughly the same size. I owe it to you."

"You don't have to do that."

"Consider it a gift to humanity, especially if it keeps you from wearing Daisy Pukes."

Yeisson grabbed his stomach and laughed, though he had no clue what I said. Which made us laugh all the more.

We carried the carton to the tent, where Red Goth stood

nearby. She smiled at James, then turned toward me with a serious gaze.

"I need to show you something, Pace." She switched on her camera monitor. "You're into animal biology, right?"

"Yeah. What's up?"

"I was taking pictures today and caught a shot of something that looks…" She paused. "A little scary."

"Scary?"

Red Goth's face showed concern. "It's unlike anything I've ever seen. Maybe you can tell what it is. *Look*."

She turned the screen toward me, and the breath left my body.

18

I blinked at the picture with my mouth open.

The finer details appeared blurry because of shadows and fast movement. It looked strangely reptilian. What in the world? My brain ran through the encyclopedia of Amazon animals, but nothing matched what lay before my eyes.

The animal looked much larger than a black caiman or a giant otter, two of the most common river creatures. I studied closer at the details. Its head was buried underwater, and two blackened bumps jutted out of the water's surface with a distinct spotted pattern, like a leopard's. One bump revealed a thick middle and two humongous pairs of fins, while the other suggested an abnormally long and thin neck, as if attached to a strange prehistoric beast.

If my eyes weren't fooling me, it was the largest marine predator I'd ever seen — perhaps fifty feet in length. The fact it existed in the Amazon River made it even more mystifying.

Could it be … the Sea Creature? No way.

With only one purported Sea Creature picture, which many

considered a hoax, what were the odds of not only catching a glimpse, but also snagging a photo in midday? And did Red Goth just happen to get the shot by pointing her camera at the right place at the right time?

There had to be a logical explanation. Maybe she was pranking me.

"Is this a joke?" I asked.

Her posture grew rigid. "Why would I joke about this?"

"Did you see its head?"

"No. It disappeared quickly and never reappeared, like it knew I was watching."

Staring closer at the picture, I zoomed in until the image pixelated. If the YouTube videos were accurate, the supposed monster had caused many deaths over the years, easily overturning large passenger boats and causing massive destruction. But how could a mysterious creature exist in the 21st century without detection?

Maybe I should tell Jose. Then I thought about Scotland's Loch Ness Monster. No serious scientist, or level-headed person for that matter, gave any credence to such preposterous ideas. He'd think I jumped on the crazy train. For now, I'd keep this between me and Red Goth.

"I'm not sure what this is, but let me think some more." I scratched my head. "There's no reason to get everyone scared."

"Too late," she said. "Whatever that thing is out there, it scares *me*."

"I'll ask the locals. They know the area and its creatures better than anyone. Maybe they have an explanation."

Red Goth clutched her hands, but eventually nodded in agreement.

I was worried, too, but tried not to show it. The last thing our missions team needed was a wild-haired alarmist. *Hey everyone, there's a deadly cr..cr..creature in the ri..ri..river! Run for your li..li.. lives!*

A half-hour later, dusk settled upon the village. The long line of A-framed thatched huts dotted the landscape, barely an arm's reach from one other, each built several feet off the ground for flood protection. Small ladders leaned into every hut and gave access to the elevated front doors. A couple of wall openings made crude open-air windows. And behind the village, the massive jungle canopy hovered like a green tidal wave, frozen in its highest point.

The villagers lived as a tight community, from the proximity of their homes to their shared clothes and food. The men and boys often wore no shirts and busied themselves with activity near the shoreline. Many of the children played naked. The women dressed in simple shirts and thin dresses, probably gifts from humanitarian groups that visited before us.

James pointed out several villagers wearing NFL t-shirts,

most notably ones declaring the Kansas City Chiefs as 2021 Super Bowl champions. The Tampa Bay Bucs actually won the game, but apparently the Chiefs were overconfident with their pregame shirt orders. Egg on face. Not wanting to waste clothes, missions organizations distributed the misprinted garments to needy communities around the globe. It was weird seeing a slice of America in a remote jungle.

We ate a late dinner in the middle of the village, a meal called farina. Made in a large metal pan over a fire and stirred by a boat oar, it smelled like fresh hay. It was warm and bland, but filling, and tasted better mixed with fruit. Jose said it offered a great source of dietary iron; nutrition we needed before tomorrow's busy day.

Yeisson ate beside me and gladly gobbled my leftover food. My heart went out to him since he seemed lonely and starved for attention. Where were his parents? I'd get a translator and talk with him soon.

After we finished eating, Lola stood and addressed the group, wearing a camouflage bandana and military pants. She looked ready to kick butt. Somehow, the Amazon transformed her from real estate agent to Xena Warrior Princess.

"It's about to get real busy." Her voice cracked a little. "So here is tomorrow's Word of the Day now. It's *Evanescent*. Everybody repeat it."

The group mumbled the word in response.

"It means 'to last a short time or go away quickly.' Your work here tomorrow is hard, but *evanescent*. It will be over in a blink, but your impact lives on forever."

Lola pointed toward our docked boat. "For the next few days, that's your floating hotel. Girls sleep on the third floor and guys on the second." She glanced at me. "And for your safety, stay on the boat all night. There's a bunch of creepie crawlies all around this place in the midnight hours."

After cleaning our dinner plates, we made our way to the boat, with Yeisson following. Jose waited on board with Squiggles wrapped around his shoulders, stroking her gently while addressing the team.

"So you know, Squiggles here doesn't have a cage. She moves around freely at night. Some people have a guard dog, but we have a guard snake. But just don't step on her, she'll throw a hissy fit."

He stopped and smiled. "Get it? A *hissy* fit."

A few groans from the group.

I turned to C-Lo, who stood beside me. "Does it bother you? A snake slithering around without a cage?"

"Me? Afraid of a snake?" She raised her eyebrows. "I've got a rattlesnake tattoo on my left butt cheek."

"Yeah, whatever." I pointed to my rear. "And I've got one of Papa Smurf."

"You don't believe me?" she asked. "Then sneak up to my hammock tonight and I'll show you."

I lifted my hands in surrender. "Whoa, I believe you. Keep your snake in its cage."

She formed a slight grin. "That's what *she* said."

Awful, that girl. As everyone headed for the hammocks, Yeisson stayed by our side. He wanted to sleep on the boat, but Jose wouldn't allow it. Tapping Yeisson's shoulder, he spoke gently but firmly, in a language sounding like a mixture of Spanish and Portuguese.

Yeisson nodded and blinked away tears.

But before walking back to the village, he waved goodbye and held his fingers out toward me in the sign language expression of love. So sweet and innocent. After only a few hours, the kid already pulled on my heart strings.

It didn't take long for everyone to find a restful place for the night. Each floor overflowed with colorful hammocks, all swinging in the breeze, their support ropes stretching down from the ceiling and forming a spider web. I'd never slept all night in a hammock, but judging from my peaceful afternoon nap, I'd have no trouble.

The evening turned chilly, so I slipped on a sweatshirt and snuggled in my hammock cocoon. Pale moonlight washed across the deck as the swaying ropes creaked. Below, water lapped against the metal hull.

James broke the silence. “Can you believe we’re sleeping on a boat on the Amazon River?”

“It’s awesome.” Big Country frantically waved the air around him. “But these bugs are driving me crazy. Anyone got more spray?”

A moment later came the loud whoosh of bug spray, followed by what smelled like a toxic chemical spill. “Much better,” he said, wheezing. “And that’s one of the questions I’m asking God one day. Why did he create these dang-blasted insects?”

I couldn’t resist. “Bugs actually have a great purpose. They pollinate fruits and flowers and sometimes eat each other, helping control the bug population. And many people around the world eat bugs since they’re a source of protein.”

“Gross.” James scrunched his nose. “Someone once dared me to eat a lightning bug, and it tasted like death. I can do without that kind of protein.”

Banks rolled to his side. “Speaking of questions for God. Where do missing socks go? You put two in the dryer, but one always disappears. It’s like the Twilight Door opens and sucks them in.”

I lowered my voice. “Deep thoughts.”

“I wanna ask God about belly button lint,” James said. “Where does it come from?”

“It’s created from all that bacteria you told me about,” I

answered.

Big Country crossed his legs, which were elevated higher than his head. "If I could ask God anything. I'd ask about the next winning lottery numbers. A lot of good could be done with that money. Could buy a nice boat, too."

"Ever wondered why psychics never win the lottery?" James asked.

"I dunno, but it reminds me of a joke." Big Country croaked in his husky voice. "What do you call a fat psychic?"

No one answered.

"A four chin teller!" He chortled so hard his belly bounced, shaking his drooping hammock up and down.

We laughed more at Big Country's reaction than his actual joke.

Banks piped up. "I'd ask God about Elvis. Is he still alive? Or is he really dead and in heaven?"

"And what about the serious questions," I said. "Like, why do bad things happen to good people? And why is there poverty, and what is God doing to fix it?"

My questions must have sucked the life out of the conversation, since nobody spoke for a while. In the silence, I thought of the sicknesses in the village. The poverty, the shacks. Yet somehow the people seemed so happy. How could I have everything yet not have their happiness?

Big Country finally spoke. "God *has* done something about the world's problems. He sent you, Pace. He sent all of us. Our purpose is helping people. That's his love in action."

Wow. I had seriously underestimated Big Country's tender heart. Beneath his country boy exterior lay a deep philosopher and theologian. Like a Shakespearean John Wayne.

"I've got one more deep thought," James whispered. A moment passed, then he let loose a rip-roaring fart, one that must have blown a hole in his cloth hammock.

"That should get rid of the bugs," Banks said.

After calming down from the gas blast, the guys eventually fell silent. But I couldn't go asleep. My mind raced. Red Goth's picture was stuck in my head, and that thing, that creature, whatever it was, swam around somewhere outside of our boat.

A slithering sound.

I raised slightly and grabbed my flashlight. Switching it on, I pointed the beam toward the ground.

Squiggles.

An unlucky rodent squirmed helplessly in the snake's enlarged mouth. Dinner time. I watched, fascinated, as the cycle of life and death played out in front of me. The victor and the victim; the hunter and the hunted. Maybe I needed to see it, because in a strange way it prepared me for the next day.

The day that changed my life.

19

Sunrise on the Amazon, one of the items on my bucket list.

And, believe me, it didn't disappoint. The sun transformed the sea into a burnt sienna, spreading a blanket of oranges and reds and yellows. Stretching behind fluffy clouds, the sky mirrored the fiery water as if the two melted into one another, like watching heaven give earth a soft kiss.

I rubbed the sleep from my eyes and licked my lips. Morning dragon breath. My mouth tasted like a dirty linoleum floor, or like something had crawled on my tongue and died overnight. It happens when I sleep hard.

The other guys stirred beside me, and Big Country's hammock drooped so low on the floor that he resembled a letter V wrapped in nylon. James and Banks groaned as they slowly awakened because of Jose's wake up call.

Already it felt like an oven with the air warm and sticky. I ran a hand through my hair and thought about the day ahead. That's when it hit me. *Apprehension*. It lodged there on the inside, uninvited, and I wasn't sure why. Maybe it was the dread of a long, hot day. Or having to face the staggering needs of the village people. Or coming to terms with my own insecurities.

Hopefully, a good breakfast would help. Our cook whipped together a meal on the boat's first floor. When we arrived, everyone else was already there, including Sage.

She looked her usual stunning self, without a hint of fatigue on her face, dressed in cuffed shorts and a striped crop top. When God made her, he poured a perfect mixture of drop-dead-gorgeous into the perfect mold.

We ate a meal of papaya fruit (tasted like cantaloupe) and an assortment of breads and white and yellow cheeses, washed down with a local beverage made from something called naranjilla. The breakfast wasn't Carolina biscuits and gravy, but it filled the hole.

The second-best part of the meal time (with Sage being the best part) was James wearing his newest t-shirt, another from his emergency purchases in Leticia. Bright green with orange letters, I almost fell out of my chair laughing at the big, bolded words: AIN'T NOBODY GOT TIME FOR THAT!

His replacement shirts were hilarious and made with cheap material, but to his credit, James rocked them with attitude. It actually endeared him to other team members since the cheesy shirts spurred lots of humorous conversation. And I was happy he wore a pair of my loaned shorts.

Taking a last gulp from my drink, I stared ahead at the awaiting village. Their primitive homes of cane and bamboo, supported by tropical timbers and covered with palm fronds, stood alongside our large blue tents.

Sick and infirmed villagers already formed long lines awaiting help, including many pregnant women carrying toddlers in slings across their bellies. Other villages, some much deeper in the jungle, must have heard about our presence since dozens of people arrived either on foot or by canoe.

Twenty minutes later, we stepped off the boat and opened the medical ministry, with team members spread across the village. The circus had officially come to town.

I helped wherever needed, like a glorified school nurse, bouncing around to the different health stations, expecting our medical care to offer simple band-aids and aspirin.

But it only took five minutes to see otherwise. We may have looked ragtag, but our team operated as a medical brigade. The volunteer doctors were rock stars. Our rough-and-tumble clinics offered a sight to behold: IV catheters, minor surgeries, dental extractions and fillings; first-aid for a litany of injuries, rashes, cuts, and infections; treatments for malaria and yellow fever; testing for tuberculosis; and well-baby checks.

An elderly woman had an ingrown toenail removed; a young woman had her molar pulled; a middle-aged man had an encysted wood splinter removed from his shoulder; a teenager had an emergency appendectomy.

Mind blown. All this happened because of creativity and skill.

The major procedures took place back on the boat, in a special area with better lighting and sterilization. Since we couldn't import much medical equipment, our anesthesiologists performed conscious sedation for the serious cases and used a mixture of medicines to block the pain during treatment. Rugged but effective.

Because of the heat and high humidity, our team also distributed rehydration salts. The lack of clean water, a precious commodity, created tremendous challenges for proper health and sanitation.

The villagers drank little water due to the river's bacterial dangers and instead relied on lots of guayusa tea made from rainforest holly trees. Big problem. The drink contained more caffeine than coffee, which caused greater dehydration.

The problem was finding clean water. Something I never thought about. Why would I? Back home, water abounded. Clean tap water, hot showers, indoor toilets. But after today, seeing the plight of these villagers, I'd never take it for granted again.

And then the smaller, yet important things: parasite meds for stomach ailments; vitamins for children and pregnant women; school and hygiene supplies for families; eye safety and pure water programs. We even gave haircuts, to the delight of the little girls.

Not so much the boys. They were more interested in playing ball than sitting in a chair.

My respect for the Amazon people grew exponentially. They were fighters. No complaining or screaming when the doctors worked on them. Their pain threshold proved almost unbelievable, which shouldn't have surprised me, since they built their homes with bare hands and planted and harvested their own food and survived for generations on scarce diets won from a hard and unforgiving land.

And yet, these makeshift medical infirmaries would change their lives. A limb saved. A baby born healthy. A deadly infection stopped. The ripple effect impacted these villagers for decades.

They knew it, too. Sheer joy spread over their faces, coupled with a deep gratitude, like they had received the most valuable gift imaginable. And none greater than when we treated their children, with thankful mommas shedding big, happy tears and giving hugs to nurses.

If only I had the money to fly the villagers out of there, away from the challenges, to America's conveniences and comforts. To clean water.

I caught myself. My privileged American thinking.

Would they even want to leave? The Amazon embodied their home, their identity, the hallowed ground where their great great grandparents had lived and died, where their babies were born, where their worship songs had filled the night skies, a place as much in their DNA as North Carolina was in mine.

They didn't need outsiders bringing first-world heroics. They needed friends. People who helped not only with out-of-reach resources, but offered training that built on the village's natural skills and tapped into their strengths. I'd bet the villagers could teach us more than we'd ever teach them.

Slowly, things were changing inside me. My reliable belief system of global politics and social justice was wobbling and swaying, its foundations crumbling away. And this after only a few hours in a remote medical clinic.

Across the village, James waved me over. A dozen kids, including Yeisson, congregated around him playing soccer. Whenever Yeisson wasn't at my side, I always found him competing in his favorite sport, played on a grassless field.

And that's where my greatest epiphany was about to happen, where more of my old school beliefs still had to fall, like a giant rainforest tree crashing hard to the ground.

20

Soccer truly is a global sport.

A group of village kids, mostly teenagers, played with passion and skill on a makeshift soccer field. They kicked a shiny new ball, compliments of our missions team. To the side, a handful of children tossed a tattered and deflated ball, no doubt a gift from visitors long-ago.

Yeisson, though much younger and smaller, played with the older kids. His skill and speed gave the bigger boys fits, so they used their muscle to nullify his advantages.

Every time he'd dribble the ball and break loose in the open field, an outclassed larger kid would throw a shoulder to his side, sending Yeisson sprawling to the ground. It was unfair and against the rules, but accepted as part of the Amazon game.

After one vicious hit, Yeisson crumpled to the ground holding his ankle and wincing in pain. The game stopped, and the boys gathered around him.

I started to run over, but James stopped me. He put his hand on my chest. "Just wait."

Yeisson eventually stood, hobbling, bent at the waist. Agony washed across his face.

After a few moments, he dusted the dirt off his yellow soccer shirt, the same one he wore the day before.

That's when the older boys got distracted. They weren't ready when Yeisson kicked the ball away and raced down the sidelines like a colt freed from the gates, with a huge *I gotcha* smile etched on his face.

He booted the ball into an unguarded goal — a netted goal, also donated by our team — and lifted his arms in triumph, sprinting along the sidelines in a victory lap. The gumption of that kid. His exuberant personality shone through even on the soccer field.

James cupped his hands over his mouth and yelled, "*Goooaaall*!" as the opposing players lowered their heads in disbelief.

But Yeisson wasn't done celebrating. He peeled toward the river and jumped in, fully clothed, yelling and slapping at the water as his teammates ran toward him.

After their congratulations, he hurtled from the river and gave James a passing high-five. Then without breaking stride, he darted toward me with his arms wide open, expecting a big hug.

I'm not a germophobe, but Yeisson was wet and muddy. So

instead of embracing him, I grabbed his outstretched arms and swung him around, avoiding close contact. We settled for a safe fist-bump.

"Did you know he was faking that injury?" I asked James.

"Yeah. He's a smart kid. And a little mischievous." He motioned toward the field. "Hey, would you mind playing with the kids for awhile? I'd like to check in with the medical tents."

"Yeah, sure."

"There's a bag of sports supplies over there." James pointed to a mesh bag as he walked away. "Have fun, bro. They'll love you. But be aware that many of these kids haven't been treated yet for lice."

Lice? Like the tiny bugs that lay eggs in a person's hair? My head itched from the moment he mentioned it, probably a weird physiological reaction.

I decided to keep my distance. A safe and respectable distance. Pulling a frisbee from the bag, I threw it toward a group of smaller children. It landed at their feet, and a free-for-all scramble ensued.

This repeated over and over, as a child would run it back to me, since they couldn't throw it accurately, and place it in my hand for another throw. Each time brought a new delightful scrum.

The kids loved the attention and constantly tried to embrace me, their dry and rough skin pulling at my hands. It was hard keeping them at arm's length. I felt bad about it, but who wants lice?

It reminded me of Mrs. Boswell's third grade class and the lice epidemic at Grove Park Elementary. It was a mess. The classroom had to be fumigated, hair shampooed, sheets stripped, clothes laundered. If possible, I wanted to avoid that happening ever again.

A safe and respectable distance.

Then a beautiful voice arose from behind. "Should I take cover from your frisbee throws?"

I turned. Sage. *Incandescent Sage.*

"Definitely." I dropped the frisbee. "Because you know how I lose composure around beautiful women." I added a quick clarification. "Spoken from the Friend Zone, of course."

The smile on her face revealed she didn't mind. "Flattery will get you everywhere."

"I'm sure you've heard it all before from your legion of male admirers and boyfriends." I picked up the frisbee and threw it to waiting kids.

Sage pushed the hair from her eyes. "This might surprise you, but I've never had a boyfriend. I'm waiting for the right one at the right time."

A guy can dream. "If you ever need expert love advice," I deadpanned, "then *don't* ask me. I'm more Barney Fife than Don Juan."

She laughed. "I'll keep that in mind."

Several kids stampeded toward me, with one holding the frisbee high in the air like a trophy. Lice alert. Taking several steps backward I grabbed the disc and waved them away, careful not to touch anyone while readying for another throw.

"Why aren't you hugging the kids?" Sage had an odd tone in her voice.

"James said they have lice."

"And?"

"And lice freaks me out."

She didn't immediately respond, which made my words hang in the air, heartless and cold and heavy.

Sage darted her eyes to the kids, then back at me. "It's not like they can help it. They really need our love more than our medicine."

Uh-oh. My actions, or more accurately, my lack thereof, obviously struck a nerve. In our short friendship, I already realized Sage was a justice fighter, one who defended the silent ones and the oppressed. She placed others first and consequences second. My hesitation must have been like fingernails on a chalkboard to her.

I tried defending my position. "I'll let them get closer once they're cleaned up."

She didn't buy it. "Seriously, Pace? We're here to help them, but you're worried only about yourself. Protecting your own hide. What are a few bugs? They can't kill you. They wash away. Love conquers all fear."

For a minute, I thought she might slap me with her pink arm cast. But instead, she lifted a village girl in her arms and squeezed a big bear hug. "Love people and let the chips fall where they may."

I drooped my head, feeling like the world's biggest jerk. She must have viewed me as an indifferent scumbag, someone who joined a missions team only to be exposed as a selfish prick with zero direction in life. I couldn't disagree. And I needed to hear it. At least she had the guts to confront me, though her words felt like a brick upside the head. Honesty stings like a mother.

"How did you get so brave?" I asked.

"I'm no braver than anyone else." She lowered the girl back onto the ground. "But I fear inaction more than failure."

"Jose said that."

"Wise words from a wise man." Sage arched one eyebrow. "So here's your opportunity. Look at all these dirty, lice-infected children. What are you going to do about it?"

Sweet. Baby. Jesus. Decision time. In front of us stood a smudged hodgepodge of smelly kids, smiling and waiting, with heads of hair chocked full of bugs. Cameron's words came to mind, the ones she had spoken back home. *Helping people can help you.*

The time had come: time to jump into the proverbial deep end.

And plus, I didn't want to be a total wuss in front of Sage. I looked at the frisbee in my hands, then the children.

"If I do this, will you help get the lice out of my hair?"

Sage's eyes twinkled. "My honor. I have lots of experience."

"So it's a date?"

She let out a mock sigh of defeat. "Sure."

"I'll take what I can get."

And with that blessed assurance, I tossed the frisbee, straight and true, into a sea of brown faces. And following the pattern, the children scrambled for the disc, a lucky child recovered it, and then they all rushed toward me in a cloud of dust and dirt.

All I could imagine was Oprah Winfrey shouting one of her giveaways to an excited studio audience, "You get lice! And you. And you. Everyone gets lice!"

I knelt and waved them forward, bracing for the impact, the shrill happy screams rising in volume. *Embrace it, Pace. Embrace them.* And it happened. An ocean wave of hugs and kisses and laughs and tickles. Losing myself in the moment, they piled on me in a sloppy, shifting, messy mountain of love.

What a feeling. So utterly, completely alive; letting it all go, pulling the ripcord and saying screw it. Bugs be damned. They say great journeys often start with small, intentional steps. For me, a new journey had begun.

I stole a glance at Sage. She stood with a hand over her

mouth, tears in her eyes, and a soft expression toward me I'd never seen before.

And all I could think to myself was, "Goooaaall!"

21

The sun shifted into its late-afternoon position and sent a warm glow across the parched ground, like staring at an old picture with a sepia filter.

Inside the village, Sage found rusted containers with rainwater and enlisted me and a few bigger kids to haul them to the riverbank.

“It’s time to clean some scalps.” She opened a shampoo bottle. “There’s medicine in this shampoo that kills the lice.”

“Okay.” I took a deep breath. “Let’s do it.”

A long line of children waited for treatment, and Sage motioned a small boy over. She sat him on the ground, leaned his head back, then looked at me.

“I’ll show you what to look for and how to clear away the lice. Then we can divide and conquer.”

After placing on surgical gloves, she examined the boy’s scalp. “Yep, I found some.” She waved me closer. “Take a look.”

Sure enough, attached to his hair strands were tiny bugs, pale in color, some no bigger than a pin point, others three times the size.

"Most of these are nits — lice eggs." She pointed. "They're easier to spot in dark hair. And several of these other buggers have been here for awhile."

Sage poured rainwater over the boy's hair, then applied the shampoo, massaging it throughout every inch of his scalp while carefully keeping it out of his eyes. The medicine smelled like a citronella candle, and after a cleansing rinse, a special comb cleared away the lice and eggs. She gave a final inspection, then moved to the next child.

Sage shampooed a small girl before turning to me. "Okay, you're my apprentice. Let's see how you do."

I slipped on some gloves. "I'm honored to have my own personal lice coach."

"I've been called lots of things, but never that."

"Maybe you could print up some business cards, create a logo."

She led me through the first couple of kids, until I became semi-proficient with the process. It wasn't as bad as I thought, and soon, I was on my own. Checking, shampooing, rinsing, combing.

For the next hour, we stood beside each other, talking and washing scalps. Who would have guessed? Cleaning lice out of children's hair beside the Amazon River, with Sage by my side.

Truth is, without her guidance I wouldn't have even tried.

Yeisson's turn. He'd waited for me.

As I lathered the shampoo into his scalp, a big smile stretched across his face. Every so often, he turned and gleamed at me. His eyes seemed to say *Thank You* and *This Feels Good* and *You're All I Have*. We enjoyed a unique way of communicating with each other, even without language.

It felt wonderful treating those kids, once I got the hang of it and overcame my fears. Helping them made me feel... *alive*. I exhaled. How many years had I wasted chasing the wrong things?

But the truth was even worse. How many years had I wasted chasing nothing at all?

After dinner, the Amazon offered a breathtaking view of the night sky.

Due to the absence of light pollution, the stars twinkled with intensity, like God had placed a dixie cup over the planet and poked pinholes in it, allowing small beams of Himself to shine through.

What a day. We had helped nearly two hundred villagers, plus all the kids with their lice. The evening offered a needed break, not only from the heat, but from the high-energy ministry demands.

Jose led a teaching time in the middle of the village, catered to the adults, while the children enjoyed a special program coordinated by other team members. Skits, face painting, and balloons. Even Yeisson temporarily left my side to enjoy the fun.

It offered the perfect time for me and Sage. We carried a flashlight and a rainwater bucket down to the river as the scent of blooming jasmine emanated from the darkened rainforest. After treating the kids all afternoon, it was time to check each other for lice.

Or, as I liked to call it, our first official date.

"Have you ever had lice?" I realized it was the worst opening line of any conversation, ever.

"Almost every time I've gone on a missions trip. And this is my fifth one." She sat next to the water. "It's not easy with thick hair like mine."

I plopped down beside her. "Your hair is awesome."

"It's a handful, kind of like me." She paused. "Hey, sorry that I came on so strong today about you and the kids. You should've told me to shut up. I need to be more patient. This is your first trip, after all."

"No, I deserved it. You kicked my butt into gear. It helped me to have one of the most unforgettable experiences of my life."

Sage stared ahead at the river as it coursed under the moon's golden gleam. "It's amazing what happens when we're pushed outside of our comfort zones."

I scratched my scalp. "Yeah, that's where you find the critters."

She laughed, then pointed to my head. "Let's see how you're doing up there."

Lifting the flashlight, she gently ran her fingers through my hair. In any other circumstance, Sage playing with my hair would've been reason for yelling, *Mamma Mia!* and singing Italian opera in a loud, falsetto voice. But I couldn't fully enjoy it, being nervous about what she might discover. My dream girl potentially finding bugs in my hair? I prayed a quick, silent prayer for a lice-free head.

She leaned closer for a better look. "Yep, I see a few. There they are, hanging on for dear life. Building a little bug village." She sounded a little too excited.

I guess my prayer didn't work. Could it get any more humiliating? I felt so unattractive sitting beside her, like a humpbacked ogre with a disgusting head disease.

"Congratulations." She lowered the flashlight. "You've officially made the transition from tourist to missionary."

Leave it to Sage to put a positive spin on it. I gave a sarcastic smile. "I would've preferred a certificate. Or maybe a nice box of chocolates."

"Nah. You get something better. A shampoo, from me."

Well, when she put it that way. Thank you, God, for unanswered prayer.

Sage poured rainwater on top of my head, then massaged the shampoo through my scalp, her fingernails scratching and rubbing all the way from the nape of my neck to the crown of my head. Pure, unadulterated bliss. Goosebumps ran up and down my body. If I was a dog, I would've been involuntarily kicking my hind leg.

After the rinse, I could barely speak. "That was totally worth the lice."

"You're terrible." She slapped me playfully on the shoulder.

I pointed to her head. "Now it's your turn."

Sage let her hair down and shook it loose. I swallowed and felt my mouth drop open. She looked stunning. I coursed my fingers through her thick black hair. True confession: for the first several moments, I didn't even look for bugs. I just enjoyed the guilty pleasure of simply touching her. There's something about rubbing someone's head that's indescribably intimate, especially hers, with her full and luscious hair.

Even if she did have lice in it.

"Found some," I said.

Sage groaned. "It figures. I'm a magnet for those bugs."

"No worries. I was trained by the best nitpicker of them all."

I washed her hair, repeating the steps she taught me. With a soft but firm touch, I kneaded and rolled her scalp, watching the water roll down her hair and across her neck. The moonlight highlighted her gentle features and perfect bone structure, and I swear an angelic choir sang and bestowed upon me the favor of the Father, Son, and Holy Spirit.

The best day of my life.

I never imagined lice could be so romantic.

22

The next day offered a more relaxed pace, since Jose encouraged us to focus on building relationships with the villagers.

People skills were his secret sauce. He lived by the guiding principle of not only serving people, but spending unrushed time with them; honoring them with intentional conversations and undivided attention, learning their names and family connections and daily rituals.

It flowed from his deep love for these oft-forgotten villagers, forged from faithful visits over the years. Jose built his ministry the right way: with love and trust. And plenty of salvations and baptisms and wedding ceremonies along the way. He was a noble man who had found and embraced his life's purpose.

If only God's mysterious, elaborate plan for my life would cartwheel down from the secret wisps of eternity and slap me upside the face. If only.

During the morning with Yeisson by my side, I interacted with many villagers. But communication proved a struggle since all our translators helped others. It didn't matter; friendliness worked without language.

Every few minutes, a new child ran up with a squeal and lovingly squeezed my waist before darting off again. The kids trusted me. Yesterday's frisbee game accomplished more than I realized.

So I shook rough hands and hugged creased necks and walked the dirt paths hewed centuries earlier. The rustic village slowly grew on me; it felt like living within a large family.

What a contrast. In only twenty-four hours I had connected more with those villagers than with my own suburban neighbors. The family on my street two doors down. Who were they? Outside of a passing wave, we gave no extra effort in our land of automatic garage doors, television, and the internet. For all the good of technology, it concealed a dark side. It alienated people.

Yet this village on a distant shore of the Amazon River didn't know diddly-squat about Google or Facebook or smartphones. They seemed better for it, and ironically, more connected.

Deep thoughts. My head hurt.

For lunch, our team ate plantains and piranha. *Yes, piranha*. The little fishies featured in James Bond movies who eat people. I almost opted for a peanut butter sandwich, but reminded myself of the rare opportunity to experience local cuisine. I'd always have Turdburger cheeseburgers back home, but piranha?

Our team chef fried the fish in hot oil and served them on a plate, two at a time, in their full fishy shapes. Head, eyes, everything. They looked like two mean, overgrown goldfish. Their mouths open, the crispy piranha revealed their infamous razor teeth, yet they tasted like any other white fish; good, but bony. The plantains, also a first for me, resembled green bananas though more starchy than sweet.

In the early afternoon, Yeisson and I visited the medical tents as our doctors gave follow-up care to their patients. James worked there, helping the physicians. He served with proficiency and skill, displaying kindness toward the villagers. After our first awkward encounter at the church, I never would've imagined he had it in him. *But look at him now*. Underneath James's alpha dog exterior resided a big squishy gummy bear.

Outside the tent, a shirtless Jose worked in a nearby garden and tilled the soil with a hoe. He glanced at me and Yeisson, then waved us over. I assumed he needed help, but when we approached he lowered the tool and motioned us to sit beside him.

"Watch out, you're entering the *seedy* part of town," he said to me.

"I didn't know the king of puns was also a gardener."

"Yeah, I *dig* it." He smiled mischievously. "I get so excited I wet my *plants*."

I grimaced. "Ohhh. Those are groaners. What are you

harvesting?"

He pointed toward a cluster of green leaves. "It's called cassava, a major part of the Amazon diet. Better known to Americans as tapioca. It's drought-tolerant. Comes out of the ground looking like a skinny potato."

"How does it taste?"

"It depends if it's raw or cooked. My son loves it either way."

"I didn't know you had kids."

"One boy. He's about Yeisson's age." He motioned to Yeisson. "So your new buddy is still following you around?"

"Yeah, and I've taught him a few words. Let me show you."

Looking at Yeisson, I lifted a hand to my mouth in an eating motion.

Yeisson studied my actions, then spoke in a thick accent. "Chocolate."

I nodded, then placed a hand over my heart.

"I love you," he replied, a smile on his face.

Then I made a kicking motion.

His eyes lit up. "Soccer!"

Jose laughed. "He's a good athlete, you know."

"And a good actor." I bear-hugged Yeisson. "He could have won an Oscar yesterday faking a soccer injury. And he scored."

"He's a smart kid. And resilient." He paused. "Anyway, I called you over so I could translate. Anything you want to ask him?"

I thought for a moment. "Ask him about his family. Where are they?"

Jose didn't turn and ask Yeisson. Instead, his voice lowered a notch. "He has no family, at least not immediate. His mother died at childbirth and malaria took his father several years ago. He lives with distant cousins. They provide a roof for him, but they're not involved in his life. So I've sort of adopted him, especially on these trips."

I marveled at Yeisson's survivor instinct. A kid, basically on his own in the wild Amazon. No one comforting him when sick or injured; no one pushing down the stubborn cowlick on his head; no one supplying his food or clothes or education. Except for Jose.

And though Yeisson didn't act angry or aloof, a hint of sadness hid behind his wide eyes.

Jose playfully dug dirt with the hoe. "Normally he follows *me* around everywhere. But there must be something about you. Maybe he sees your kind heart."

I shook my head. "There's a lot more people kinder than me."

"I don't know. Yeisson's very discerning. Wisdom beyond his years. He often travels with our teams to other villages and is a big helper. He's well-known throughout these parts. Kind of a lovable stray. Everyone claims him as their own."

He then spoke to Yeisson and the little boy responded.

Jose smiled. "He going with us to tomorrow's village."

I gave Yeisson a thumbs up. "Ask him what other fun things he likes doing."

Jose asked Yeisson, and he answered.

"He loves climbing trees and catching snakes," Jose said. "I've seen him do both. He's actually very good."

"Snakes?" I bristled. "Isn't that dangerous?"

"Believe me, I've given him plenty of warnings. But he has a stubborn streak."

"Maybe *that's* what he sees in me. I've got a stubborn streak, too."

Yeisson talked.

Wrinkles creased around Jose's eyes. "He says he loves hunting things. And he wants to catch a bushmaster viper. There are quite a few in this area, or *matabueys* as the locals call them. Cruel snakes with fatal bites."

Oh yes, the bushmaster. Any second-rate animal biologist could tell you about it. The most aggressive snake in the world. If one of those vipers bit you, lights out. The Grim Reaper. A first class ticket to a horizontal phone booth. But it also reminded me of another dangerous beast.

"Ask him about the Sea Creature. Has he ever seen it or hunted it?"

"You've heard that crazy story?" Jose crinkled his brows. "The creature is only a legend, Pace."

"I know, but ask just for fun." I hadn't told him yet about Red Goth's picture.

After Jose asked Yeisson, the boy's expression changed immediately. He nodded and spoke with seriousness.

"He says he's seen it before." Jose played along, like explaining the Easter Bunny. "A magic creature with great power. The ultimate hunt."

We sat there for a moment, silent. Then Yeisson muttered something and pulled a small knife from his pocket.

Jose translated. "He wants to bury that knife with you. The next time you come, you can dig it up together. Like a time capsule. And he also wants to show you where he sleeps."

I placed a hand on Yeisson's shoulder. "Tell him I'm honored."

Yeisson spoke again, with a playful look.

"And he saw you last night with Sage." Jose's face brightened. "All alone, by the river."

"That little gossip. Tell him it was innocent." I pointed to my head. "She shampooed my lice away."

Jose told Yeisson, but the boy smiled and shook his head like he didn't believe me.

"The last couple of years, Sage has done a lot for him." Jose pat Yeisson's knee. "But he's still shy around her."

I turned toward him. "Why are you shy with Sage?"

Jose asked my question, and Yeisson answered while

covering his eyes.

"He said it's because she's so pretty." Jose winked.

I didn't say a word, only nodded in full agreement. Yeisson stood and spoke something, then motioned for me.

"He wants you to follow him," Jose said.

I stood. "Okay, where he leads, I'll follow."

Jose rose with us, giving my arm a loving squeeze. "Pace, thank you for giving him attention. It means more than you know. He needs positive male figures in his life."

"I'm not sure I qualify, but happy to help."

He rubbed Yeisson's hair, then pulled an apple out of a nearby bag and gave it to him. "This kid loves apples."

I couldn't resist. "Maybe it's because he's *hardcore*."

Jose gave an affirmative nod. "Oh, nicely done. I'll have to remember that one."

At sight of the plump fruit, Yeisson's eyes widened and he took it gladly, cradling it into his hands before sliding the apple into a back pocket.

My chest caved. *Look how excited he is about an apple.*

A skinny orphan boy without a family who wants to bury his special knife with me. Maybe I was sent all the way to that one overlooked part of the world, to that one overlooked village, to that one overlooked kid.

Maybe God had a purpose for my life, after all.

23

Yeisson's hut reached barely eight feet tall.

Held together by mud and sticks and palm branches, it actually smelled pleasant, like a mixture of deep flora and wet grass.

On top of the straw-strewn dirt floor stood a makeshift chair, and to the left and right, animal skin mattresses covered two wooden beds. The thatched roof had fallen in halfway.

Yeisson showed me the hut with a gleam in his eye, like giving a mansion tour. I smiled and nodded approvingly, though the abject poverty made me lightheaded. My God, I earned more in a week as a lowly busboy than these hard-working villagers made in a year.

Placing both hands on one side of my face, I gestured to Yeisson, asking where he slept. He understood the silent question and walked past the bed and motioned toward a pile of ripped blankets in the corner; a hardened, unforgiving space of only four feet.

Doghouses in America are bigger than this. The kid didn't even have a proper bed, much less a pillow. How many other people crammed into the two-bed shelter?

Yeisson lifted a tattered blanket and revealed a dozen snake skins of all sizes and patterns. His trophy case. He pointed at his chest, communicating he had caught and skinned them. The reptile skins represented some of his only earthly possessions.

Then he smiled and raised his knife, motioning outdoors.

Time for a burial ceremony.

Yeisson walked all the way to the rainforest border.

And with a quick glance back at me, he entered confidently, encouraging me to follow.

I hesitated, remembering Jose's — and Lola's — repeated warnings about not going into the jungle. But Yeisson signaled we'd go inside only a few feet. Uggh. If not for my debacle on the Leticia docks the first night, I wouldn't have thought twice.

Looking around at the village behind me, everything seemed calm. Several villagers gardened and fished, children played, some women carried water buckets. At least I wasn't neglecting any duties. Jose had encouraged us to build relationships, and he already knew Yeisson's desire to bury the knife.

The jungle. In and out. We'd make it fast.

I stepped inside, under the canopy of the wooden giants, immediately conjuring to life all the fantastical tales stored in my brain: the hidden cities of gold; the legend of El Dorado; the female warrior tribes filled with beautiful but deadly women.

The rainforest overflowed as the world's largest containment of biodiversity, a wild cauldron of life. Geek out time. The tree-choked mazes invited us deeper, with a fragrance of mandarin hovering above the forest floor. A curtain of leaves, washed in shadows and fused alongside wurly-curly vines, revealed unexplored pathways. The whole atmosphere felt dangerous and alive, buzzing with nature's power.

In the treetops, flittering wings suggested a vast number of unseen creatures. The chip and chirk and chack of birdsongs surrounded us, led by the screaming piha, the noisiest of all rainforest birds. In the distance, butterflies the size of coffee saucers shimmered above jagged branches, glowing in their colors like tie-dye t-shirts with wings.

The jungle offered surprising finds at every turn. Along our path lay a gigantic flower with red-spotted petals, an orange center, and a hole in its middle. I had no idea the name of it, since my specialty was biology, not botany. But its three foot wide blossom sat on top of a crawling vine and smelled like rotting flesh.

Life and death. The rainforest offered them both, along with an assortment of unpredictable sights and sounds and smells.

Yeisson kept his promise of a shallow jungle entry. A few feet inside, he stopped at the trunk of the first massive tree and pointed upward, making motions with his arms and legs. He wanted us to climb.

Straining my neck above, the tree crown opened like an umbrella nearly two hundred feet in the sky. I shook my head in doubt. *Ain't not way I'm climbing up there.*

But Yeisson pinched his fingers close together, indicating a short ascent. I studied the tree closer, the thick trunk sprouting spines arcing toward the ground, and its horizontal limbs creating a natural ladder.

Taking a deep breath, I remembered my neighbor's treehouse. Twelve wobbly steps on the side of an old Oak tree led to a rustic room and a waiting pitcher of orange kool-aid. *Think of this as another treehouse.*

So I convinced myself. Climbing a Kapok tree in the Amazon rainforest? Seize the day. Yeisson scrambled up the tree, fast and nimble, obviously from lots of practice. He was a natural climber. And though I didn't have his skill, my upper body strength came in handy. Those gym leg squats paid off, too.

We climbed maybe twenty-five feet, enough to make me nervous. One misstep and I'd experience a bad day. Broken arm, leg, neck. A serious injury in the Amazon wasn't on my wish list.

Yet the new perspective from our height took my breath away, and I gazed again at the treetop as it stretched and disappeared into the sky. What must the jungle look like from the top? I didn't intend on finding out.

A strong wind blew, and the Kapok's peak swayed back and forth. I imagined all the exotic creatures sharing that same massive tree with us. Perhaps macaws perched high above, their feathers adding splashes of maroon and blue; or titan beetles so large their mandibles could snap a pencil in half or rip into flesh; or maybe — just maybe — a uakari, a furry monkey with a bright red and hairless face resembling an old man's.

Yeisson leaned on a branch and smiled, his arms crossed, thoroughly enjoying the moment. I pointed to him, then upward, motioning if he had ever reached the crown.

He seemed to understand and nodded nonchalantly, as if scaling one of the world's highest trees was a daily occurrence. The kid lived fearlessly.

But then his expression changed.

He straightened and stared toward the ground, at a leaf pile near the tree bottom. Pointing his finger, he whispered reverently, "Matabuey."

Matabuey. The local term for a bushmaster pit viper.

It took a moment to see it, but there it lay, a grand specimen of a snake, camouflaged in the dense bushes and tree leaves. The reptile had a triangle-shaped head and a thick, golden body washed in black blotches. Easily twelve foot long. The legendary bushmaster.

Just as Jose had warned, it was a creature you never wanted to meet. And staring at it reminded me of the scary details: many considered it the jaguar of the reptilian world.

It was the jungle's silent assassin, infamously known as the "cigarette snake" because once you get bitten there's only time for smoking a cigarette before you die. If you're lucky enough to have anti-venom administered quickly, your chances improve slightly.

A clever serpent, the bushmaster waited for its prey, often staking out an ambush spot. A patient killer. Known to linger in the same spot for days or weeks at a time, the creature would strike a potential victim aggressively and ruthlessly.

Experts reported it as one of the rare snakes that chased humans. Making matters worse, it was also heat sensing. So hiding didn't work. If you emanated body heat, the viper would find you.

We had unwittingly stepped into its trap. Thankfully, we didn't encounter it on the ground. And at least we sat high in a tree, safely removed from its treacherous fangs. Bushmasters didn't climb trees, or so I read. But the snake could wait us out; it had nowhere to go. How would we get down?

It's almost like the serpent instinctively knew it had an

advantageous position. Head moving from side to side, its long body lunged across the forest surface, pushing and bending, extending and heaving.

Both graceful and horrifying to watch, the reptile rolled in a wavy motion from neck to tail and seduced us with its beauty. It stretched and glided along the earth below us, contracting its muscles, creeping and taunting, like a great white shark circling hapless swimmers. The evolutionary dance of hunter and hunted. No wonder the locals loathed that snake.

And then it happened.

With a ripple of muscular movement, it gripped the soil and pushed down with force. It thrusted toward the tree and attached to the trunk in a surprising burst of speed and strength.

Flinging its dragon-like scales against the Kapok, it winded its way up the smaller vines and boughs like a barbershop pole, bunching the middle of its body into tight bends, pulling its back end and springing upward for a new grasp.

It climbed angrily and steadily with the same sinister motion: throwing its head forward, the body following, then throwing its head again.

The blood drained from my face.

Bushmasters *did* climb trees.

24

That snake wanted me for dinner.

My heart raced, about to explode, and a spike of dizziness made my legs and knees shake. The worst fear imaginable: being chased by a ruthless creature that desires you dead.

Everything in me screamed *run*. Or, because we hunched in a tree, *climb*.

Grabbing onto a higher cluster of branches, I braced for a frantic scurry to the two-hundred foot treetop. A faulty plan, though. What would happen after reaching the crown? At best, climbing only delayed the inevitable.

But Yeisson held my arm. "No." One of the few English words he knew.

Pulling out his knife from a pocket, he cut several smaller branches and threw them in the direction of the fast approaching viper, motioning me to do the same.

So we pelted the bushmaster with everything we found. Sticks, small limbs, fruit pods. Maybe the snake could be slowed, injured, or best case — dislodged from the tree.

But after several attempts, it became apparent our efforts weren't working.

The snake grasped the trunk with a supernatural grip. Making matters worse, the viper behaved more aggressively the harder we fought, rearing its head and letting out an evil hiss.

But Yeisson hunched with the knife in one hand and a long stick in the other, prepared for a face-to-face confrontation with the jungle's most feared enemy. Really? Fighting a bushmaster with only a pocket knife and a skinny piece of wood?

Our situation deteriorated by the second.

We crouched in the tree, not sure what to do, like our feet were stuck in cement, silently debating whether to fight and hold our ground or retreat upward.

The viper bobbed and lunged toward us, a beast obeying its reptilian DNA, its body as thick as my thigh, moving like a shining phalanx of armor and spears and pikes, its scales making a loud sawing sound.

I looked into its eyes. Cat-like pupils, vertical slits, large and unblinking and constantly staring.

My body shivered. The snake's black forked tongue danced wildly as it climbed closer into striking range.

And then Yeisson dropped his knife.

In his moving and defensive positioning, our one weapon

slipped from his hand, bouncing off branches and landing on the ground far below.

Unbelievable. It was like a scene out of a movie when a helpless victim runs from a chasing boogie man, only to fall down trying to escape.

What was I thinking when I followed him into the forest? My life rested in the hands of an eleven year old. I wanted to yell at him, but somehow held back my anger. Time for surviving, not arguing.

My face must have shown the pent-up emotion, though, because Yeisson looked at me and tears filled his eyes.

We had no protection, and the fast-climbing snake would eventually overtake us. For a moment, I thought we should jump. But a thirty foot drop? The landing would be dangerous, if not fatal, and it wasn't a clear fall due to the jagged branches below.

Climb. We both knew it was our only option, so with Yeisson going first, we scratched and pulled and scraped our way upward.

I glanced toward the forest edge where we had entered. Village children played in the open, fifty feet away, their legs and feet visible through the foliage.

I yelled for help, over and over, until my throat stung.

Yeisson did the same, but to our dismay the kids didn't notice. Why couldn't they hear?

The bushmaster gained on us. I wondered about previous

viper victims. What did they experience in the final seconds before being bitten? I'm sure it was terror. The same feeling I had, paralyzing my own body and mind.

Yeisson stopped.

"Keep climbing!" I screamed.

Instead, he reached into his back pocket and pulled out his apple. *What's he doing?*

Yeisson squared his body toward the jungle edge, facing the village, and heaved the apple with surprising speed and accuracy.

A perfect throw. It landed in the open and rolled near the feet of a child.

A village girl picked up the fruit and stuck her head into the rainforest, curious.

We shouted again.

The child's gaze found us in the tree, and when she saw the snake climbing below us, her eyes filled with panic.

Yeisson screamed hurried instructions and she sprinted toward the village.

The thrown apple. Quick thinking by Yeisson. But could the girl find help in time?

We climbed frantically yet made slow progress, looking both upward and downward, aware the bushmaster closed in fast.

The viper revealed its long fangs, its main weapon designed to penetrate deeply and inject toxic venom. Its tail vibrated, a sign of imminent attack.

I feared the danger of a lightning fast surge, followed by the snake's ability to strike numerous times in rapid succession.

We had to keep moving. With muscles screaming, sheer adrenaline pushed me ahead.

But poor Yeisson slowed.

I yelled, "Faster!" but the little guy's arms and legs wobbled. He was scared.

At least I was between him and the snake. It would strike me first, giving Yeisson more time to climb higher.

Where was the help? I shouted again toward the village while flailing my arms at Yeisson, desperately wanting to push him higher, faster. Time was running out.

A loud yell from somewhere behind.

Jose barged through the jungle entrance with garden hoe in hand and several villagers following. He saw us, and without hesitation, climbed several bottom branches and reared back the hoe's sharp edge.

With a mighty swing, he severed the bottom third of the bushmaster.

The reptile unleashed a devilish hiss.

He swung again, this time higher, at the snake's midsection, a powerful slice that sent the viper falling from the tree, almost hitting Jose on the way down.

As the snake landed on the ground, Jose leveled another powerful blow on its triangular head.

A direct hit. Decapitation.

For several seconds, the dismembered head continued moving and jerking and jumping. The reptile offered a vicious fight to the end.

Jose nudged the creature with his bloodied tool, and the other villagers searched the surrounding area for more hiding snakes.

Eventually, he looked up at us. “It’s safe.”

Descending carefully, my right ankle throbbed, and my arms and legs shook from the near-death experience. Our actions had placed numerous lives in danger.

I dreaded facing Jose, so as we stepped onto the ground, I decided to make light of the situation.

“Quite a swing you’ve got there,” I said, limping away from the tree.

He stared at the bushmaster. “Three seasons of minor league baseball comes in handy sometimes. You okay?” He had genuine concern in his voice.

“I must have twisted my ankle while climbing. Didn’t realize it until now.”

“Adrenaline hides a lot of pain. The doctors should take a look at it.”

Then Jose turned to Yeisson, speaking in the boy’s language.

Yeisson nodded, verifying he wasn't injured, I assumed.

Jose pushed the snake with the outstretched hoe. "Never get too close to a dead snake. Residual reflexes can result in a bite. And its venom is still dangerous."

Yeisson said something.

Jose nodded, then turned to me. "He wants me to help him skin it."

I studied the dead body. What a specimen. "He always dreamed of catching a bushmaster."

"But not in this way." Jose lifted his gaze from the bushmaster and leveled his eyes on me. "What were you doing inside the jungle?"

I swallowed, knowing the answer sounded paper-thin. "Yeisson wanted to bury his knife in here."

"Were you planning on burying the knife in the tree? What if you had fallen? Or were bitten?"

My head lowered. "Yeah, we got distracted."

"Getting distracted in the jungle usually means death. You're fortunate this viper didn't kill you."

"It was stupid. I'm sorry." A pause. "Do you have to tell Lola? I've already got one strike against me."

"You scared of Lola?"

"Terrified may be the better word."

Jose pointed at my ankle. "I'd advise you to get it wrapped.

But eventually she's going to ask why you're limping."

"Yes, sir."

Jose spoke sternly to Yeisson, and the boy slumped his shoulders and retreated toward the huts.

I wanted to hug him and say everything was okay, assure him I wasn't mad. The kid didn't need any more rejection in his life. But sadly, we never buried his knife, his only one, since it was lost somewhere on the jungle floor.

I hobbled to the snake, keeping a safe distance.

The bushmaster's muscular body lay motionless on the ground, its open mouth revealing fangs that looked like two hypodermic needles.

Jose nudged the snake again with the tool. "At least the matabuey wasn't a total loss. We'll put the meat in a soup."

Yeah, but when Lola heard about our misadventure, she'd have *me* for soup.

25

It saddened me to leave.

Our team stood inside the boat and leaned against the rails, shouting early morning goodbyes to our new friends.

The entire village had gathered on the shore, waving and smiling, the crowd bursting with fresh slings and crutches and bandages. It felt good to have helped so many. If only we had extra time.

But our work wasn't finished; another village awaited with more sick people. Yet no matter where else we traveled, that first village would always be dear to my heart.

Would I ever see the place again? It was where I fell in love with the Amazon people…where Sage helped me overcome fears… where I met Yeisson.

And where I almost died.

I hobbled around, my ankle throbbing from the tree injury and hurting worse than the previous day. Stubbornness kept me from using crutches. Several people called me *Hop-a-long* or *Peg-leg*, but I preferred *Wobbles*.

At least I had a kick-butt backstory, but a missions trip was no place for a bum leg. It limited me from carrying supplies and assisting the doctors and playing with the kids. What a pain, literally.

But it could've been much worse. Encountering a killer viper often ends with more than a twisted ankle.

One bright note, however, was Sage's sympathy. The evening before, after learning of my injury, she brought me a flower and a protein bar. A simple act, but it made my night. Because... she thought of me.

I told her what had happened and she listened with a concerned look. I wanted to ask, *Since I have an 'owie,' can we kiss and make it better?* But that would've violated our blessed Friend Zone.

Instead, she held my hand and prayed for the ankle to heal quickly. A girl had never prayed for me before, much less a hot one. Her tender touch and sweet voice offered a religious experience in itself, helping the pain become more bearable. But it didn't give me better rest.

Later that night, I struggled sleeping because of recurring snake nightmares, several times awakening in a cold sweat a split second before the viper's long fangs sunk into my leg. The bushmaster had shaken me to the bootstraps, even in my dream subconsciousness.

I guess a brush with death does that to a person. I wondered how Yeisson was coping since he experienced it, too. Ever since the incident he had kept his distance from me, disappearing during the evening crusade. Was he mad? Maybe he felt responsible for putting us in danger. I didn't know.

But at least he arrived for the morning boat ride, traveling with us to the new village. It was a relief seeing him, though he clung to Sage's side, finally overcoming his shyness with her. Hopefully the ride would give us an opportunity to connect again.

The previous night, I had planned on visiting Yeisson's hut before bed, but then Lola found me, giving me the Mike Tyson verbal butt-kicking I so richly deserved. Angry that I'd wandered off into the jungle, she lectured me again on the Amazon rules, raising her voice and turning red in the face. She almost hyperventilated.

But then she paused and her lips quivered, and the next second she started crying before embracing me with a bear hug.

"You're my lovable problem child," she sputtered, through her tears.

Pace Howell, the loose cannon.

But a new day had dawned. Time for redemption. No more wandering away from the group, since both times had turned out less than stellar.

The next village was an hour away. Jose said his teams had

never visited there, and the villagers had little contact with outsiders. Sounded like a set-up for a bad horror movie. Would they be welcoming? Hostile? We'd find out soon enough.

A refreshing breeze hit my face as the boat chugged downriver, following the meandering river curves, the water resembling molasses and smelling like smoke. Beside the shore floated giant water lilies, six foot in diameter, and a black caiman lay on top of one, lounging in the sun.

A few moments later, we glimpsed another unexpected treat: pink dolphins. Famous for their habitation in the river, and named for their unique rose-colored skin, the friendly creatures playfully dove in and out of the water.

Everyone snapped pictures. The Amazon's grand amusement park never failed.

But despite the jaw-dropping beauty of our surroundings, my eyes still favored Sage. She wore a white sleeveless top with a cute knot tied at the waist, and olive drawstring pants. *Is it hot out here or is it just the Amazon?*

She relaxed near the back of the riverboat, playing cards with Yeisson. I noticed their newfound easy relationship, the smiles and laughter and conversation. Unlike me, she spoke Spanish and easily communicated with him.

The rest of our group sat at the front of the boat and pestered me about the snake encounter. So I recounted the story, giving them all the gory details. Many had never heard of a bushmaster pit viper, and they marveled at Yeisson's ingenuity and Jose's courage.

I finished the story and said, "It was the scariest moment of my life."

Everyone stared in silence before Big Country spoke. "I've worked outside all my life, with every type of farm animal. But I don't trust anything that slithers."

"Amen." C-Lo slid to her seat edge. "And caterpillars also scare the hell out of me. They're like worms in fur coats. How many feet do they have? A hundred? All marching toward you, bent on destruction. Those things can crawl into your mouth."

"Don't be so hard on them," Red Goth said. "Caterpillars represent potential, how new life can exist inside a body that has yet to experience second birth."

"That's an interesting point, very true." James gave a contemplative nod. He wore a t-shirt that read, NO COFFEE, NO WORKEE.

Red Goth blushed at his compliment, showing more emotion than I'd ever seen from her.

"I know this sounds weird," Banks said, "but Dr. Seuss characters give me nightmares. Think about them: Foo Foo the Snoo. Nizzards. Thing One and Thing Two. Was the doctor smoking crack when he invented those creatures? Horrifying."

"Are you scared of Muppets, too?" C-Lo's voice dripped with sarcasm. "Fozzie Bear a little creepy?"

"You should know, your role model is Miss Piggy." Then he imitated the character's voice. *"Moi doesn't like caterpillars."*

"Now, children, keep things civil," James interrupted. "I think clowns are scary. Especially killer clowns carrying axes."

"Anything carrying an axe is scary." C-Lo blinked rapidly. "And I'll tell you what else is frightening. Public restrooms. How many other butts have sat on that same toilet seat? Hairy butts. Acne butts. So I use public restrooms only if it's a five-alarm emergency. And that's with double-lined toilet paper covering the seat."

"*Moi buttocks must not get dirty*," Banks imitated, "*I'm a piggy prima-donna*."

"Shut it up, Lorax, or I'll karate chop you in the throat," she answered.

I honestly couldn't tell if they were joking or serious. Those two had a strange love-hate relationship going on.

"I'm terrified of oncoming trains." Red Goth added no explanation.

Everyone glanced around awkwardly.

"Okay, I'll bite," Big Country said. "Why do trains scare you?"

Red Goth seemed annoyed. "It's obvious, isn't it? The noise and pure power. The surge of wind that sucks you closer. A five thousand ton metal shell rolling at a high speed on a skinny rail. No thanks. I won't get close to one, not even to take a picture."

It reminded me of her mysterious snapshot from the last boat ride. "Did you guys see the picture she took of the creature in the river?" I asked the group. "It's freaky. Whatever it is."

Banks looked at me. "You mean the renowned animal expert can't identify it?"

I shrugged. "It's unlike anything I've ever seen. Maybe it's the scary sea creature we've heard about. The Hipupiara."

I expected them to laugh, but no one did. Instead they clamored around Red Goth's camera screen and gawked at the picture.

While they studied the image, I limped painfully to the opposite end of the boat toward Sage and Yeisson. She glanced up and smiled, but he barely acknowledged my presence.

"How much money do you have riding on the card game?" I asked.

"I'm not that crazy," she said. "I'm better at checkers than poker. And Yeisson's a great player. He's already beaten me several times with his poker face."

I gave Yeisson a pat on the shoulder, but he didn't respond.

Sage noticed. "He thinks you're mad at him for what happened in the jungle."

My head tilted. "No, I'm not mad at all. We were in the wrong place at the wrong time. And tell him it was his quick thinking that actually saved our lives."

As she spoke to Yeisson, an idea hit me. Telling Sage I'd be right back, I walked to the front of the boat and found Jose sitting by the decorative shrunken head. Asking if I could borrow Squiggles the snake, he looked overjoyed at my request.

It took everything in me to wrap that boa across my shoulders since my trust in reptiles was at an all-time low. But I did it. And with snake in tow, I hobbled back to Yeisson and knelt beside him.

His eyes lit up. What the boy saw in reptiles I'll never know.

I opened my arms and he fell into my embrace, a big hug with me and Yeisson on the outside and Squiggles on the inside. Somehow, supernaturally, we shared a deep brotherly bond though separated by age and geography and language.

Sage stood. "I'll let you boys get reacquainted."

As Yeisson continued hugging, I whispered a silent *Thank You* to her.

I placed the snake on Yeisson's shoulders, and for the remainder of the trip we played more poker. He beat me every hand. Maybe I was distracted by the staring boa.

We arrived at the next village an hour later, and everyone crowded at the rails for a closer look. It was much smaller than the last one.

As the boat neared the shore, our team waved at the assembled villagers. But they returned only blank and distrusting stares. Several children hid behind their mother's backs.

And I noticed something else, something peculiar.

No one in the village looked sick or injured; the complete opposite from the previous village. Their bodies appeared strong and vibrant and healthy.

How could a remote, isolated people show no outward signs of sickness?

Strange.

26

The villagers watched quietly, pensively, following our every move, on edge against us encroaching their homeland.

I didn't blame them. We were quite the sight: a hundred foot, open-air, three-deck boat with sixty people clamoring at the rails, gawking. It was like a coach bus pulling up to my front yard with all the passengers staring from the windows. Uh, awkward.

No doubt the villagers had seen these boats pass in the far-off distance, but none had docked at their shore. I half expected them to pull out poisonous darts and shoot at us.

The male villagers, shirtless and holding pointed sticks, stood defensively. Scattered around them, scowling women wore coarse and hand-loomed dresses, with many cradling nursing toddlers. Not exactly a feel-good ticker-tape parade. Their facial expressions looked like someone had yelled, "*Free enemas!*"

The temperature felt hot and humid, suffocating, like a fat dude riding on my back. A sweet pineapple smell wafted through the air, making it more bearable.

The village itself looked much smaller than the previous one, a quarter of the size. Its huts were simple and solid: thatched straw and stilted A-frames constructed from bamboo, palm leaves, and wood. Sparse, but they did the job.

While Jose talked to the tribal leaders, Lola gathered our team for a quick pep-talk.

"Our Word of the Day is *perspicacious.*" She spoke fast, bobbing around like she had drank too many Red Bulls. "It means having insight and deep understanding into things. It's like saying, 'She has perspicacious judgment.' We'll need it as we step into this new village. Be extremely careful. These villagers don't trust us yet."

"Are these people dangerous?" C-Lo asked.

"I told you in Leticia, everything in the Amazon is dangerous." Lola looked at me. "Right, Pace?"

I pointed to her. "Stay out of the jungle."

She smiled. "See? The boy has learned something. He's growing in perspicaciousness."

I wasn't so sure about her assessment, but I finally acknowledged the need for crutches. My ankle had grown increasingly painful, mainly because like an idiot I kept walking on it. Ibuprofen brought little relief, and several doctors considered a cortisone injection if there wasn't soon improvement. I hated needles, but maybe Sage would lay her hands on me and pray again.

"Okay gang, bring it in." Lola motioned us to huddle. "We're here to kick butt and take names. Give it your best and love these people like there's no tomorrow."

We placed our hands together and lifted them with a whoop.

"Who Da Mom?" she yelled.

"You Da Mom!" we shouted back.

After Jose gave us the go ahead, we disembarked and tried connecting with the villagers. Nothing worked. It felt forced, like we intruded on their privacy. Though Jose had talked with them beforehand, we were a strange looking boat of gringos.

But after several minutes, many villagers returned to their daily work, apparently comforted that their tribal leaders had given us their blessing and we showed no aggression.

Village life buzzed with activity. Many able-bodied youngsters helped the adults with fishing, rowing out into the river in thin and wooden canoes, anticipating a catch for a future meal. Others worked in the fields beside the men, cutting grass using only a machete. But several villagers glared at us with curiosity, especially as we unloaded the horde of supply boxes and equipment.

Being unable to walk, all I could do was sit and watch the medical set-up, feeling emasculated. Every day, the natives survived Amazon dangers, but I couldn't manage a sprained ankle? Maybe I had a condition known as *wimpitis*.

At least it gave me a chance to observe. The last village had many big-bellied children, due to worm infestation. But this new village showed no evidence of those issues, surprising since the nearest hospital required days of rowing to get there. What was their secret?

Without needing to treat imminent injuries or sicknesses, our team changed strategy, instead focusing on prevention, such as educating moms about boiling water before giving it to their children. We'd disperse toothbrushes and toothpaste, distribute mosquito nets, and show them how to build better latrines.

As our tents raised, the villagers gasped at the slick and shiny material, watching our strange huts being lifted in the air and built in mere minutes. Magic from the modern world. But instead of it endearing us to them, our oddness separated us even more, and they shuffled back several steps, perhaps fearful of our contraptions.

Except for one villager, a young man probably in his twenties. He stepped from the retreating crowd and addressed us in his language. Puffing out his chest, he pointed toward the bottom of nearby trees.

We all stared. Two separate ant hives stood against the trunks, both knee-high.

Using my crutches, I approached closer, noticing black insects crawling in and out of the dirt cones. Immediately recognizing the species, my breath hitched.

The villager rubbed his arm and motioned toward the ant hills. I looked for Jose or Lola, hoping for some insight, but they stood across the village talking with others.

Then the man yelled something else, in a booming voice.

I turned to Sage. "What's he saying?"

"He's daring us to battle him in an ancient ritual."

"What kind of ritual?"

"It's where two people stick their arms into ant hives. The last one to pull it out is the winner."

I flinched. "That guy's crazy. Those aren't ordinary ants. They're bullet ants."

Four times the size of average ants, bullet ants resembled wingless wasps and packed a venom-filled sting. The insect inherited its name for its powerful puncture, one of the most painful experiences known to man, like being shot with a bullet. Guaranteed to knock you on your butt.

While not usually fatal, a bullet ant's sting resulted in twenty-four hours of excruciating pain and a temporarily paralyzed body limb. So sorry, buddy, we're not that stupid. Keep your rituals to yourself.

"I'll do it." Big Country's voice.

I turned and saw him stepping forward. He must've overheard Sage's explanation and decided on taking the challenge. Was he bluffing?

I tried persuading him otherwise, but he wouldn't listen. He had no idea the power of the awaiting sting.

"On the farm, I've encountered much worse than ants." He rolled his sleeves up to his shoulders. "Plus, I've got more fat than the other guy. I'll be okay. Maybe it'll help us win their respect."

The villager smiled and waved Big Country forward. The man smeared a dark coating on Big Country's arm and hand, what looked like charcoal, then rubbed it on himself. Did they really think that stuff would be an adequate protective covering?

I grabbed Big Country by the arm. "Look, it's not worth doing this. Trust me, we'll earn their respect another way."

"Listen to Pace," Sage added. "There's no reason getting hurt doing something like this."

Big Country turned and spoke with seriousness. "Let me do it. Where I come from, we accept challenges because otherwise you're labeled a pushover." He stared at the skinny villager. "If he can do it, so can I."

"Yeah, but he's been raised here." I pointed to the man, who was busy slapping his arms. "He probably eats those ants. Maybe he's developed a resistance."

Big Country didn't answer, only shook his head and smiled, stepping toward the tree. Both men knelt in front of their respective hives as the dirt hills buzzed with agitated ants.

Tension filled the air. They lifted their coated arms, and with a mutual nod, thrust their hands inside, up to their elbows.

I grimaced, barely able to watch.

But nothing happened. Maybe the strange coating somehow stunned the ants and made them unable to sting.

Five seconds, ten.

And then it happened.

Both men screamed simultaneously. The surrounding villagers, a couple dozen, began swaying and singing, like in a bizarre religious ceremony.

Meanwhile, the two men beat the ground with their fists, howling in pain, doubling over and shaking violently, too stubborn to give up.

Twenty seconds, twenty-five.

They eyed each other with anguish, the haunting song of the villagers growing louder, each man focused on outlasting the other.

With every passing second, they crouched closer to the ground, convulsing, barely managing the shockwaves of stings. A high-stakes game of chicken. Who would blink first?

Big Country grasped his submerged arm with his free one, forcing it to remain inside, not wanting to lift it involuntarily.

Beside him, the villager looked shocked at his worthy opponent, a man double his size with an amazing threshold for pain.

Forty-five seconds, fifty.

With a shriek, the villager pulled his arm from the hive. A second later, realizing his victory, Big Country lifted his free.

The village song stopped. Both men fell on their backs in agony, pictures of misery and torture, and trembled with cold sweat.

Their skin blistered quickly with red, swollen spots resembling chicken pox. They needed immediate help.

I yelled for our doctors, but none stood nearby. And then an older man appeared from the crowd wearing an elaborate headdress made from an assortment of orange and red and yellow feathers.

All heads turned.

His dark face was painted with intricate designs and shapes, from his forehead to his chin. Gray hair protruded from the headdress, covering his ears and accenting bushy eyebrows. He carried a decorative bowl and stirred the contents with a crude brush.

He was a medicine man, the spiritual leader, one with a deep knowledge of the jungle's biological treasures. A *shaman*.

Unruffled by the contortions of the men, he stroked the moist brush on their hands and arms, singing underneath his breath in a deep baritone chant.

Almost immediately, the two men calmed. Seconds later, they

sat up, catching their breath, their chests rising and falling as if they had completed an epic wrestling match.

In minutes, the swelling and redness miraculously decreased.

Big Country slowly rose, dusting off his shirt and pants.

"See?" He looked at me, his voice shaken and eyes unfocused. "Rednecks always win."

I stood in shock. What just happened?

And could that potion stuff work on my ankle?

27

Big Country did us good.

His bullet ant "plan" was foolish and dangerous, but somehow it worked. Strike one up for the country boys.

After his victory, the villagers reacted differently toward us, like we had passed an unspoken test. They began treating us as family, welcoming our team into village life. Once they trusted us, the villagers showed kindness and generosity. But they remained a quiet, introverted bunch; more subdued than the first village.

We responded by inviting the people onto our boat for an impromptu tour. They loved it. Jose said the villagers had never stepped on a large vessel before, and they gawked at its sheer size.

Red Goth took pictures of everyone, and the villagers looked confused over the black box flashing in her hands. Probably the first and only photos of their lives.

After she snapped the shots, she showed them the preview screen of their lifelike images, and the villagers gasped and pointed in amazement. From visiting a three-deck boat to discovering a digital camera, it proved a memorable experience for that remote tribe.

Throughout the rest of the day, our team traded within the village. We offered clothing and snack items in return for their crafts and baskets and painted tribal masks. I'd never seen people so excited over protein bars and chips.

But the food wrappers presented a unique problem. Apparently they'd never eaten food requiring the removal of packaging, and more than once we caught them chewing the chocolate bars, wrappers and all. They didn't seem too embarrassed.

In terms of medical help, outside of prevention, the only priority was a young pregnant woman. I wanted to ask her, "Can I rub your buddha belly?" but thought it might be borderline creepy.

The doctors believed her birth could happen at any time, but she showed no imminent signs of labor. They watched her carefully, though, and suggested she utilize the boat for monitored rest.

The day passed into evening, and the team prepared for a night crusade. But I was concerned. My foot had swollen larger and felt more sensitive to the touch. I wouldn't be of much use.

Then a thought hit me: what if I stayed on the boat with the pregnant girl? Our physicians needed a break, and I needed to rest my ankle. A win-win. If by some small chance she went into labor, I'd send Yeisson to grab our doctors.

When I told Jose my idea, he agreed.

Surprisingly, James overheard and offered to stay awhile, too, in case his medical training could help.

Tajuana's orange-flowered dress flowed to her ankles, and the sunny color contrasted against her brown skin, giving her a healthy glow.

Her youth surprised me. About sixteen years old with strikingly beautiful features, she wobbled up the boat's gangway holding her stomach, which looked like a beach ball ready to pop.

James, Yeisson, and I were the only ones on the boat. Due to the language barrier, James and I said our names and shook her hand. She smiled and nodded.

Yeisson, however, carried on a short conversation with her, speaking freely in the village language that sounded mostly like Spanish.

We led Tajuana to a large, somewhat unlit room we affectionately called "The Operating Room" because it contained an examination table and shelves crammed with medical supplies. It resembled an outdated high school lab. All it lacked was a creepy doctor holding a squirting syringe. The room granted better sterilization than an open-air tent environment, and our physicians reserved it for the serious cases.

She stretched out on the bed with a groan, looking tired, and we settled into chairs against the wall.

I wondered why Yeisson remained on the boat when the children's outdoor crusade offered fun and games. Then it dawned on me. He loved soda and probably thought he could score a can by staying behind. Why disappoint the kid?

When I grabbed the drinks, Yeisson's eyes grew big. He chugged twenty ounces in ten seconds, almost in one long gulp, then erupted a room-shaking, physics-defying burp.

"Why fart and waste it when you can burp and taste it?" James joked.

Yeisson wiped his mouth with his arm and smiled in triumph.

"Thanks for hanging with me," I said to James as I leaned my chair on its rear legs. "Haven't seen you much today."

"Yeah, I was with Sarah."

The name *Sarah* sounded odd, since I only thought of her as *Red Goth*. A gleam sparkled in his eyes. "I helped her organize the villagers for their pictures. She's a talented girl, with a lot of interesting philosophies on life."

"Definitely a deep thinker."

"She encouraged me to stay here with you for a little while," he said. "To be a part of this girl's birth song."

"Birth song?"

"It's her poetic way of describing the pregnancy and child birthing experience."

"To me, there's nothing poetic about it. It's like squeezing a watermelon through a slurpee straw." I rubbed the back of my neck. "But whatever. I don't think the birth song is happening tonight. Why don't you take off and enjoy the crusade?"

"I'll go in a few minutes." James looked at Tajuana. "Man, childbirth is a miraculous thing, isn't it? A human being coming out of another human being."

"I'm amazed at doctors who deliver babies every day. I'd be a nervous wreck."

"I use to feel the same way. But then I realized delivering a baby is a lot like playing football."

"*Football*?" I asked.

"Yeah, lots of similarities. Think about it, starting with a uniform. Football players wear jerseys and helmets, baby doctors wear gowns and gloves. Got to be prepared for all the baby juices."

"Baby juices?"

"It gets messy." James finished his soda, then crushed the can in his hands. "But that's okay. Nature knows what it's doing. But it can get intimidating, like facing a defensive blitz. A seasoned quarterback stays cool under pressure. Delivering a baby requires the same. Don't panic. If the mom sees you panic, she may panic."

I laughed. "So delivering a baby is like playing quarterback?"

"Absolutely. We're after the Super Bowl trophy, which is a safe and healthy birth. And it all begins under center at the line of scrimmage."

He stood and imitated a quarterback crouching, ready to receive a hiked football. "And when the game's on the line, you've gotta be confident. Respect the defense."

"The defense?"

"See Tajuana's face?" James pointed to her. "Always watch a woman's face. During childbirth, it tells you everything. Don't be fooled. If you misread and disrespect a birthing momma, she'll rise up and snap you like a twig. Anyone who can push an eight pound baby out of a tiny hole is a Billy Badass, in my opinion."

He sounded dead serious, which made it funnier. I'd never heard someone relate football to childbirth, but if anyone could do it believably, it was James.

"Okay." I tried controlling my laughter. "So I need to stay focused and confident, watching the woman's face. Eyes on the prize."

"Football's a rough sport, Pace. You might get punched in the throat. Likewise, when it comes to delivery, be prepared for anything. It can get rough in the trenches. Yelling, cursing, blood."

"And baby juices."

"Yes!" he exclaimed. "The baby's head comes out first, and you must gently guide it with your hands, like a quarterback cradling the ball. Once the shoulders slide out, the rest of the baby comes fast."

"And that's it?"

"No. You've got the ball in your hands but you need to cross the end-zone. When you finally lay the newborn on the mother's chest, you've scored."

"*Delivery* in the clutch."

James loved it. "Perfect way to describe it. See what I mean? *Football*. Oh, and remember, at first babies don't look like they do in the movies. They have cone heads and look like they're covered in mayonnaise."

"Gross."

"Don't ever say that to a new mother. Or an old mother. To a mom, there are no ugly babies."

"Point taken," I said. "But I'm curious, how many babies have you delivered?"

"Oh, well, none. Not yet. But in school we've watched a lot of videos."

Uh, okay. It was like taking Drivers Ed from someone who had never driven a car. But I loved his confidence.

James stayed for a bit longer, probably because he sensed

my nervousness with the expectant mother in our midst. I appreciated it. But after a while, when an imminent baby encounter seemed unlikely, he decided to visit the crusade and urged me to send Yeisson for help, if needed.

So the two of us waited. I drank bottled water, while Yeisson downed the sodas and rattled more burps.

Apart from Yeisson's supernatural belching ability, he amazed me with his compassion towards Tajuana. Whenever she moved uncomfortably on the bed, moaning as she changed positions, he'd hurry to her side, placing a wet cloth on her forehead and holding her hand.

Eventually, Tajuana drifted to sleep, forcing us to remain quiet. We played several hands of cards, but soon Yeisson grew restless. Probably the loads of caffeine.

He pointed to himself, then in the direction of the crusade. "Yeisson. Sage." He held his fingers close together, indicating he wouldn't be long.

He was growing more attached to Sage, and he wanted to see her. Couldn't blame him.

I glanced at the sleeping mom-to-be. Still no baby action. What would it hurt if he made a quick crusade visit? As long as he checked back soon.

I nodded and held my fingers to indicate a short trip.

Yeisson seemed to understand, and with a wave, he quietly

darted out the door.

In the distance, the crusade music danced along in the air from the middle of the village. A moment later, I sat alone on the boat with a very pregnant woman.

Please rest well. And long.

A sleeping pregnant woman meant no baby. And I'd be off baby watch soon.

Even in sleep, Tajuana's arm cradled her belly, protecting her unborn child, her face looking pretty and serene. The calm before the storm.

But why was she alone?

And where was her family?

28

What a boneheaded move.

Tajuana had been asleep for fifteen minutes, off in peaceful la la land. That's when I woke her. Not on purpose.

My crutch leaned against the wall, and as I stretched my leg — *BAM* — the crutch fell over and banged into a metal countertop and clanged like a church bell.

She awakened with a jolt, a startled look in her eyes. Then she clutched her stomach.

Thankfully, the crutch had missed her, but the sudden noise kickstarted a contraction. This was why people don't put me in charge.

Tajuana grimaced, riding a wave of intense spasms. Then, just as quickly, her body relaxed.

I did, too. That was a close one.

She glanced at the crutch on the floor, then me.

My face grew warm with embarrassment. "Sorry," I said, not knowing if she understood.

Barely a minute passed. Another contraction.

It seemed fiercer than the one before. Uh-oh. I looked toward the door. Where was Yeisson?

The doctors needed to be here, not me. Did Tajuana think I was a physician? She probably wondered why I sat there glaring at her with a dumb look on my face. At least she didn't know I was a flunk-out busboy. Sometimes a language barrier is a good thing.

She screamed, gritting her teeth, and for some reason my mind flashed to old TV episodes featuring women giving birth. Someone would inevitably ask for towels and hot water. I understood the towels, but why the hot water? For brewing coffee? A spot of tea? I could've used a stiff drink, that's for sure.

The contraction gradually weakened, and things returned to normal.

We stared at each other awkwardly, two strangers thrown together in one of life's biggest moments. Her expression showed loneliness and fear, unsure of what was to come. I didn't know who looked more nervous, her or me.

Another contraction. Tajuana shrieked and bolted upright, holding her belly and back.

I wasn't sure where to stand or how to help, but she definitely needed comfort. Yeisson, at eleven years old, was more natural at it than me. I thought of James's football analogies. *Stay calm under pressure*. Yeah, easier said than done.

With a deep breath, I hobbled beside her, and after her contraction ended, I gave her a soda and dabbed her face with a towel.

For a few moments, everything calmed.

Then more contractions erupted in violent surges.

Where was Yeisson? I held her hand, the vice grip almost unbearable.

Her pain crested and subsided, before crashing back again with electric force, like her insides were being twisted and squeezed. She wailed as her back seized, so I applied pressure and rubbed her back and whispered encouragement.

She had moments of loud screams, followed by short, silent periods of panting and exhaling.

A clock ticked on the wall, a noise I hadn't noticed before. And oddly, the *tick-tock* grew in volume between every contraction, booming like a timpani kettledrum, the beat mirroring the unabated advancement of life.

Tajuana released my hand and gripped the table. She squinched her eyes and a vein rose on her forehead. If I touched her, she screeched and growled.

The reality finally hit. The baby wasn't waiting for a doctor; that baby locomotive was barreling down the uterus train tracks straight toward me.

I slipped on gloves. *Football players wear uniforms, so do baby doctors.*

Her body dripped with sweat and she turned toward me and yelled angrily.

Couldn't understand a word. I'm pretty sure she said something about my mother. I didn't mind, though. If I was giving birth, I'd probably say much worse.

I felt sorry for her, a young girl all alone. Where was the baby's father? She should be yelling at him, not me.

Or what about Tajuana's mother? It didn't seem right for me to be there, experiencing the once-in-a-lifetime event, intruding on someone's most private and precious moment.

Another scream; it sounded different than the others. She started pushing. *Dear God in heaven.*

I stood behind her, rubbing her shoulders and back, as her body shook and convulsed. Then she lifted the bottom of her dress and spread her legs.

Should I stand in front of her? Would it be awkward? She lay spread-eagle, after all.

But I instantly realized there was no other option; I had to deliver the baby. The adrenaline kicked in and I forgot my ankle pain.

I knelt in front of her like a quarterback behind center, her nether regions in my face. It seemed perfectly normal and primal and medical.

As she pushed, Tajuana worried me. Her body drooped from exhaustion and the natural childbirth brought her unrelenting agony.

Several times she tried fighting the contraction, but I encouraged her to keep going. The baby was near.

Panicked questions ran through my mind: what if she or the little one faced an emergency situation? What if the baby breeched? What if the cord wrapped around the baby's neck?

The day before, I had feared death; but now I feared life.

After only two or three pushes, I could see it; the baby's head, a patch of black hair.

My heart thumped wildly. *Be confident, you can do this*.

I found peace in remembering childbirth had taken place billions of times, in billions of places. Many without doctors.

I placed my hands gently around the baby's emerging head, and a moment later, a scrunched face appeared.

From that point forward, the birth resembled a dam bursting, emptying and exploding and spraying, with a blood pool collecting on the bed.

James had warned about the bodily fluids. But not the sounds. Fortunately, I had a strong stomach.

Tajuana pushed again and the baby's shoulders slid out, followed quickly by the torso, and in a blink, I held a newborn in my arms.

A boy.

And he looked like he was covered in mayonnaise.

The baby cried, and cradling the tiny body, I wiped his face with a clean cloth and placed him on Tajuana's chest. He calmed immediately.

In a split second, everything changed from traumatic to peaceful. The old was gone, the new had come. The greatest moment of my life.

Tears flowed down Tajuana's cheeks and she kissed the baby's forehead, wrapping her arms tenderly around him and smothering him with a mother's love.

Then she closed her eyes, wearied, and the three of us sat in the beautiful, messy aftermath, the tick of the clock pounding away above us.

29

Footsteps on the boat, approaching the room. *It's about time, Yeisson. You're a little late*.

Tajuana and the baby rested comfortably, with the umbilical cord still attached. No way I was cutting it.

The steps stopped at our door.

It wasn't Yeisson, but the shaman; the same man who rubbed the voodoo ointment on Big Country. He carried a fan of dried leaves and exuded a calming presence. Nodding at me, he spoke softly to Tajuana and knelt by her bed while rubbing the baby's back.

He waved the fan over their bodies and uttered in a monotone voice, like some sort of prayer, then reached inside the fold of his tunic. Pulling out a tiny container, he opened it and lifted it to his lips.

He drank without swallowing, then slowly spray-blowed the liquid onto both the baby and Tajuana while again waving the fan leaves. An ancient village blessing, I assumed. Mom and child settled into a peaceful rest.

Then he left abruptly, his work apparently done, silently acknowledging me on his way out.

What a weird ceremony. But how did he know the infant was born? The entire village attended the crusade, and the newborn had barely cried. Yet the shaman arrived at exactly the right moment, like when the wise men followed a star and visited the baby Jesus. But instead of gold, frankincense, and myrrh, he sprayed stuff on them. Go figure.

I walked outside and stood by the railing, watching him step off the gangway and disappear into the night, down a dirt path toward a hut in the middle of the empty village. An eccentric loner.

In the distance beyond the huts, Jose's crusade was finishing and Yeisson emerged from the shadows running toward the boat. He saw me standing by the railing.

I yelled to him, "Doctor! Baby!"

He understood and turned around, sprinting back toward our team.

A few moments later, Yeisson and several doctors hurried onto the boat and darted into the Operating Room. They glared at Tajuana and then at me, expressing both surprise and shock. I shrugged.

The doctors examined the mother and child, handling the afterbirth details while I stepped outside for fresh air, with Yeisson by my side.

I stared at him and lifted my hands as if asking, *Where were you?*

His face flashed guilt. “Yeisson. Sage.”

With a hug, I let him know everything was okay; only eleven years old, cut the boy some slack. Sage was quite the distraction. How could I blame him?

News of the birth must have spread quickly because we watched the entire village leave the crusade and stream toward the boat. In minutes, the crowd pressed on board, wanting a glimpse of the newborn.

Our missions team went nuts when they saw me, making a big deal about the delivery. Embarrassing, really. Given the situation, they would’ve done the same thing, but it felt nice making a contribution since my ankle had sidelined me for a full day.

James was the first to offer a celebratory hug. “You did it! You won the Super Bowl! Now you can teach me a few things.”

I pointed back at him. “The *murse* gave me great coaching.”

“That’s my boy!” Lola followed right behind him, jumping up and down like a whirling dervish. “God knew what he was doing when he kept you behind. Is the baby okay? The mom? You? Can I do anything?” Somehow her mouth had to keep up with her hyperactive brain.

Jose gave a fist bump. “Well played, Pace. This birth is your *crowning* achievement." He laughed hard. "Get it? *Crowning*?"

Red Goth entered the Operating Room with her camera and snapped pictures of the mom and infant from all types of artsy-fartsy angles. Probably the first village newborn ever recorded on camera.

Then Banks and C-Lo arrived, offering their unique brand of encouragement.

"You really know your way around a vagina." She patted my back as she walked by. "Congratulations."

I wasn't sure how to respond. *Thanks*? "A dollar for every time I've heard that," I finally said.

"You're a real hoohaw whisperer," Banks added.

"I prefer baby whisperer." I tilted my head. "And *hoohaw*? Really? Is that what your grandmother calls it?"

He ignored the comment. "Too bad we can't celebrate with Cuban cigars. That's what real men do after a birth."

"That's a sexist statement." C-Lo stood by the foot of the bed and admired the baby. "The women push the babies out, but the men smoke stogies. I'd bet a hundred bucks you couldn't handle a cigar."

"And you could?" he asked.

"I'd smoke you under a table," she sneered. "And I'd do it *while* giving birth. To twins."

"Oh really?" Banks didn't back down. "Be careful. They say

cigars grow hair on a chest."

She motioned toward her ample bosom. "If only you could find out."

Big Country thankfully interrupted and gave me a high-five. "Proud of you, Pace. I've helped deliver a few calves, but never a human. You should be awarded a honorary degree."

C-Lo couldn't resist. "Yeah, let's start calling him Dr. Oppenwider."

"Or Dr. Pappy Smear," Banks said.

They both laughed. Since they weren't putting each other down, I suffered at their expense.

"So is the baby healthy?" Big Country asked, showing no ill effects from the bullet ants, the bites barely visible on his arm.

I nodded. "Yeah, thankfully. The baby resembles a wrinkled potato with a patch of black hair. Like a troll doll, but very cute."

The sentence barely left my mouth when Sage walked up. Her presence always felt like pixie dust sprinkled from heaven.

She kissed my cheek. "I heard the news, Dr. Pace Howell. And I'm impressed."

I'll never wash that cheek again. And at least she didn't call me Dr. Spreadems.

"Thanks. I was scared to death, but everything turned out fine."

After Sage caught a glimpse of the baby, we walked outside

to the deck, alone, since people crowded the room.

“And you were the guy afraid of lice.” She leaned against the railing, her eyes narrowed. “But look at you now. Going and delivering a baby. You faced a fear and overcame it.”

“Sometimes you don’t have a choice.”

“But you embraced the moment. Childbirth is a scary experience, I’ve witnessed it over and over.”

“You’ve delivered babies?”

“No, but a few years ago I worked at the hospital as a candy striper.”

“You… striped candy?”

She laughed. “It’s a term for teenage girl volunteers. We wore red and white striped jumpers that looked like candy canes. I served hours in the maternity ward.”

“Then you know how incredible it is, witnessing a birth,” I said. “My mom deserves a bigger Mother’s Day present. Didn’t realize childbirth was so gruesome. I’m just glad the baby and Tajuana are healthy.”

“They’re definitely blessed.”

Blessed. The word reminded me of the shaman blessing the baby. “Do you know anything about the village shaman?”

“The guy who healed Big Country?” she asked. “No, not really. A shaman tends to be mysterious, even a bit elusive.”

“It was strange. He arrived here minutes after the birth. How did he know?"

"Coincidence? Maybe he was checking on her."

"I don't think it was a coincidence. He came prepared for a blessing ceremony."

"Shamans serve that role in their villages," Sage said. "They're masters of their craft and claim a deep connection with nature as a source of their healing powers. Some say they're hucksters, but it's hard arguing with results. Like what happened with Big Country."

"Have you ever talked with one?"

She paused. "I don't think so."

"Could you translate if I talked to him?"

"I could probably manage it, since these villagers speak a loose form of Spanish. But what do you want to ask him?"

"Lots of questions. From the healing stuff to…" I paused. "Other things."

She burrowed her eyebrows. "What other things?"

I felt embarrassed saying it out loud. "I'm wondering if he knows anything about the Sea Creature."

"The Sea Creature?"

"I know, it sounds crazy. But you saw Red Goth's picture. That kind of stuff fascinates me."

"That's why you're my favorite animal biologist." She smiled. "So yeah, if you want to ask him about it, I'll help you."

I glanced around at the boat teeming with people. “Everyone’s awake for a while. Want to go now?”

She looked surprised. “Now?”

“I know where he lives. A quick conversation. Come on, it’ll be fun and maybe educational.”

Sage stared out into the village, like fighting an internal debate. She finally exhaled in surrender.

“Okay, Pace Howell. I’m a bit leery since drama follows you around lately. But lead the way.”

That’s all I needed to hear.

No one noticed as we slipped off the boat and stepped into the darkened village, just the two of us, hoping answers awaited in a tiny, thatched hut.

30

The front door didn't exactly scream *Welcome*.

Draping the entrance were reddened chicken bones with holes bored into their bulbous ends, held together by a string of vine. A splattering of painted circles, each with a dot in the middle, covered the wood-planked door. Not the ideal place to sell Girl Scout cookies.

Sage smiled half-heartedly in a way that seemed to ask, *Why did you bring me here?*

There wasn't a good answer other than curiosity. Or insanity. But how many chances do you get to visit a real Amazon shaman?

After knocking on the door, a shuffling noise came from within. Nothing happened for a moment, and then the door swung open.

We stepped back.

The shaman, his hair pulled in a ponytail, glared at us silently as a necklace of ornaments drooped across his chest. I elbowed Sage to say something, anything, and she addressed him in his language.

They conversed back and forth in short, stilted conversation. More silence and awkward stares. He finally backed away from the entrance and motioned us inside, flashing a tooth ring on his finger. Whatever Sage had said, it worked.

The hut's interior had a cadaverous appearance, resembling the aftermath of a crime scene. An acidic odor hit my nostrils; the nauseating smell of steaming herbs or maybe the sulphur smell of cooked cabbage. It stunk to high heaven.

The room was droopy and dark, except for a small fire flickering in the middle of the floor. On each side of the fire pit stood a thick Y-shaped branch holding one end of a log stretching across the flames. The firewood crackled and snapped, the smoke wisps escaping out of an opening in the thatched ceiling.

Goosebumps rose on my arms. A human skull rested in the dirt, silently observing the proceedings through hollow eyes. Maybe it had belonged to a former patient or a foreigner who once visited unannounced.

More bizarre decorations dangled from ceiling strings, like demented wind chimes. Crooked shelves lined the walls, stocked with jugs and gourds and hand-carved images. Probably local deities.

Around the base of the hut lay a graveyard of animal hides and tusks, drums and rattles; along with bone spears, antlers, and a peculiar collection of smoking pipes. The man definitely had a Gothic decorating style.

We followed the shaman's lead and sat on the dirt floor beside the fire, on the opposite side from him.

The orange glow of the flames danced on his face, highlighting his coal eyes and carved age lines. It sorta freaked me out. I imagined his deep ancestry, the long family tree of mystics and healers and storytellers who had passed their necromantic knowledge from generation to generation.

He and Sage talked in short sentences, and after a moment of silence, she turned to me.

"He's willing to answer our questions out of gratitude for helping his village. You talk, I'll translate."

Turns out, she was a remarkable translator. Though some phrases had to be repeated and clarified, I talked to the shaman with little difficulty.

"Thank you for inviting us inside," I said.

He drew a deep breath. "You come with questions?"

He wasn't a man for small talk, so I got straight to the point.

"You healed one of our team members from the bullet ants. And the entire village is remarkably healthy. How do you do it?"

"Your friend was brave, but foolish. I spared him much pain." He looked at my wrapped ankle, then at Sage's arm cast. "Are you also brave and foolish?"

“Foolish most of the time,” I responded. “But not very brave.”

He stoked the fire with a long walking stick, rarely making eye contact. “You are indeed brave, otherwise you would not ask a shaman about his healing practices.”

“I’m sorry.” Five minutes and I’d already ticked him off. “Just curious, that’s all.”

“You do not know what you ask. Have you ever communicated with the spirits?”

I wondered how to answer the translated question. Sage smiled and shrugged, probably happy I was on the hot seat and not her.

“Spirits?” I asked. “No sir, I’ve never talked to spirits.”

He lifted his gaze from the flames, his eyes burrowing into mine. “Do you believe in spirits?”

Whatever. Ghosts and palm readings and seances. The spirit world. All a crock of bull. But I didn’t want to offend him.

“If you mean talking with dead people, I’m not sure.”

The shaman wielded his walking stick like a pitchfork. “Then you will never understand my healing practices. The spirit world is life, not death. Health, not sickness.”

“Can you show me the spirit world?” My unplanned question popped out, a challenge for him to persuade the unconvinced.

Sage bit her lip, seeming uncomfortable as she asked him my question.

A slight smile formed on the shaman's face. "Only if you drink from the yaje."

"A yaje?" I didn't have a clue about a yaje. "What happens if I drink it?"

"That is for you to discover. It opens deep layers of the mind. What cannot be explained must be experienced. Do you want to try?"

After Sage translated, she leaned over and whispered. "I've heard of this drink before. It's made from a jungle vine. Extremely powerful, like a drug. You could get very sick."

A part of me wanted to try it, but it would risk getting ill and becoming a further hindrance to the team.

"I'm afraid of getting sick." I held a hand to my stomach.

The shaman laughed. "But you are already sick." He pointed to both of our injuries, my ankle and her broken arm. "Fortunately you do not need to see spirits to be healed." He paused. "You came here for healing, did you not?"

After Big Country's miraculous recovery, I considered asking the shaman to do the same *voodoo-hoodoo* on my ankle. But the day's busy events, including the unexpected childbirth, had distracted me. I hadn't come to his hut for healing, but for answers.

"No, sir," I said. "We're not here to get anything from you. Only answers to questions."

A thunderous beating sound started; heavy rain pelted the

thatched roof, and Sage and I jumped at the noise. Water dripped inside, but the shaman stood and adjusted the roof covering with his walking stick to divert rain from the fire.

"So you do not desire healing?" He stood with his shoulders drooped.

My mind raced. "Yes, we do desire healing, but we didn't come here expecting it."

"Why not? You must live with expectancy." He walked to a leaning shelf by the wall and lifted a basin the size of a large bucket. "You want answers? I will give you the greatest answer. The secret of the village's health is found inside this vessel. A *drink*." He sloshed the liquid. "But it is almost gone, and the village faces a dark future."

"The village's health is because of a drink?" I asked. "Can't you make more of it?"

He stared, unblinking, for several moments before answering. "You do not know what you ask." More silence. "But I will give you and your friend the last of it."

Sage and I looked at each other, surprised. We couldn't take the final amount from these villagers.

"You're very kind, but we must refuse." I waved the drink off. "Please save it for your people."

"For decades, my people have benefited from this tonic. It has given much to us. It is now our turn to give."

A quandary. It would be highly offensive to reject such a generous and sacrificial offer. But also a risk to drink it, much like the yaje.

The shaman seemed to read my mind. “No worry. Unlike the yaje, it will not make you sick.”

“But aren’t there others who need it more than us?”

“That is not for you to decide.” His eyes flashed anger. “I am the steward, and I choose you.” Then his voice softened. “For I am grateful.”

“Grateful?”

“You delivered my grandson. Delivering the family member of a shaman is a high honor.”

“Tajuana is your... *daughter*?”

He nodded. “So you both must drink.”

We had no choice, though Jose warned us not to eat or drink anything local. If I got sick, it was one thing. But not Sage. I brought her there and felt responsible.

I whispered to her, “You don’t need to do this.”

“Yes, I do,” she answered with resolve.

Placing the container on the ground, the shaman shuffled to the other side of the hut, sliding on an elaborate headdress and fastening a leopard cape across his shoulders. My heart thumped at the unknown.

He carried a dented pot to the fire and hung it from the log above the flames, stirring the concoction by slowly rotating a thick stick between his palms. The vapor smelled like turpentine and menthol.

He performed an elaborate ceremony; haunting and strange and oddly beautiful. Muttering baritone words, he sang and chanted a flurry of incantations while dancing across the hut and waving feathers over us.

I stole a glance at Sage. *What have we gotten ourselves into?*

Next came the pounding of an animal hide drum, followed by the shaking of an odd-sounding rattle in four directions, north and south and east and west. He gave us dried tobacco leaves, not to smoke, but for squeezing tightly in our hands. Why, I had no idea.

After a few minutes, he took the crumpled tobacco back, rolling and stuffing it into a pipe. When he blew its smoke over us, I stifled a cough.

Examining our injuries, he lifted from the steaming pot several green strips of slimy leafage resembling seaweed. He draped long bits on my injured ankle. It seared like a hot rag, at first burning, then stinging, before finally cooling and causing a shiver. It reminded me as a boy whenever my grandmother slathered topical cream on my congested chest.

He did the same for Sage, but since the arm cast blocked her skin, he squeezed the herbage at both ends of the plaster, letting the juices drip and roll underneath. Judging from her expression, she experienced the same hot-cold tingling sensation.

Turning back to the large container, the shaman poured the last of the mysterious healing balm into wooden cups, until his container was bone dry.

"You must drink." He handed the liquid to us. "Drink it all."

He sat across the fire from us again, his body shuddering until he settled into a trance-like state. I gazed into my cup; the frothy potion resembled egg nog. I sniffed it, but no fragrance. *Here goes nothing.*

With a deep breath, Sage and I raised the cups to our lips.

Who knew? After we drank it, maybe *our* bones would be the ones hanging on the front door.

31

The cup offered barely enough for a sip or two.

How could that tiny amount really make a difference? I hated myself for doubting, but even with all the surrounding evidence it didn't seem logical.

Sage clutched her cup tightly and paused for a moment before tipping it upward, squeezing her eyes as she swallowed. Obviously not a pleasant taste. But by drinking first she showed less hesitation than me, and after a long exhale, she rubbed the residue from her lips and stared at the fire.

My turn. I thought about faking it, letting the goop touch my lips without swallowing. What awaited inside the cup? Smushed fish organs or crushed monkey brains? I remembered my dad once drank a terrible-tasting concoction to prepare for a colonoscopy. He sat on the toilet the entire day. I really didn't want the runs in the Amazon.

But after watching Sage, I couldn't be a wimp. Not in front of her. And the shaman waited for me, observing with a wild look in his eyes.

Remember, Pace, this was your idea. I should have stayed on the boat and basked in the birth celebration. But instead, we sat in a shaman's weird Halloweenie hut holding his abracadabra healing drink.

Just do it. Carpe Diem. Geronimo.

Like throwing back a shot glass, I swallowed the contents in one gulp, the thick liquid oozing down my throat as slime, the taste resembling a mixture of glue and grease. Another sip and I would've spewed.

But the effect was immediate. It felt like a soft and warm blanket draped over me, accompanied by an intoxicating feeling of lightness and the sensation of floating in the air on a billowy cloud.

The room spun. The slightest stimuli charged forward in vivid detail, sights and sounds and smells, all somehow unlocked and amplified by the mysterious tonic. And this wasn't even the yaje drink he told us about.

Sage blinked rapidly with an unfocused gaze. Then her eyes darted to mine, an expression that said *Help!* but with heavy eyelids showing her body relaxing. Whatever was happening to us, we experienced it together.

For a few moments, everything turned fluid; a dream, time slowing down, like being underwater without the water. I wanted to both scream and laugh, at nothing in particular, while the liquid plowed its way through my blood stream, a stimulant and sedative all at once. We needed some Pink Floyd tunes to complete the trippy experience.

An energy pulsated in and around me, the frightening sense that someone or something else had wrested control with devilish vigor. A relentless pressure pushed against my forehead, chest, legs. Muscles tightened and enlarged.

Then came a poking vibration, a tingling, like pins and needles prodding and exploring, restricting and constricting, invisible fingers pinching troubled areas. The injured ankle felt numb to the touch, but my mind worked clearer than ever.

The shaman broke the silence and spoke.

Sage translated, her voice wavering. “He says by tomorrow morning we will both be healed.”

If only a camera could have recorded Sage’s face and mine. *Skeptical*. Was the guy crazy? Was he screwing with us gullible gringos?

“But she has a broken bone.” I pointed to her pink cast. “How can a bone mend overnight?”

The shaman leaned closer. “The drink can restore broken bones, chase away diseases, heal cuts and gashes. But it cannot revive a dead person. It becomes less effective the closer one gets to death. Though it has been known to happen.”

I touched my forehead. A cold sweat. “How many other

villages use this drink?"

"We are the only village."

"So no one else knows about this?"

He shook his head. "There are many secrets along the river."

I stared into the heart of the fire, needing time to reflect. It seemed too good to be true. How could a remote village possess a medicine more advanced than modern hospitals?

Time would tell if the wonder drink really worked on us. And if it did? A discovery of this magnitude would forever shake medical history. It promised cures for major injuries and illnesses, maybe cancer or diabetes or HIV if what the shaman told us proved true.

But the drink was gone; he had served us the last drops.

"Do you have anything else to ask him?" Sage sounded anxious to leave.

"Actually, yes."

I had one more specific question; it was the reason I initially wanted to visit, though I felt nervous about his response.

"What do you know about the sea creature?" I asked.

Before she translated, Sage shifted and shot me a side glance. With a grimace, she asked him the question, and the shaman jerked back and narrowed his eyes.

Wow. Mentioning the sea creature really got a reaction, like bringing up politics or religion.

He responded in a challenging manner. "Why do you ask?"

"Just curious."

"How much do you know?"

"Very little." The effects of the drink were still strong, like a Mariachi band playing in my chest. "But I've seen reports of the boating accidents the creature has caused. And the hunts for it."

The shaman scoffed. "When people don't understand, they invent stories. The Hipupiara is as much a part of the Amazon as the water itself. It is the snake of the river."

"But apparently an angry snake. Many people have lost their lives because of it."

"She is a powerful creature, but intelligent." His voice lowered. "Her violence is not without cause."

We were getting somewhere. "You know a lot about this creature."

"Enough to have respect." He lifted the empty container of the healing drink. "She brings fear, but she also brings life."

Wait. What? "The drink... is from the *Hipupiara*?"

I was shocked about the connection.

"Indeed." A slight smile from his thin lips. "You now have the power of the river snake working inside of you."

Sage gasped. My brain couldn't fathom the implications. Things got weirder by the minute. If true, the village had been miraculously sustained by the Sea Creature for decades.

"How did you get this drink from the creature?" I asked.

"Why do you ask?"

His favorite question.

"Because I love animals and I'm intrigued by nature," I answered. "And now I'm fascinated by the spirit world of which you speak. If the Hipupiara has healing power, then it needs to be protected and not hunted. Appreciated and not hated."

"Yes." He gave a crisp nod. "That is the right answer, young man. You have a pure heart. Something that cannot be said for many."

He stood and grabbed another pipe, stuffing it with leaves. We declined when he offered us a smoke; my body didn't need anymore strange substances.

"The true story of the Hipupiara has not been shared outside this village." He lit the leaves, then puffed and exhaled a full-bodied fragrance of jasmine and cedar. "Do you want to hear it?"

I nodded, but Sage wrinkled her forehead and remained quiet. It felt like preparing for a ghost story around a campfire, except the shaman's tale was real. I was surprised he wanted to offer so much, almost like he had waited years for someone to ask.

He crouched again by the flames, blowing a smoke ring that rose and dissipated as an apparition.

Creepy hut? *Check.* Spooky shaman? *Check.* Loud rainstorm? *Another check.* Sage slid closer, her shoulder touching mine.

He began his tale.

As I was about to discover, it was a story that profoundly changed his life — and a story that would forever shape mine.

32

A born storyteller, the shaman's delivery sounded almost like a song, drawing us into his tempo and capturing our imaginations.

The power of his words held us in a trance, even with Sage translating every couple of lines.

This is how I remember his story:

Our village did not originally begin here; we lived several hours up the river. My grandfather served as the village shaman, and over time, he became increasingly concerned over the failing health of his people. The village suffered greatly.

During an evening yaje ceremony, he communicated with his ancestors. And to his surprise, the spirits directed him on a sojourn, promising an answer to our needs. So he packed provisions and set off, unaware of his final destination.

He traveled the jungle for six days, finding nothing, and wondered if he had understood correctly. Exploring remote areas, the journey proved harrowing, and at one point he fell and gashed his arm badly. Thick blood saturated his shirt.

Ready to give up and return home, he heard a loud, sliding noise. He investigated an overgrown section of the river bank, and that's when he saw it… a magnificent and frightening creature slid out of the water and into the underbrush, unlike anything he had ever seen.

The length of twenty-five men, the reptilian monster slithered and roiled across the river bank. It possessed a coiled neck and an extremely long tail, with yellowish stains blotting a thick and muscular body.

Slitted eyes perched on top of its triangular head, and a forked tongue stabbed between needle-like teeth. From its midsection protruded four fins, which served as forelimbs and hindlimbs, enabling the creature to move lightning fast whether in water or on land.

The creature turned and hissed, sounding like pent-up wind. My grandfather shuddered, frozen in terror and disbelief. Before him prowled a living nightmare, a behemoth of terrible proportions. And by accident, he had stumbled into its nesting ground full of eggs, at least two dozen, each the size of three coconuts.

Fully realizing the danger, he ran for his life, finally hiding a safe distance away. But oddly, the creature didn't pursue him and eventually slipped into the river and swam away.

Did his shamanic ancestors lead him there? My grandfather snuck toward the nest. He desired an egg from the magnificent creature, to study it, since he experimented with natural resources from the jungle, whether fruits or vines or dead animals.

Lifting two eggs cautiously, still favoring his bleeding arm, he carried them from the nest. And walking away, satisfied with the discovery, he instinctively glanced over his shoulder.

His breath stopped.

To his horror, the creature's head lurked slightly from the water a few feet from the shore, watching, like an alligator skimming the surface.

He feared for his life, but surprisingly, the creature didn't attack; it allowed him to inch away, eggs in his arms. Why didn't it strike?

In that moment, he believed a supernatural connection resided between the inhabitants of the spirit world and that monster in the river. He whispered the name, *Hipupiara*, which means dweller of the water. A name we have used ever since.

Taking note of the location for a later return — and noticing the curious swarm of birds — he departed for the village, carrying the eggs safely home.

Back in his hut, he cracked an egg and cooked it over the fire.

But to his dismay, the yolk burned almost immediately. Unusable.

Breaking open the second egg, he changed his approach, slowly adding boiling water and stirring softly, until the liquid thickened into a froth. Ten parts water to one part yolk. But was it safe to drink?

He understood the dangers of consuming jungle poisons, in their many forms. So for weeks he waited for direction, with no answer from the spirit world, amazed the peculiar substance remained intact without spoiling.

One day a village dog, a beloved pet of the children, was bitten in the jungle. It struggled back to the huts, shaking and dying. Sensing an opportunity, my grandfather secretly poured the egg drink into the dog's mouth, almost the entire amount.

And then he waited.

To his amazement, in minutes, the dog recovered and wobbled to its feet, completely healed. It proved the power of the drink, but would it work on a person? He needed more eggs.

Not long after, a child in the village became violently sick, and none of the shamanic healing treatments had any effect. Death was imminent. Desperate for eggs, he hurried to the nest, taking two men with him.

When they arrived, the Hipupiara was nowhere to be seen. The nesting ground contained numerous eggs, though some were cracked open by hungry birds, who fed on them savagely.

Though my grandfather warned the men of the dangerous creature, the two rushed into its lair, their greed for the eggs blinding their caution.

They did not see it coming.

In seconds, a large black shadow emerged from the river and lashed out, snapping its spindly tail like a whip, pulling their bodies into the water and instantly killing them, spraying my grandfather with their blood.

He watched in shock. The creature submerged in the water with its eyes bobbing on the surface, staring directly at him. Why didn't the creature attack him on the first visit? Would it kill him like it did the other men?

The boy, and the village, needed those eggs.

But after an hour, the creature hadn't moved. Summoning his courage, my grandfather approached nervously, a few steps at a time, eyes focused on the water. Easy steps.

Entering the nest, he slowly picked up two eggs. As he straightened, he held his breath, waiting for the deadly strike of the tail, prepared to sacrifice his life for the chance of saving the boy.

But surprisingly, no movement from the watching creature. Eggs in his arms, my grandfather backed out, matching the Hipupiara's glare the entire way.

The creature remained as still as the night. Perhaps the river snake desired to bring health to the village; perhaps the spirits of ancestors inhabited the creature; perhaps only a holy man, a shaman, was granted access into the nest, nature's holy of holies.

Rushing back to the village, he prepared another drink. And after performing a short ceremony, he poured a tiny amount into the dying boy's mouth, unsure of the human reaction to the unusual substance. The answer came quickly.

In an hour, the boy blinked open his eyes. Three hours later, he sat up in bed. And by the next morning, the boy played with the other children, like nothing had ever happened. A miraculous healing.

That child was my father.

Word soon spread, and others in our village sipped from the strange tonic with the same incredible results. Gnarled backs straightened, damaged limbs reformed, blind eyes opened.

But after learning of the death of the two men, they grew more fearful of the creature. Though the people were grateful for the egg potion, no one dared travel to the nest with my grandfather.

Meanwhile, he learned how to portion the drink to last longer, eventually using one egg to sustain the village for an entire year. But every autumn, he repeated his long journey, restocking for the future. Fresh eggs always awaited, and the Hipupiara always watched.

In time, he took my father with him, training him as an apprentice, though my grandfather insisted on retrieving the eggs.

But after he grew too old for the difficult journey, he passed the sacred duty to my father. It was a successful transition. When my father first entered the nest, the Hipupiara observed with the same dangerous, but willing, eyes.

This continued for years, and the village's health prospered. Growing older, I traveled there with him, learning and respecting the reverent process he learned from his father.

The future looked promising. But like anything good, the people took the power of the drink for granted. A new generation arose, one which had never known life without the healing tonic.

Then two decades ago, the village experienced severe flooding. Our people decided to move downriver, to the higher ground of our current home. And while we no longer battled rising waters, the village was much farther away from the nesting area, making the annual journey for the eggs more treacherous.

Eventually I became the shaman and traveled alone to the nest. And because of the distance, I stockpiled an egg supply. But time changes all things.

I am now an old man, with no sons. The trip has become too long and too difficult for me. My strength has waned, and it has been several years since I journeyed to the nest.

And now we are out of eggs. When I was young, I begged men to travel with me, with the hopes of training a successor. But no one ever accepted. Fear has deep roots.

But there is hope. A future shaman was born tonight. In the meantime, both he and the village face uncertain days.

The Hipupiara is alive, but the drink is gone.

"That's an amazing story," I whispered, wondering how many others had ever heard the tale.

"There are many stories that amaze." The shaman spoke with his eyes closed. "But do you believe it?"

Though my rational brain said *No*, my heart said *Yes*. Maybe because of the second-hand effect of whatever he was smoking.

"I do believe," I stammered, "but your story raises more questions."

He opened his eyes. "Such as?"

"Your wife, your family. How do they feel about this?" I assumed he was married, since he had a daughter and a newborn grandson.

A tinge of pain flashed across his face. "My wife is now in the spirit world. The drink extended her life, but could not save her."

"I'm sorry."

The shaman nodded and clutched his walking stick.

"Are there certain things the drink cannot heal?" I tried

sounding respectful.

"It cannot persuade a person's heart." He took a deep breath. "After some time, my wife refused to drink it. She wanted to depart this place, desiring the next life more than this one."

"Do you also wish to depart?"

"With all my soul. But my work is not yet finished." The shaman lifted the empty drink container and his voice softened. "Or perhaps now it is."

"Maybe we can help. We have a boat, after all. We can take you to the nesting area."

When the words came out of my mouth, I realized the difficulty. How could I ask sixty people to travel hours downriver in search of magical eggs? And Jose didn't even believe in the Sea Creature.

"No." He shook his head. "The responsibility lies on the people of this village and no one else."

At least I offered. "Where is the location of the nest? How far away?" I'd keep asking questions until he stopped answering.

"It is in Guyerma's Well, the deepest part of the Amazon. By boat, hours from here. By foot, several days. People have passed it for many years, but do not see it. The Hipupiara builds it in the remote grasses, under the covering of twigs and mud and leaves."

My mind struggled to make sense of it all. "Is there more than one Hipupiara? With eggs, there has to be, right? It must reproduce somehow."

"A hen lays eggs without a rooster." The shaman made a circle in the dirt with his walking stick. "There is only one Hipupiara."

I turned and spoke to Sage. "Which means the eggs are unfertilized. Once this creature dies, its species goes extinct."

A rush of concern. The creature offered untold treasures; what a tragedy to see it wiped from existence.

"The eggs benefit any rainforest creatures who consume them," he continued. "The power of the eggs brings life to the Amazon, and the Hipupiara seems to understand this. So it is unfortunate that people view her as a killer when she actually gives life."

"But what about the two villagers you said were killed by her? And the boating incidents she was blamed for?"

"Nature has its reasons. Not only is the Hipupiara mysterious and spiritual, but wild." He exhaled another long smoke from his pipe. "Blood repels death."

I wasn't sure what he meant, but undoubtedly, the Sea Creature was incredibly important. If someone found its eggs, they could use them for selfish purposes and become rich beyond their wildest dreams. And what if scientists studied the egg yolk and duplicated its properties? It would become a wonder drug on a scale never before seen.

"The discovery of those eggs would change the world," I said. "Imagine the amount of healings."

"But man has always killed that which he fears. People have searched for the Hipupiara, but have never found her. Not yet."

"But no one else knows of its eggs?"

"If old age has taught me anything, it is that secrets are hard to keep." He rubbed his wrinkled forehead. "I worry that some people have grown suspicious and are looking for the eggs. Bad people with wrong motives."

"Then why did you tell *us*?" I asked. "You don't even know us."

"I've known of you for a long time."

"But we've only been here two days."

Another puff of the pipe. "You underestimate the power of the spirit world."

Spook alert. My body tingled a little. Sage's face looked pale, and then I realized I had kept her in the hut much longer than she anticipated.

"I'm ready to go." She clutched her hands.

We stood, thanking the shaman for his story and the healing ceremony. He remained sitting on the ground, staring at the dying flames.

"Remember our village," he said. "The future is dark."

With nods, we opened the door and faced a heavy rainstorm.

My hand got soaked when I plunged it from under the hut's covering. Without an umbrella, it would be a wet walk to the boat.

I turned to Sage. "Sorry about the rain."

"I could care less about the rain." She gave a narrowed glance, visibly upset.

My chest tightened. Wait. What was she mad about?

33

We stood outside the shaman's front door, underneath a covering, with a driving rain falling around us.

The dirt paths deteriorated into mud, though the wet smell of soil offered fresh air from the hut's stifling pipe smoke.

I took a deep, cleansing breath. In the river a hundred yards away, the boat looked clear of visitors. The villagers must have settled into their huts for the night. Hopefully Lola wasn't worried since we had been AWOL for over an hour.

Sage stood with her hands on her hips, like she wanted to say something. But she didn't. Instead, she abruptly darted into the beating rain, disappearing into sheets of water.

I followed her, but my crutches slowed me, the rounded ends sinking and sliding in the mud. She must have forgotten about my ankle.

Glancing back, her shoulders fell when she saw me struggling. Turning around, she grabbed my arm and guided me back under the dry covering of the shaman's hut. Wet clothes matted our bodies, and we were soaked to the bone.

"I forgot you couldn't keep up." She wiped the dripping water from her eyes, sounding somewhat irritated. "It's too slippery, especially with your crutches. We should wait for the storm to slow."

And then she mumbled under her breath.

"What did you say?" I asked.

She acted surprised I'd heard.

"I was thanking God for my grandpa." She clutched her necklace charm. "God rest his soul."

"Your *grandpa*?" It seemed an odd time to think of a deceased family member.

She cut her eyes toward me. "He was the only man I've ever met who would consistently stand up for a woman. No other guy does it. None." Her tone carried a sense of betrayal.

Was she angry at me about something? But Lord Almighty, she looked smokin' hot when mad. It made her eyes even more striking, and with the raindrops streaming down her face and moistening her lips, I wanted to pull her close for a long kiss.

She said something else, but it was all white noise. *Focus, Pace, you're not listening to her.*

"You're not listening, are you?" An edge to her voice.

I snapped back into reality. "Heard every word."

My thoughts raced, replaying the last hour. What offended

her? Had I not stood up for her? It must have been a doozy since she invoked the memory of dear gramps.

"Did something happen that I missed?" I asked.

Sage tilted her head, like I had asked a dumb question. "What happened in there was weird. And that story? I had to repeat his every word. It scared me. You didn't notice?"

The shaman creeped me out, too, but I didn't realize she had gotten that unnerved. I'd obviously failed Sage. Time to step up my game.

"It's my fault," I touched her arm. "I should've paid better attention. His story distracted me. I'm sorry."

She shook her head and turned away, then snapped her gaze back at me. "Why are you so fascinated with the Sea Creature, anyway?"

I shifted, uncomfortably. "What do you mean?" She made me sound like a nerd who still played with plastic light sabers. "I'm only curious."

"Sometimes curiosity causes problems. We shouldn't have visited the shaman. I knew better. And we shouldn't have drank that drink."

"You didn't have to drink it. You could have refused."

"No." Her jaw clenched. "We've worked hard to develop relationships with these villagers. Entering someone's hut changes the dynamic. Refusing their hospitality is an insult."

I hadn't thought about it that way; she had a point.

"Did the drink make you sick?" I asked.

"The sensation from the drink felt odd, but I'm fine. And the whole healing ceremony thing, all the spirit world talk, it freaked me out."

I felt terrible. "Why didn't you say something?"

"Are you kidding? You were on a roll. And you ignored all my signals. You really need to learn how to read women."

"Signals? You gave me signals?"

She raised her eyebrows. "Lots of them."

"I'm not an expert on women. If something needs to be said, then say it."

"Okay, then." Her posture stiffened. "We didn't come on this trip to hear fairy tales or drink magical drinks or chase fanciful creatures. We came here to help villagers."

When she put it that way, it sounded like I should be fitted for a tight white coat without any sleeves. But I pushed back.

"True, but what if we're here for another purpose? Something… *larger*. What if the shaman's story is true? Maybe we should check it out."

She stepped closer, a fixed stare. "You want Jose canceling our medical mission so we can go on an Easter Egg hunt? Mind you, one that's based off a blurry photo and a guy who talks to his dead family members."

"Yeah, it sounds crazy," I said. "But you never know, maybe there's something to it."

"You're getting sidetracked again, Pace. Like you did in Leticia by the docks and in the jungle with Yeisson. You're a dreamer. And that's fine. But there's a big difference between dreamers and doers."

Ouch. I hadn't expected the brutal honesty, but she was right. Doers don't flunk out of college and become busboys.

We stood in silence for a long moment, the sound of pouring raindrops pounding her words into my heart, like seeds melting into soft soil.

Sage's body relaxed and her voice softened. "I'm sorry. That was rude."

"I asked for it." I looked away, still stinging from her words.

"My passion sometimes affects my tact." She touched the tips of my fingers. "But if the sea creature story is remotely true, it changes everything. It's a lot to process, that's why I'm so scared."

"Sorry I blew it. I always want you to feel safe with me."

It sounded cheesy, but I meant it.

She looked to the ground with a slight smile. "You're a good guy, Pace. Even if you do miss my signals."

"Guilty as charged." I paused. "By the way, how's your arm? Any miraculous healing from the magic drink?"

She moved her cast up and down. "Not much of a difference

yet. But it's not hurting. What about your ankle?"

"Still numb."

"Well, it's only been a few minutes. We'll give it the benefit of the doubt." Sage turned and studied the storm. "Doesn't look like the rain is slowing anytime soon. Should we make a go for it?"

"You run ahead. You've seen how slow I am on crutches. I'll be fine."

"I'm not running ahead this time, I promise. If you're getting drenched, so am I."

"Then hold on for a second." On a whim, I pulled my wet t-shirt off and handed it to her, leaving me bare-chested. "Use this and cover your head. I'm gonna follow in grandpa's footsteps and stand up for a woman."

She busted out laughing. "You're a nut. But I'll never turn down a chivalrous act." She glanced at my chest. "Or a great view."

Did she call me a great view?

We stepped into the rain shower with Sage holding my yellow shirt over her head, and me limping along topless, both of us slipping and skidding and splashing in the mud. Quite the sight.

Shuffling along side by side, her arm cradled my elbow, giving me support. It was a moment I wanted to pause forever, us squinting and blinking away the water, giggling, getting drenched under a torrential jungle rain.

Sage's hand eventually slid from my elbow. To my forearm.

To my wrist. And then she grasped my hand, our fingers intertwining, helping me across the slick ground.

Was the hand-holding a friendly gesture or something more? The girl was hard to read, which made her even more tantalizing.

Maybe it was another one of her so-called signals.

I couldn't wait to find out.

34

Music blasted from the boat's speakers as the sun faded into the horizon.

After a full day of prevention clinics, we had packed away our tents and supplies, preparing for a new village the next morning. A heaviness grew inside my chest, realizing I'd probably never see my new Amazon friends again. Saying goodbye really stunk.

But in the meantime we partied, and the villagers stood with widened eyes as our strange music played. Jose said they'd never heard recorded songs. We didn't hold back, giving them a heavy dose of 70's disco with Bee Gees falsetto harmonies blaring through the jungle. Saturday Night Fever in the Amazon. If only I had packed my platform shoes and skin-tight gold pants.

Yesterday's rain had dried away, making for a beautiful evening. A large bonfire crackled as the entire village gathered for a farewell party and feasted on cricket kabobs. Apparently a local favorite, each skewer contained four of the dry roasted insects, heads and all, alongside pineapple and peppers.

Our team stuck with a tried-and-true meal of chicken and rice and bottled water. The village men offered us a drink called chuchuhuasa, but Lola gave us a stern warning to steer clear of the powerful liquor.

But the best part of the evening: a painless ankle. During the day, the swelling completely decreased, enabling me to walk without crutches. Coincidence? Maybe the strange shaman drink had actually worked.

Our doctors gasped at my miraculous recovery, though I didn't mention the Hipupiara concoction. Lola would have been ticked to learn the shaman had performed his *voo-doo-hoo-doo* medical services on us. Sage… how did her arm feel? I couldn't wait to see her. We hadn't talked the entire day due to different assignments.

I found her playing soccer in a nearby field with the kids. Her hair pulled back, she wore a casual red-and-white baseball tee, its rounded neckline highlighting her petite yet athletic shoulders. Dark skinny jeans hugged her toned figure. Who needed any chuchuhuasa? Staring at her offered plenty of intoxication.

She dribbled the ball off her feet and knees for several minutes without dropping it, schooling all the boys. They watched with dropped jaws. Standing beside her, Yeisson studied her abilities and tried imitating the skillful moves.

But when I walked up, he dropped the ball and plowed into

me with a huge hug. Sage turned with a glowing smile.

I winked at her. “Don’t embarrass the boys too much with your soccer skill.”

“They’re so sweet.” She rubbed one of the boys’ heads. “And they’re good players, in another year or two I won’t be able to keep up.”

“Translate this for me,” I said to her, then turned to Yeisson. “Is she a good soccer player?”

After she asked him the question, he smiled and answered.

Sage gave his response, lifting her eyebrows with a smirk on her face. “He said I’m a great soccer player, and he wants to be as good as me one day.”

“Really?” My eyes narrowed. “How do I know you’re not changing around his words?”

She blinked. “You not only doubt my soccer skills but also my translating?”

Yeisson spoke again before I could answer.

“He hopes to be as good a snake hunter as I am a player,” Sage translated. “His exact words.”

I asked him, “You’re still chasing after snakes, after our close call?”

She translated his response. “He says there are lots of snakes in this area, and he wants to catch one before we leave.”

“Just be careful.” I offered him a high-five.

"I love you." Yeisson spoke in broken English, one of the few phrases he could speak.

"Love you, too." I playfully punched him in the arm.

Sage covered her mouth with her hands. "Awww. You two are so precious."

"He's my forever buddy."

The boat's music grew louder and people cheered and applauded by the fire. Whatever was going on, it sounded fun. Curious, we led the group of kids toward the party, like pied pipers.

Sage pointed at my ankle. "You're not using any crutches. I'm amazed."

"Must be our mystery drink. No swelling or pain. How's your arm?"

She moved it freely. "Feels great. And I'd give anything to remove this cast. It's getting on my nerves."

"If you have an itch, I'm here to scratch it."

She turned, a pained look. "That's the worst pickup line in the history of mankind."

"It wasn't a pickup line. Friend Zone, remember?"

She half-grinned. "I'm watching you, Pace Howell."

Approaching the fire, we discovered the cause of the commotion. Our team formed an impromptu dance line, ready to display their best cheesy moves to the song, "Celebration" by Kool & The Gang.

First to boogie down the line, C-Lo performed a stirring-the-butter arm move before gyrating her legs in her version of the Stanky Leg. Banks followed with his best rendition of a stiff robot, then imitated a sprinkler by placing one hand behind his head and rotating the other.

The crowd went wild.

James, wearing a bright blue t-shirt that read, I'M GOING COMMANDO, brought the house down with a MC Hammer "Can't Touch This" shuffle. Then Red Goth demonstrated seductive "cat's eyes," making horizontal peace signs in front of her eyes from the movie *Pulp Fiction*.

Not to be outdone, Lola jumped into the action and to our utter embarrassment and laughter, she twerked her way down the entire dance line, her glasses bobbing on the bridge of her nose.

Then Big Country did something he called the "Bus Driver," where he imitated rotating a big steering wheel and honking the horn. And finally, Jose surprised everyone with the classic "Running Man" routine, a move with his arms stretched out while he ran and shifted in place. All we lacked was a disco ball.

The song switched to the groove classic "YMCA" by the band named, appropriately, The Village People. C-Lo led the dance routine, teaching the villagers how to form the Y-M-C-A motions with their arms. By song's end, the entire village waved and swayed, both old and young, with some particularly gregarious villagers adding their own flair, probably due to too much chu-chu juice. If only I had a video camera.

I looked for Yeisson but couldn't find him, thinking he was in the middle of the party somewhere; but being a loner, he often drifted away following his own whims. He was probably kicking a soccer ball somewhere, even in the dark.

The song ended and segued into the famous ballad, "My Girl," by the Temptations. It reminded me as a kid at the Roll-A-Bout skating rink when the lights lowered and the announcer said, "Couples Only." When the music turned soft and romantic, I never had the guts to skate-dance with a girl. It was too risky, so I'd hang out at the video games until the song mercifully ended.

We encouraged village couples to slow-dance, and even our team formed into their own partners. Lola and Big Country innocently danced together, looking hilarious since he towered over her both in height and width. Banks and C-Lo acted way too comfortable, all pressed together. Perhaps their playful banter had turned into something hot and heavy? Leave room for the Holy Spirit, kids.

But most interesting was James and Red Goth, who stared into each other's eyes quite a bit. Was there more behind their slow moves? They'd spent a lot of time together recently. He looked all *Hey Girl* and she seemed all *Hey Boy.*

But like in fifth grade at the skating rink, I watched from the sidelines. Puberty all over again. Sage stood ten yards away, gleaming like the North Star to a weary traveler, too shiny to be standing alone. And we were the only team members not dancing. A golden opportunity. I dreamed of holding her close and calling her *My Girl*.

Strolling toward her and ready to extend an invitation, her gaze turned toward me and those pretty eyes met mine. My sunshine on a cloudy day; a sweeter song than the birds in the trees. Deep breath, head up, confident smile. Everything felt so right.

And that's when a little village girl tugged on my pants leg, lifting her small hands toward me, wanting to dance. Talk about terrible timing.

I looked down at her, then back at Sage, who smiled when she saw what happened. I exhaled. Just my luck. Dancing under the stars with Sage would have to wait.

Turning back to the girl, I placed her tiny feet on top of mine, and we danced for the remainder of the song, bobbing up and down as her face beamed. It actually felt nice, seeing the joy it brought her. As the song ended, she lovingly wrapped her arms around my waist, her head pressed against my stomach. My heart melted into a blob.

But what happened next was a blur.

A scream. Gasps. Panicked murmurs.

The crowd parted, and in the distance a male villager ran from the woods, cradling a child in his arms. As he drew closer, it became clearer.

He carried the limp body of a boy.

Yeisson.

A wave of nausea crashed over my body, making me lightheaded and weak in the legs. I tried moving my lips but my mouth was too dry to speak. He resembled a helpless rag doll.

A shudder traveled up my spine; I knew what had happened. Only one reason he would leave a party and venture into the jungle. A snake hunt.

The shaken villager laid Yeisson's body on the ground near the fire, and our physicians rushed to help.

I couldn't believe my eyes. Energetic, vivacious Yeisson, unresponsive and bleeding, semi-unconscious, his breathing labored.

His teeth chattered, and his right arm swelled with black-blistered flesh and oozing blood. Wiping the fluid away, they discovered what I feared: two defined, deep punctures.

Fang marks from a large snake.

Like stepping into a nightmare, horrendous images flashed back to me again, remembering our close call with the bushmaster; that attacking serpent, its cold and calculating face, the forked tongue and long viper fangs.

The venom would work quickly in Yeisson's skinny body. But thankfully, we had amazing doctors. Several had already ran to the boat and returned with an armful of emergency supplies.

Every second mattered. Yeisson's body jerked with compulsive spasms in his abdomen area and saliva poured from his mouth. A few moments later, he vomited.

The physicians injected a syringe needle of antivenom in his hip. Large doses would be required to keep him alive. They worked furiously, placing a constricting band on his arm above the bite marks.

Yeisson needed a miracle. How could life be so cruel? A young boy, healthy one moment and dying the next.

The shaman stood close behind, waving colored feathers and uttering incomprehensible words, and to their credit, the doctors parted and allowed him to apply an ointment to Yeisson's forehead and arm.

Guilt rolled through me. If only there was one more sip of the Hipupiara drink. Sage and I had drank the last drops, wasting it on our relatively minor injuries.

After stabilizing Yeisson, the doctors carried him to the boat, no doubt to the Operating Room, his eyeballs rolling back into his head.

No no no. My brain revolted in a million protests, trying to make sense of it all.

35

Jose bowed his head, running his hands through his hair.

The team gathered with him to pray for Yeisson while sitting in chairs on the boat's top floor. Several group members circled around me and placed their hands on my shoulders, sensing I needed extra comfort.

After the prayer time ended, we sat quietly, still shocked over how quickly the village celebration had turned somber. Jose cleared his throat and broke the silence.

"Obviously, this changes some things with our trip." He clasped his hands, shoulders slightly drooped. "Our first priority is getting Yeisson to a hospital. Problem is, the nearest one is back in Leticia. The poison in his snake bite is extremely powerful. And while the doctors have stabilized him, he needs comprehensive medical care. More than we can provide here."

"So keep praying, gang." Lola acted more subdued than I'd ever seen her. "The trip back to Leticia is five hours. This is a critical time for Yeisson."

"The next passenger boat doesn't pass by here until tomorrow afternoon," Jose said. "That's too long to wait. So I radioed around and discovered a cargo boat is coming our way. It's headed to Leticia, and they've agreed to stop and take Yeisson along. As long as I feel good after meeting the crew."

"You're putting him on a cargo ship?" My voice sounded confrontational, and I didn't care. "That's only slightly better than floating him upstream on a log. There's got to be another option."

"I agree, it's not ideal." Jose spoke softly, avoiding a similar tone. "But it's the fastest way of getting him to the hospital. Otherwise, we'd have to skip the next village, load the entire team, and all go to Leticia. Our mission would be over."

My anger rose. "If we need to cut our trip short to save his life, then let's do it. What's the problem?"

The heads of team members watched the back-and-forth conversation like spectators at a tennis match. It felt like having a private conversation in a group chat. Both Lola and Jose looked taken aback at my stubbornness.

But to his credit, he remained calm. "I understand what you're saying, Pace. But think of the hundreds of people in the next village — especially the children — who are in dire need, too. We only visit that village once a year. They're expecting us. They *need* us. It'd be a tragedy if we don't go."

I shook my head. "Those villagers have to understand we

have a bigger tragedy."

Lola took my hands in hers. "Yeisson will have great care. We're sending one of our doctors back on the boat with him."

"A doctor? Which one?" I asked.

"Dr. Walt."

Dr. Walt Williams, a physician from Tennessee. I barely knew him, but he was a soft-spoken guy who possessed an easy smile. He had a lanky build and a thick head of hair, parted down the middle eighties-style, and a brown beard with a slight hint of gray. His John Lennon glasses gave him the look of a hippie professor.

"As Dr. Walt takes Yeisson to the hospital," Jose said, "we'll finish at the next village. When we're done, we'll travel back to Leticia, too."

The next village. How could they think about it? I couldn't imagine trying to work while Yeisson fought for his life. How could anyone focus?

Lola stared into my eyes. "Pace, we've got to trust everything will be okay."

Something in me snapped. "*Trust*? You're putting him on a boat with strangers? A kid is dying, so instead of pausing your little medical trip, you're throwing him on a cargo boat? Where's the compassion? I thought this was a Christian group."

Tension filled the room. I didn't mean to show Lola or Jose any disrespect, but it came out sounding that way.

Jose exhaled, seeming to carefully choose his words. "I know this is deeply personal to you. It is for me, too. But the cargo boat is our best option. It will travel all night and arrive at the hospital by early morning. Please understand we want the best for Yeisson."

"Fine." I was losing my case. "But I'm going on that boat with him. He needs a familiar face. He doesn't really know the doctors."

The entire time, Lola continued holding my hands. She squeezed them tighter. "Honey, I know you want to go, and I love that about you. But we need you on the team. You're a valuable member. So I insist you stay, for many reasons. But most importantly, it's dangerous traveling the river at night. I can't handle calling your parents if something happens to you."

I dropped my hands from hers. "That's ridiculous. It's just as dangerous for the doctor, but you have no problem sending him. I'm an adult, too. I can make my own decisions without a permission slip. So with all due respect, I'm going whether you like it or not."

Every head in the room swiveled toward Lola, waiting for her response.

She shook her head. "There's nothing you can do, Pace."

"I've always done nothing." My heart thumped, filled with righteous anger. "I'm not living like that anymore."

Another awkward, silent moment. And then an unexpected voice.

"You need to let Pace go."

It was Red Goth.

"His presence will comfort Yeisson." She fiddled with her camera, not speaking to anyone in particular. "Experts say unconscious people can hear the voices around them, even if they're unable to respond."

Her words shocked me. Normally quiet and reserved, I could hardly believe she argued on my behalf. Then, surprisingly, Banks spoke.

"Yeah, Pace and Yeisson have a special bond." He leaned back in his chair, arms folded. "If Pace stays with us, he'll be miserable."

James spoke to Lola. "One of your 'words of the day' was *perspicacious*. Remember that? I think Pace has some *perspicaciousness* about this — deep insight. Let him follow his heart."

The team voiced their approval. I wanted to give them a group hug. And from Lola's expression, she looked overjoyed someone had actually remembered a Word of the Day.

Then she regained her focus. "But Pace doesn't speak Spanish." She shot Jose a wary glance. "It's not good traveling without knowing the language."

"What about Dr. Walt?" I asked. "He doesn't speak Spanish but you're letting him go."

Sage spoke. "I'll translate for both of them."

All heads turned toward her.

"I can translate *and* help comfort Yeisson." Sage nodded toward me. "If Pace goes, I go."

Pick me off the floor. In a million years, I wouldn't have expected her to say those words. And her opinion carried more weight than anyone else on the team.

"So now we're sending *three* team members?" Lola's voice pitched high. "I don't like it, not at all."

She looked at Jose, as if silently pleading for his help as the group mumbled.

He spoke with reassurance. "Relax, everyone. The whole purpose of this trip is for team members to love and help people. That's what matters in the end. Pace, I'm touched you feel as strongly as you do. Love is about sacrifice, and when people are willing to sacrifice for others, it's a noble thing."

He focused on me and Sage. "If you both want to go, then go. But on one condition. I'm talking with the cargo crew first. I need to make sure everything on the boat is above board. If it's not, you don't go. Deal?"

We nodded, and Lola seemed resigned to Jose's wisdom.

My blood pressure returned to semi-normal. But the more I calmed down, the more I felt bad about my mega-meltdown temper tantrum.

Forty-five minutes later, a bright light appeared downriver, emerging from the darkness. As it approached, the three-floor cargo boat heaved forward under the sound of huge diesel engines. A staring crowd gathered on the shore.

Eventually, the boat stopped parallel to the village a safe distance away, careful not to run aground. Each of its three floors stretched longer than the one above it, giving the illusion of a stairwell. The extended back of the bottom floor contained huge mountains of tarped and roped supplies.

At the shore, a few bamboo rafts offered the only access to the cargo ship, so Jose and a villager rowed one toward the vessel.

Another half-hour passed.

I paced with a loud imaginary clock in my head, knowing every minute mattered in Yeisson's life-or-death struggle. We needed to get moving. The hands of time ticked away.

Finally, Jose returned in the raft, a satisfied look on his face.

"It's all good." He stepped onto the shore. "And you're fortunate. There are no passengers aboard, only a dozen crew members. So there's plenty of room."

During the agonizing wait the team loaded another couple of

rafts, with one holding luggage and basic supplies such as bottled water, hammocks, and snacks. They thought of everything. Doctors carried Yeisson from our riverboat and placed him on the second raft, his body limp and unresponsive and wrapped in a blanket.

Jose and Lola insisted on riding with us to the cargo ship, so we gave goodbyes to the rest of the team. We'd see them in two days. Pushing off from the shore, a couple of villagers rowed our rafts, with Lola, Sage, and myself on one, and Jose, Dr. Walt, and Yeisson on the other.

Big Country waved as we drifted away. "Praying for you guys."

"Love those kids in the next village for us," Sage yelled back to the team.

Everyone smiled and waved. I already missed the team.

As we drew closer to the cargo boat, it looked much larger than it did from the village. Its large spotlights attracted insects the size of small birds, and the diesel exhaust made us cough. It made me even more nervous.

We boarded and met the crew, who appeared friendly and helpful. They gave us a brief tour. The belly of the ship contained a maze of pipes, along with heaps of mattresses, cement bags, bananas, and crates of every size. Several open cabins were available, and we placed Yeisson in one of them. Not wanting to inconvenience the crew, we refused any additional rooms and hung our hammocks from metal rods on the ceiling.

So far, so good. Yet something nagged at me — a sense of responsibility for Sage, realizing I had placed her at risk on a strange boat. She wouldn't be there if not for my embarrassing hissy fit back on shore.

Jose interrupted my thoughts and motioned me to the side.

He pulled out Yeisson's knife. "I want you to have this. I found it on the ground by the Kapok tree you climbed." He placed it in my hand. "Figured you could give it back to him when he gets better."

"Thank you." With all the frantic activity, I'd forgotten about the treasured knife, the one Yeisson wanted to bury in the jungle.

I rubbed my fingers over the knotted handle. Holding it stirred both sadness and joy, and I dreamed of soon placing it back in his hands.

Jose gripped my shoulder. "I'm contacting Carlos back at his hotel in Leticia. He'll look for your arrival and have several rooms ready."

"Thank you. But before you go, I need to apologize to both you and Lola."

As they stood together, I took a deep breath.

"I'm sorry for losing my temper tonight. Yeisson's injury has made me a little wacko. I trust your leadership and didn't mean to undermine it. Please forgive me, I'm an idiot."

"No hard feelings." Jose patted my back. "It's emotional for all of us."

"You'll always be my favorite problem child, no matter what." Lola gave me one of her mama bear hugs. "Now just make sure you get to that hospital in time. And get that damn poison out of him."

It took a second for her to realize she had cussed, then she covered her mouth, embarrassed.

"Don't worry." I smiled and winked at her. "I hear you damn well."

With a final wave, they stepped off the ship and back onto the bobbing rafts. Moments later, the cargo boat chugged forward with the whine of engines and puffs of thick smoke.

I wished it had a turbo button to whisk us high-speed to the hospital. But instead, we meandered along at twenty miles an hour, the crew carefully watching the river depths. Five hours to go. At least we moved forward.

I felt good about things until another man walked toward us from the top floor, one we hadn't met yet. He looked Russian, and I recognized him immediately; he was the man from the Leticia docks my first night, when the angry fishermen accosted me. He had passed by on a boat.

And one weird detail stuck out more than any other.

On his head he wore the same white fedora hat.

36

We stood on the boat's second floor, leaning on the rails, and watched the river move like tar.

Behind us, the dying fire in the village poured smoke and sparks into the night sky, while in front of us stood the short, thick man with a cigar in his mouth.

Along with pale skin and a strong chin, his middle-aged face looked abnormally wide, as if a sculptor spread the clay too thin. Sunken eyes made his gray pupils look distant and uninterested, and his eyebrows were almost invisible, creating the illusion of an emotionless cyborg face. A cyborg wearing a white fedora hat.

Before we spoke, a butterfly fluttered onto a nearby rail. I immediately recognized it. The *periander* species, the kind featured in many wall displays. Its wings glowed a neon blue, and a black outline transversed its body, like someone had taken a permanent marker to its edges. Orange splotches rested near the bottom of its wide tail.

To my surprise, the man crept toward the butterfly, like a cat on the prowl. The oblivious creature flitted its wings.

Inching closer, the man slowly lifted his hands and spread them apart. What was he doing? I realized it too late.

In an instant, he slapped both hands together, the fragile creature caught helplessly in the middle. Crushed in his palms.

A smirk appeared on the man's face as he wiped the crumpled wings and slime from his hands.

Sage and I stood speechless, disgusted. I wanted to slap him upside his head and say, *See? It doesn't feel too good, does it?*

"I really hate these buggers." He rubbed his hands on his pants. "Don't let the pretty colors fool you. They're disgusting insects. Underneath is a beady-eyed worm."

He spoke good English, though with a strong accent, and when he talked his mouth barely opened and only his thin upper lip moved. He rolled his R's and a guttural growl escaped from his tightened throat. Extending a hand, he offered a formal greeting.

"Vlad," he said, with a blank expression.

I wasn't shaking his hand, not after the butterfly incident.

"How about a head nod?" My tone wasn't warm. "You still have smushed periander on your hands."

Pausing for a moment, he sized me up. "Suit yourself, son. But this is the Amazon. We don't mind getting dirty out here."

His eyes flashed toward Sage, looking her up and down, undressing her with a long stare. I already didn't like the guy.

I spoke to divert his attention from her. "From your name and accent, I'm guessing you're Russian."

"A proud Communist." He took an extended puff on his cigar, blowing smoke that smelled like leather and black cherry. "I love saying that to Americans." He didn't smile. "What happened to your young friend? He looked pretty bad when you brought him on the boat."

"Snake bite," I said. "Happened about two and a half hours ago. He's in great danger."

"That's a shame. Too young to die." He glared at Sage again. "So how did two attractive people find themselves in the deep Amazon?"

My chest tightened. My friend lay dying in the next room, but Vlad only had the hots for Sage.

She spoke to him for the first time, in a matter-of-fact air. "We're on a medical mission. Helping people physically and spiritually."

Another drag from the cigar. "Peddling God to the needy villagers, huh?"

"Excuse me?" Her eyebrows crinkled.

"How do you come to terms with religion, especially in the Amazon?" he asked. "All the crime, the poverty. And there are violent men in this jungle. Men you can't trust. Men with violent appetites. So where is your God? He let your friend get bitten by a poisonous snake. I'd say your deity has a few problems on his hands."

"He sends us here as part of the solution." She stared him straight in the eyes, unblinking.

Vlad laughed. "Solution? You come, you leave. Nothing changes. The river keeps on moving. The jungle keeps on killing." He leaned over the rail and spit into the river. "And why did three of you come with the kid? Isn't one doctor enough?"

"The kid's name is Yeisson." I said, growing more ticked with each passing second. "We want to be here for him. And Sage is a translator."

"Sage. Such a pretty name." He spoke in Russian. "*Etot paren' tvoy paren'? Yesli net, to my dolzhny vypit'.*"

She sounded unimpressed. "I only translate Spanish."

"What a shame." His voice like ice. "Russian is the mother tongue."

"But Spanish is the mother tongue of the Leticia hospital." Sage turned away from him and focused on the water. "That's all I care about."

I changed the subject, wanting to avoid more awkward conversation. "How well do you know the river?"

Vlad pointed at the containers on the back of the ship. "I've transported goods on the Amazon for years."

"Have you ever heard of a spot called Guyerma's Well?" My

question popped up completely unplanned.

Sage turned her head sharply, like she didn't want me mentioning the location of the Sea Creature's nesting area.

"Guyerma's Well?" The name seemed to grab his attention, and he thought for a moment. "There are a dozen names for every river section, depending on who you ask."

"Just wondering." I shrugged. "It's a place a shaman told us about. Some legend about a special nest. We've got a friend in Leticia who may know where it's at."

"This friend of yours has a boat? And directions?"

"Yeah. He grew up on the river."

Vlad's eyes narrowed. "Sounds like that nest is pretty important."

"Long story." If only he knew, but I wasn't about to tell him. Time to change the subject again. "What are you guys transporting?"

He exhaled thick smoke in our direction. "There's a rule on the river, kid. Never ask what a cargo ship is carrying."

I gave him a side glance. "Almost sounds like you're hiding something."

Two could play the game. If he wanted to stir the poop pot, I'd make him lick the spoon.

His facial expression changed. "If we were hiding something, we wouldn't have stopped and picked you up."

Sage sounded like a mom stopping a fight. "We're very grateful." She shot me a corrective glare. "Yeisson has a fighting chance because of your generosity."

"We're not the generous ones, honey," Vlad said. "Your friend, he's the generous one."

"Who?" I asked. "Jose?"

"Yeah, he paid my crew a handsome amount for this transport. And for our protection."

I thought the crew had offered the boat ride as an act of compassion. So naive. And the price probably doubled when Sage and I decided to tag along. Jose paid it out of his own pocket and didn't mention it. I felt terrible.

Sage leaned forward. "What do you mean by protection?"

"River pirates." Vlad watched our faces closely, as if looking for a response. "Attacks happen all the time, especially at night. Passenger boats are the easiest targets. But sometimes criminals get brave and chase cargo boats. But don't worry." He lifted his shirt and revealed the grip of a gun. "We're ready."

I got the feeling he wanted to show us his gun, river pirates or not. And for the first time, I understood Lola's hesitation about us traveling alone.

In the wee morning hours Sage and I rested in our hammocks, the breeze off the water turning chilly. Except for the boat's front light, the outer darkness seemed oppressive and gave the feeling of entering into a tunnel, with the jungle hidden by the black curtain of nightfall.

After the talk with Vlad, we couldn't sleep. Two hours had passed since we boarded, but progress was hard to measure. We could have been idling in place and wouldn't have known the difference. So we talked, mostly about small stuff. I loved hearing the sound of her voice in the dark.

And then her expected questions. "Why did you bring up Guyerma's Well to Vlad? Are you planning something I should know about?"

No point in dodging; she'd discover my plans sooner or later. "Once we get Yeisson to the hospital," I said, "there's no reason to stare at the waiting room walls. So I thought about searching, you know, for the eggs."

She popped up in her hammock. "The *eggs*? Are you crazy?"

"Carlos once mentioned he owned a boat. Maybe he can give me a daytime ride down the river. Nothing too extensive. But if I don't at least look for those eggs, I'll wonder about them for the rest of my life. And just think, what if we find them?"

"*If* they truly exist. And what if you find them?" she asked. "Are you strolling into the nest and grabbing them? The shaman said men had died trying that."

"I'll figure out that part later." My voice softened. "Yeisson needs all the help he can get. Maybe that drink can do for him what it did for us."

In time our conversation quieted, and the hum of the boat's engines finally lulled us to sleep. It was a comforting feeling, falling asleep with Sage nearby. But way too short of a rest.

Sometime later, we jolted awake due to the sounds of the crew preparing to dock in Leticia. Our three-hour nap felt like fifteen minutes.

I immediately checked on Yeisson. Dr. Walt sat faithfully beside the bed and described his condition as unchanged. *Hang on, Yeisson.* We couldn't dock fast enough; I wanted him in that hospital more than anything.

The crew helped us unload our supplies while Dr. Walt and I carried Yeisson carefully off the boat. Oddly, we didn't see Vlad again.

After saying thank you's to the men, we grabbed a mototaxi to the hospital, with the Letician city lights offering a welcome relief from our voyage of darkness. But an invisible clock continued hammering away in my head.

Every second counted for Yeisson's survival.

37

We rushed into the hospital, a simple, three-story flat-roofed structure.

It was the only medical facility for miles, and the inside resembled a middle school with low ceilings and narrow cinderblock hallways.

Thankfully, Sage took charge and spoke in Spanish to the nurses, explaining what had happened and introducing them to Dr. Walt. The workers quickly took Yeisson behind closed doors and allowed Dr. Walt to follow. A moment later, Sage and I found ourselves sitting in a quiet waiting room, a contrast to the frenetic pace of the last six hours.

After spending so much time in the villages, it seemed strange walking back into a real building, especially one with a strong antiseptic smell of sanitizer. And also buzzing fluorescent lights, running water, and flushing toilets. I'd always taken those things for granted, but now I saw them with new eyes. I still hated hospitals, however. The peekaboo gowns. The cold stethoscopes. The people who stick you with sharp objects.

Despite my issues, it was a relief admitting Yeisson to the emergency room, though I realized the cold, harsh truth: within those four walls he would either recover or die. Under my breath, I prayed.

The waiting was the worst part, feeling helpless and bored and at the mercy of outside forces. Maddening, really. And we were exhausted since we hadn't gotten much sleep during the overnight boat ride. I wondered about poor Dr. Walt. He surely needed more rest than us after staying awake all night by Yeisson's side.

I stared ahead, numb from it all. But out of the corner of my eye, Sage trembled.

I turned toward her.

She sniffled and rocked gently back and forth, eyes squeezed shut and body shivering. And then the dam broke. Lowering her head, she surrendered to a release of pent-up emotion, the grief bursting upward from somewhere deep within, large tears streaming down her cheeks and dropping to the floor below.

I've always felt uncomfortable whenever women cry, not knowing what to say or do. But I found a nearby tissue box, and I slid close and wrapped an arm around her. Sage lowered her head on my shoulder and buried her face in my shirt, muffling the sobs.

I stroked her hair and whispered that everything would be okay, though my eyes filled with tears, too. After hours of staying strong for Yeisson, our hearts broke together. We sat there for a long time, not saying a word, until her breathing returned to normal and the weeping became sniffles once more.

Sometime later, Carlos from the hotel arrived, carrying sodas and bags of food. He wore a flowy, white shirt unbuttoned at the top, showcasing his tan skin and a strong scent of cologne. Radiating charisma, he brought a larger-than-life presence into the room and a welcomed sense of calmness. Exactly what we needed.

After a round of hugs, I opened a cold soda, desperate for caffeine. The drink tasted much sweeter than I remembered since my taste buds were super-sensitive after days of only drinking water. But man, did it hit the spot.

He told us Pastor Jose had contacted him, and then asked about Yeisson and our cargo boat ride. After giving him all the details, Carlos said he had prepared hotel rooms for us.

I couldn't wait. The thought of a comfortable bed and hot shower seemed like guilty luxuries. We talked for several more minutes when an exhausted-looking Dr. Walt returned to the foyer.

Eager for news, we jumped up to meet him.

"They're still working on Yeisson." He spoke softly. "The doctors here know what they're doing."

"How is he?" Sage asked. "Are they able to help him?"

Dr. Walt pointed us back to our chairs and encouraged us to

sit. I hated being told to sit. Bad news usually followed. My stomach turned when I saw the pained look on his face.

"It's touch-and-go." He stared at the linoleum floors, then back at us. "Yeisson experienced severe envenomation. And while our antivenom helped, there's already been some tissue death."

Death. I despised the word. "What exactly does tissue death mean?"

Dr. Walt removed his glasses and rubbed his reddened eyes. "When there's not enough blood flowing to tissue, it can cause inflammation of the surrounding healthy tissue. Gangrene. It's very serious."

Sage asked the question I couldn't bear to articulate because of fearing the answer. "Is he going to live?"

"There's a lot happening inside Yeisson's body." He sighed and leaned back in his chair. "Viper poison packs a wallop. He has respiratory failure, hypotension, hematemesis, and abnormal coagulation. And since he was bitten over ten hours ago, it's late in the game. He needs a miracle."

The big medical terms scared me. "Yeisson's going to make it." My voice shook. "He's young and stubborn. And he's a fighter."

I needed to verbalize those words, throw them out to the universe, at least so my own ears could hear them. Medical reports be damned.

Sage placed her hand over mine, the soft touch bringing

comfort.

"It's going to take a while for the doctors to stabilize Yeisson." Dr. Walt paused, then cleared his throat. "I'd advise us getting some rest and freshening up. There's a long road ahead. It may be the end of the day before any new update."

"I agree with the good doctor." Carlos slid to the edge of his chair and dangled car keys. "My hotel is a short distance away. Take care of yourself so you can take care of Yeisson. A cargo boat trip isn't very restful. Sitting in this hospital all day doesn't do anybody any good."

The hot shower felt glorious, like washing off a layer of my former self, the film of bug spray and campfire ash fading into the drain.

It was almost a religious experience, working the grime from my hair, massaging that apple-scented shampoo into a massive bubble afro and letting it sit there until my scalp tingled. After shaving and putting on clean clothes, I stepped out of the bathroom a new man.

While Dr. Walt napped in his room, we met Carlos back downstairs in his office. As always, the newly-showered Sage glowed like a runway model. She wore high-rise denim shorts and a scarlet colored short sleeve, with a scooped neck accenting her necklace charm. Her black sneakers gave her the perfect modern-casual vibe. Her hair was pulled up, and she smelled like lilies.

Carlos's office decor reflected his personality, neat and pristine with bold accents. Wooden plank ceiling and beige walls. Black wicker seats with orange throw pillows. There was also a small circular table with a miniature carved-out canoe on top, and on the wall behind his desk hung a large satellite map of the Amazon River.

I looked closer at the framed picture. "I love this map."

"I've grown up on this river." Carlos stood beside me. "The most amazing four thousand miles in the world. Dumps more water into the sea than any other river. And notice, there are no bridges."

I searched the map for our location, but with no success. "Help me get my bearings. Where's the village we came from?"

He pointed to the right side of the map. "See this little area? That's Leticia." He moved his finger slightly to the left. "And you guys went all the way over here and back." His touch landed on a large green patch, with no visible huts due to the zoomed-out image.

"It took so long to get there." Sage studied the images. "But we only traveled a small sliver of the river."

I swallowed. That sliver of the river had profoundly changed my life.

“So much to explore.” Carlos shook his head, rubbing his chin. “So much history and culture. And legendary stories.”

“Speaking of which, have you heard of a place called Guyerma’s Well?” I asked, glancing at Sage and wondering if she had tired of my preoccupation with the Sea Creature story.

“Ah, now that’s a term I don’t hear very often.” He studied the map again. “It’s a small, deep section of the river. Matter of fact, yeah, it looks like your boat passed right by it. Why do you ask?”

I shrugged. “A village shaman told us a story about it.”

“A shaman? What kind of story?”

“Pace is fascinated with it.” Sage raised an eyebrow. “But I have my doubts.”

“You’ve got my interest.” Carlos sat in his desk leather chair and motioned us toward the wicker chairs.

I braced for his reaction. “The Sea Monster, the Hipupiara.”

His head tilted, full attention.

“The shaman says it’s real.” I leaned forward, hands on my knees. “And he claims its nest is in the area of Guyerma’s Well. For decades he’s used those eggs as a healing drink. And remarkably, no one in his village is sick. *No one*.” I paused. “Even Sage and I drank some.”

A concerned look washed over his face. “You did what? Do you know how dangerous it is drinking liquids from those villages?”

"I know, it was stupid. But it worked." I raised my leg. "It healed my twisted ankle almost immediately. A miracle."

Sage lifted her pink cast. "And I've had no pain from this broken arm ever since."

Carlos leaned back in his chair, hands together under his chin, thinking.

"One of our team members took a picture," I said. "It was totally by chance, on our boat ride. She captured a large creature partially submerged in the water, bigger than anything I've ever seen."

Carlos chuckled to himself. "All my life I've heard about the Hipupiara. It's a legend around these parts. The talk of magical eggs. There's a lot of fantastical stories but never any conclusive evidence."

"But what about *our* evidence?" I felt myself getting agitated, like trying to convince an adult about Santa Claus. "A miraculously healthy village. Our healings. And the picture."

"Do you have the picture with you?"

I was afraid he'd ask that. "No, it's on someone's camera. But I'll show you when the team returns."

"Pace, there's got to be a rational explanation." He shifted and turned his head, looking away. "It's a far-fetched story. One that's utterly ridiculous."

He must think I've flipped. A ridiculous story? Well, yeah. But I knew what I'd seen and experienced. "Do you think I'm crazy?"

"You? No." Carlos smiled, eyes turning mischievous. "It's a story I've studied for a long time. And one I happen to *believe*, by the way."

"Wait. Really?" Shock hit me like a slap across the face. "You actually believe this could be true?"

"It may not be true, but I believe in the possibility. And it's a lot of fun imagining if the Hipupiara is real." He swiveled his chair and pointed at the map again. "Let's say we find those eggs somewhere here, in Guyerma's Well. Did the shaman tell you how to prepare the drink?"

"If I remember correctly," Sage said, "it's ten parts water to one part egg." She glanced at me to confirm.

"Amazing." He shook his head. "And the entire village is healthy?"

"For now, but they're out of eggs," I said. "The shaman is old and the villagers are afraid of the creature."

"Maybe they're wise to be afraid." Carlos stood and studied the map closer.

We remained silent for a few moments and gave the map our full attention.

"I've got a boat." He turned his head toward us. "You thinking what I'm thinking?"

"That we're all delusional?" Sage's eyes bounced between us.

I looked at her. “It’s worth a shot. For Yeisson.”

“Guyerma’s Well is only about two hours away.” Carlos leaned on the desk edge. “A quick look wouldn’t hurt. There’s nothing you can do at the hospital but stare at the walls. And Yeisson’s in good hands.”

I temporarily forgot about my exhaustion as a surge of excitement coursed through my body. “I remembered you had a boat. And honestly, it was one of the reasons I came back to Leticia, hoping you’d be willing to explore.”

Sage lowered her head. “Boys will be boys.”

“I was born to explore the Amazon.” Carlos straightened, standing tall. “Lorena says the water is my mistress. And she may be right.” He checked his watch. “But we must move quickly to be back before dark tonight.”

We wasted no time. Within a half-hour, we sat in Carlos’s boat and sped away from the steamy, frontier town of Leticia, squinting into the mid-morning light as its reflection created an orange vertical line on the river like an arrow pointing us forward.

The search had begun.

38

Carlos's boat looked nicer than most of the others.

Well-worn but obviously cared for, it stretched about fifteen feet long. In the middle rose a thatched covered archway, like an open-air tunnel, perfect for shade and storing supplies. A portable one-burner propane oven sat fastened to the side.

Though only mid-morning, the heat grew uncomfortable so we slathered on sunblock that smelled like coconuts. So much for my shower. After our all-night trip, another boat ride didn't excite me. But you do what you got to do. Thankfully, neither Sage or I dealt with sea sickness, but after this trip I was swearing off water travel for a while.

Carlos seemed right at home on the river, proud of his vessel. "She might not look like much but she gets the job done," he said. "Stubborn sometimes, but when you get her going this little lady flies through the river."

The boat bobbed up and down, zipping across the surface and coating us with an Amazon mist. A montage whisked by of overgrown rainforest grass and forest-lined shores, tree canopies and drooping vines. Occasionally, villages dotted the sides and offered visual history lessons of ancient civilizations, like exotic scenes out of a James Bond movie.

Carlos proved an impressive driver, especially since the river wasn't a straightforward path. He knew the water. With sudden twists and turns, narrow waterways quickly grew wide, and vice versa, creating a murky navigational maze. We sat under the canopy, which shielded the sun and also muted some engine noise so Sage and I could talk without shouting.

"What happens if we don't find the nest?" She never minced words.

"I'll be the world's biggest idiot. But at least I'll know we tried."

She bit her lip. "I'm worried about Yeisson. What if something happens while we're gone? What if..."

"We can't think like that," I said. "He's going to be fine. And if the doctors can't help him, we'll give him a special Hipupiara milkshake."

She gave a slight smile. "I need your faith."

To her surprise, I took her hand and held it. "A friend once showed me something."

I touched her thumb: "Always worship."

Her index finger: "Ask forgiveness."

Her middle finger: "Be thankful for everything."

Her ring finger: "Pray for what you need."

Her pinkie: "Pray for someone else."

I touched her palm: "Prayer and faith work together."

"You remembered, " she said, glowing.

"I remember everything you tell me." I pointed to her neck. "For instance, that ring necklace is from your grandpa."

She rubbed the ring between her fingers, a gleam in her eye. "Before my grandparents married, grandpa hid this ring in a seashell on the beach. He took grandma for a walk and led her to the shell. She always said it was the most loving surprise of her life."

I winked. "Sounds like grandpa was a hopeless romantic."

"They were married for sixty-two years and she wore this ring everyday." Sage paused. "During her later years, she had kidney failure. It was a bleak prognosis. But guess what grandpa did?"

"What?"

"He donated one of his kidneys. Didn't think twice about it. It helped her live another four years."

I blinked. "He really set the gold standard."

"After grandma died, he made the ring into a necklace. Gave it to me, his only granddaughter. Whenever I look at it, I'm reminded true love does exist."

Carlos stopped the engine unexpectedly. But why? We didn't

have much time to waste.

"This will only take a minute." He stood from his seat. "You've got to see something. This area is famous for pirarucu."

"Pirarucu?" Sage leaned over the edge. "The fish?"

"Yeah." Carlos studied the water. "Know anything about them?"

I couldn't resist describing one of the Amazon's most famous animals. "They're giant, carnivorous fish. They can grow nine-feet long and a couple hundred pounds. Shaped like torpedoes. And their outer layer looks like armor."

"Locals often fashion those scales into jewelry," Carlos said.

"And they're known for crushing prey with their teeth." I gave an imaginary bite at Sage. "Even their tongues have teeth."

"Yep." Carlos ran his hand across the water's surface. "And their tongues are sometimes used as seed graters."

"So why are we trying to find them?" Sage stepped back and leaned against me. "They sound terrifying. I say leave them and their teeth-encrusted tongues alone."

I enjoyed her touching me, so I gave more scary facts. "Yeah, be careful. They stay close to the surface. And they make a strange coughing sound when they come up for air."

Carlos looked at me, eyebrows arched. "I'm truly impressed."

Sage tapped my shoulder. "Pace here is a walking biology book."

I'd never impressed a girl before with animal biology. It was kinda nice. Power to the nerds.

"But I bet you don't know the secret of attracting them." Carlos switched on a waterproof radio by the steering wheel. "They're drawn to music. Probably something to do with the bass frequency. But it works like a charm. May take a few minutes, though."

A ballad played on the radio, a soothing sound after the unyielding engine whine.

An idea hit me. "While we're waiting…"

I turned to Sage, offering her my hand. "May I have this dance?" We needed a quick diversion, something to take our minds off the last few hours.

A priceless expression washed across her face. "Are you always this forward with the ladies?"

She looked both flattered and skeptical, like she couldn't figure out my motive. With a flirtatious grin, she stood and grasped my hand.

I pulled her close, ready for the slow dance we didn't get in the village. She didn't balk. And to my surprise, she leaned her head on my shoulder. *Somebody pinch me.* Feeling her breath on my neck, I wrapped my arm around her lower back. I had officially died and gone to heaven.

But a loud engine sounded in the distance, growing louder.

She lifted her head. Still holding my hand, Sage stepped back as Carlos grabbed his binoculars.

"We've got visitors." The lines on his forehead creased as he focused on the approaching boat. "And I don't feel good about them. Those types of boats usually mean trouble."

I squinted ahead.

A small, fast-moving black vessel.

Carlos cut off the radio and pulled a handgun from a supply cabinet. "Just a precaution." He slid it underneath the back of his shirt.

Things had to be dicey if he brandished a gun. Then Sage dropped her hands from mine. I couldn't catch a break.

"Time to get moving." He attempting to start the boat, but it sputtered. After several attempts, the engine whirled but wouldn't turn over. Rushing to the motor, he hit it with his palm. "Come on honey, now's not the time for an attitude."

Why doesn't anything ever start when you're trying to get away from the bad guys?

Meanwhile, the growl of the black boat increased, its bow pointing aggressively in our direction, coming closer. Maybe they were stopping to help, like Good Samaritans.

In seconds, the fancy speedboat slowed and idled beside us, with two suspicious men holding guns. My pulse raced. They didn't look nice.

And they were definitely not Good Samaritans.

39

A jet black speedboat. Long and thin, sleek fiberglass, loaded with powerful engines. We couldn't have outrun it even if we tried.

"River pirates," Carlos whispered. "Let me handle them."

In the middle of the Amazon, we had nowhere to run or hide. Completely vulnerable. I instinctively stepped in front of Sage as the men in the speedboat glared at us, like hunters inspecting their snare.

They both had dark, straight hair and olive skin, a mixture of Spanish and European. One pointed a shotgun at us and shouted orders in Spanish. We lifted our arms.

Carlos talked back and forth with them, but their guns remained raised. Whatever he said, they were unconvinced.

Carlos turned to us, face tense. "Just do as they say."

One man stood guard in the speedboat, while the other stepped into our boat. He smelled of sweat and cigarettes. The man frisked Carlos and found the handgun, admiring it like a trophy before placing it under his belt. Any hope of protecting ourselves had vanished.

I swallowed hard. Why attack our small boat? Judging from their equipment, they possessed superior resources. The river pirate searched me next, finding nothing, and then focused his attention on Sage.

With roving hands and obvious pleasure, he slowly inspected her, often checking certain areas multiple times. *Don't touch her like that.* I wanted to give him a pat-down with my fists.

Abruptly, and with a wave of his gun, he ordered us overboard. *What… really? Overboard?* Did we look threatening?

At first, we didn't budge, and Sage clutched my arm.

"Can you swim?" Carlos looked apologetic, as if the whole predicament was his fault.

We both nodded.

Sage glared over the rail at the muddy, reddish water. "Is it safe?"

The pirate pumped his shotgun and chambered a bullet.

"Safer than being shot," Carlos replied.

I plunged in first, the water much warmer than expected. But as Sage prepared to jump, the pirate stopped her. He noticed her necklace, and without warning, yanked it away with sudden force.

She shrieked, then stared with narrowed eyes, her fingers rubbing her reddened neck.

A pounding in my ears. Clouded vision. "No!" I screamed.

Grabbing the boat's railing, I pulled myself halfway up. Bullets be damned. But the pirate leveled his gun at my forehead with a menacing expression, his deadened pupils like those of a killer.

"Pace, stop!" Carlos reached toward me. "Your life's more important."

Sage cupped her mouth and tears filled her eyes. The necklace. The barrel of the gun. Sage. I wanted to fight for her, defend her, save the day. But Carlos was right. What good would it do fighting an armed assailant?

Helplessness washed over me as I sunk back into the water.

Carlos and Sage leapt into the river and momentarily distracted the pirate from lodging a 12-gauge shell in my brain. We huddled together, treading water, watching as the other man joined his partner in pilfering the boat and our belongings. Humiliating.

"I'm so sorry." Carlos's voice shook as he treaded.

"What about the pirarucu?" Sage scanned the water.

"They don't hurt humans," I said.

Technically a half-truth. Pirarucu don't feed on people, but they fight aggressively if threatened, often with violent force. I didn't tell her that part.

Several minutes passed, and my arms tired from keeping afloat. Sage's chin trembled and Carlos labored with fatigue. How long could we keep our heads above the surface?

In the distance, another engine.

The thieves heard it, too, and turned their heads, shouting at each other. Maybe a good thing for us.

Seconds later a small boat appeared, sweeping around the bend, and before the two men could raise their weapons, the staccato burst of machine gun fire echoed around the rainforest trees.

Bullets slapped into the river with fountains of spray, close to us. We ducked underwater, afraid for our lives.

I stayed beneath the surface until my lungs ached, finally ascending for a frantic gulp of air, looking for Carlos and Sage. Thankfully, they weren't hit.

But a shock awaited. The two pirates had raised their hands in surrender, their guns lowered. But why had they given up so quickly? Maybe because their weapons offered no match to the high-caliber weaponry of the fast-approaching boat.

Or maybe because they were sitting ducks.

A white, outboard-powered panga boat rocketed toward us, its pointy bow resembling a floating machete. Built for speed. Three men aimed guns toward the pirates, with one wearing a white fedora hat.

I may have peed my pants. Couldn't believe my eyes.

That white fedora hat. Vlad.

A toothpick dangled from his mouth, and he chewed on it like someone relaxing on a lazy Sunday afternoon. Same icy persona, and he looked like he had done this a hundred times before.

Pulling beside us, his men lifted us from the water and into their boat, handing us towels. Vlad screamed something at the pirates. I'm not sure what he said, but they looked resigned at obeying his orders by preparing to jump into the river themselves.

"Stop!" I yelled. For a moment, everyone froze. I pointed at one of the thieves. "He has Sage's necklace. I want it before he jumps. It'll get lost in the water."

Vlad shouted again at the pirates. One of them raised the necklace in his hand, then grudgingly dropped it inside Carlos's boat. Vlad motioned to the water with his weapon, and the men jumped into the Amazon with a splash. Talk about role reversal.

Turning to the pirate's speedboat, Vlad aimed and unleashed a torrent of rapid gunfire, sounding like fast knocking on a door, and riddled their engine with holes.

The deafening metallic noise startled us, and we cupped our ears. A dark cloud of smoke rose. The pirates weren't going anywhere anytime soon.

He lowered his gun and spoke toward us. "In the Amazon, wild animals aren't the only things you need to worry about."

Carlos surveyed the bullet damage. "True. The most dangerous predators are men."

"We've dealt with this drug group before." Vlad watched the treading men. "They may look tough, but they're amateurs."

Carlos huffed. “Shotguns and speedboats don’t look amateur to me.”

“A professional drug operation doesn’t pirate on the side. Draws too much attention.” Vlad turned his focus on me and Sage. “And it looks like the mighty river has drawn us together again.”

“You know each other?” Carlos sounded surprised.

“Yeah, from the boat ride last night.” I lifted my hands and shrugged. “What are the odds?”

“How’s your young friend?” Vlad’s tone sounded more like a growl than a question.

I doubted he really cared. “Yeisson’s in good hands. But still needs a miracle.”

He moved the toothpick to the other side of his mouth using only his tongue. “So why are you out here and not at the hospital?”

My mind stumbled for a response. I didn’t want to tell him the real reason.

But Sage gave the perfect answer. “Looking for some natural remedies. We’re exhausting all the options.”

Vlad probed. “Plants? Berries?”

“Something like that.” She wrapped herself in a towel.

“Does this have anything to do with…” He shifted and looked at me. “The interesting place you told me about?”

Ugh. Me and my big mouth. “The place?”

Maybe my faked ignorance would derail him. It didn’t.

His face, stern. "Guyerma's Well."

"You've got a good memory." I was surprised he remembered the name.

"It's an old term." Vlad sat behind the steering wheel and leaned his feet on the boat's edge. "A lot of mythology surrounds the place. Though nobody really knows where it is." A pause. "Except for you, apparently."

He was on to us.

"We're desperate." Sage dried her hair with the towel. "It's doubtful we'll find anything. Probably a wild goose chase."

"A quick trip there, a quick trip back," Carlos agreed.

Vlad spit the toothpick from his mouth, a serious look on his face. "The Hipupiara. Am I right?"

Awkward silence before Carlos spoke. "Yeah, that's right. Just another group of fools searching for something that's never been found."

"Not found… yet." Vlad fiddled with the gun in his lap. "Great legends surround the Hipupiara's nest. Eggs with healing properties. Able to heal the sick and raise the dead. Whoever finds those eggs becomes extremely rich."

He knew more than I expected.

"We're not after any money." Sage pursed her lips. "It's to help our friend."

"We have different motives, but the same goal." Vlad's face

broke into a crooked smile. “But there’s no reason why we both can’t mutually benefit.”

“Mutual?” Carlos’s voice sounded doubtful. “In what way?”

“We saved you. All I ask in return is lead me to the nest.” Vlad looked at the surrounding trees, then at the pirates flapping in the water. “This area can be a dangerous place. Remote. People die here and are never found.” His thin lips gave a half-smile. “But we can provide you with protection.”

The tone sounded more threatening than helpful. But there was no way out of it. Refusing him would seem ungrateful, but saying yes would definitely give him the upper hand.

I tried hiding my frustration without much success. “I don’t think we have a choice.”

“Not true, young man.” Vlad stood from the seat and faced me, real close. “Life is full of choices. And those choices carry consequences. Both good and bad.”

He had us cornered, and he knew it.

“We’ll lead you there.” Carlos spoke calmly. “And if by chance we find the nest, we’ll both get what we need. Then go our separate ways.”

“Deal.” Vlad extended a handshake and sealed the agreement. “With one stipulation. No radio contact with anyone. We keep the purpose of our trip a secret. How far away is Guyerma’s Well?”

"About a half-hour from here." Carlos nodded toward his boat. "Problem is, we're not gonna go very far. Our engine won't start."

"That's what partners are for." Vlad directed one of his men to the problem engine. "He's an excellent mechanic."

As the man worked on the motor, Carlos pulled us away from Vlad and spoke with a lowered voice. "Are you guys okay? I'm so sorry this happened."

I shrugged. "Just another day being robbed and dodging machine gun bullets."

"And pirarucu," Sage said.

"You know we don't have to do this," he whispered. "We can forget the nest and return to Leticia."

"After coming this far?" Sage shook her head. "No way."

The girl had a fighting spirit. "Yeah. It can't get much worse, can it?" I asked.

Carlos eyed Vlad. "I hope not."

In minutes, our repaired boat roared to life. We stepped back inside and Carlos gripped the steering wheel. Back in business.

Sage found the necklace on the floor and clasped it around her neck with relief on her face. Then she embraced me with a long, tender hug.

"Thank you."

"True love," I whispered.

Pulling back, she tilted her head, gently. "Excuse me?"

I pointed at the necklace. “The reminder of true love. Your grandparents.”

“Oh, yeah. Absolutely.” Her face flushed and she swept the wet hair from her eyes. “I owe you one, Pace.”

Carlos adjusted the throttle and slipped the motor into gear. *Hipupiara nest, here we come.*

Vlad and his men followed as we cut through the Amazon River, leaving the disabled speed boat and its two treading pirates in our wake.

40

The sun had already started drying our wet clothes as Carlos steered the boat through the winding sweeps of the Amazon.

Vlad followed in his boat, with one of his men piloting and the other watching us. The two men both looked Slavic, similar to him, with wide foreheads and round faces. Big-boned and muscular, they had dull complexions, dark hair, and cattle-brown eyes.

Carlos turned to us, as we sat on a long cushioned seat beside him. “So Vlad was on the cargo boat last night?”

“Yeah,” I said, squinting in the wind.

“And you *told* him about Guyerma’s Well?”

I shifted, feeling like an idiot. “Just making conversation.”

I don’t always put a foot in my mouth; sometimes I manage to fit both.

Carlos shook his head. “For Hipupiara believers, Guyerma’s Well is a sacred term. Kind of like Mecca. It’s not listed on any maps, so many people don’t know its exact location. I’m probably one of the few.”

Sage pushed the blowing hair out of her face. "You think Vlad has always searched for the Sea Creature, too?"

"Not for the creature as much for the glory and riches." Carlos paused, as if in deep thought. "Do you find it amazing that you bumped into him again, after last night?"

"Small world," I said. "And I swear he rode past on a boat our first night in Leticia. I remember his stare, and he wore that same fedora hat."

"So you've seen him *three* times?" Carlos's shoulders fell a little. "There's an old truth, 'The second time is coincidence, but the third time's on purpose.'"

I glanced behind at Vlad and his men. "He can't be all that bad. Those pirates were dangerous. He saved us."

"Or maybe he gave the *appearance* of saving us."

His words surprised me.

Sage's chin dropped. "You think the pirates were more of Vlad's men?"

"It's a possibility," Carlos said. "Once Pace mentioned Guyerma's Well to him, I think it got his attention. Did you tell him you were going there?"

I hung my head. "Probably. But I didn't tell him what we were looking for specifically."

"You didn't have to," he said. "When you spoke of the nest's location, it branded you as someone with inside information."

“But why would he shoot the speedboat engine to smithereens?” I asked. “If they were his men, that was his boat. He destroyed the engine and shot at those guys. We saw the bullets hit the water.”

“Appearances can be deceptive.” Carlos navigated a right turn and adjusted the boat’s throttle. “Vlad has an AKM assault rifle. That’s big time. Yet no one got hurt.”

“So it was an *act*?” I asked.

“Think about it: if you were him, would you be willing to sacrifice a simple boat engine in order to gain our favor? It makes him look like the hero and we owe him our lives. I bet he has other goons helping those pirates as we speak.”

“So why did you agree to let him come along?” Sage leaned forward to speak above the engine. “We can’t trust him.”

“It doesn’t matter if we trust him or not.” Carlos darted his eyes toward us. “We have no choice. And he knows it. But I don’t think he wants to hurt us. We’re only a means to an end, which is good, because I don’t have a gun anymore.”

He opened a drawer below the steering wheel. “But I do have my machete.”

Heaviness crept into my chest. “So why was Vlad so adamant about us not using the radio? Seems a little sketchy.”

“Because others can listen to the frequency.” Carlos squeezed the steering wheel tighter. “If word got out, treasure hunters and conspiracy theorists would have a field day."

"But what if something happens to us?" Sage's countenance changed. "What if he… how will anyone find us?"

"Honey, I've been married for many moons. I don't go anywhere without Lorena knowing about it." He turned and winked. "We're gonna be fine."

Positive thinking, but I wasn't so sure. Only a few minutes before, a gun was pointed at my forehead. We could've been killed. It's hard calming down after that type of experience. And I wondered about Sage. She had a focused look on her face but worry in her eyes.

Yeisson. It was all for him. A wave of grief. *Is he still alive?* I whispered a prayer for a miracle.

After another twenty minutes, Carlos slowed the boat and cut the engine off, allowing Vlad's boat to pull beside us. We floated along side-by-side and stared ahead at the miles of thick leaves and tall canopies along the riverbank. It looked no different than other areas. The nearest shore stood a hundred yards from us, and the opposite side was three-quarters of a mile away.

"This is it." Carlos checked his gauges. "Guyerma's Well. And it stretches ahead for several miles."

"Several miles," Vlad repeated, his eyes narrowing. "And how are we supposed to find the nest?"

"Your guess is as good as mine." Carlos stood from his seat.

"I've searched for years."

Vlad's face reddened. "With miles of shoreline on both sides, we're supposed to stumble upon the nest?"

"The deal was to lead you to Guyerma's Well," Carlos said firmly.

"The deal was to lead me to the nest."

"No." Carlos shook his head. "We came to *look* for the nest. No promises beyond that."

"How do I know you're not lying?" Vlad's eyes changed. "What proof do I have this is the right location?"

Carlos pointed at the boat's dash. "Look at your depth finder. Over three hundred feet of water sits beneath us. One of the deepest parts of the Amazon. That's why Guyerma called this area a well."

"And it makes perfect sense," I interrupted. "An abnormally large creature would naturally choose the deepest section."

"A good story." Vlad made no effort in hiding his scowl. "But I'm not buying it."

"I don't care if you buy it or not." Carlos shrugged. "It's the truth. I grew up on this river, and if there's a Hipupiara nest in Guyerma's Well, it's here somewhere."

Vlad glared at me. "What else do you know, kid? You holding something back?"

"All I know is that a shaman told me he visited this area for many years." My throat was tight. "The nest is near the water, where the creature can stay submerged while protecting its eggs. It's also covered. So we must look carefully."

"I've got a better idea." Vlad raised his voice. "Let's get the shaman and have him show us exactly where to look."

"He'd never come," I said. "He's too old. And too protective of the creature. If he sensed selfish gain, he would lead us astray."

Vlad studied the expanse stretching before him. "This is damn near impossible."

"We can't debate all day." Sage sounded irritated. "Sunlight's burning and my friend is dying. So let's stop talking and start looking. Your boat can take one side and we'll take the other."

That's my girl.

Vlad's face softened slightly as he ogled her. "I love a forward, take-charge woman." He addressed his men and gave directions in Russian, then turned back to us. "They'll check the opposite side. But I'm coming with you."

"What?" Carlos flashed a sarcastic smile. "You don't trust us?"

"Trust?" Vlad stepped into our boat and observed the supplies. "We're partners, remember?" He opened a cooler and rumbled through the ice, finding only water bottles. "Got any vodka?"

"No." Carlos gave no explanation.

Vlad's eyes plunged to Sage's neckline. "Glad I got your

necklace back. It disgusts me when people take what isn't rightfully theirs." He twisted open a water bottle and drank it in one long gulp.

Carlos started the engine again, and the agonizing search moved slowly. We couldn't draw close enough to the shore to see much detail since the overhang of foliage obscured what lay beyond the water. Like looking for a needle in a haystack.

We searched for over an hour. Nothing. Using binoculars, we took turns watching Vlad's men on the far shoreline. Their search looked just as slow-going and fruitless.

Hope faded, and time ticked away. The sun had shifted and soon we'd have to leave for Leticia, empty-handed. Since we got robbed in broad daylight, I shuddered thinking about nightfall. I pounded a fist against the boat railing, frustrated to be so tantalizingly close to the nest yet no nearer than when we began.

"We have one last strip to check." Carlos wiped the sweat from his forehead. "Another half mile or so. But if we don't find anything, we're calling it a day."

He turned toward Vlad. "You and your men can stay out here all night, but not us."

Vlad didn't answer, his face set in stone. We continued prodding along, staring at the mind-numbing monotony of tangled sprigs and sticks and logs. It was hard to stay focused, and my eyes felt like they had crossed.

Wait.

Something finally caught my attention, hanging from the branches above. I squinted.

Two dozen drooping baskets. Woven from sturdy vines and about four feet in length, they resembled gourds. I smiled and knew exactly what they were. And sure enough, moments later came the unmistakable timbre of a melodic, pan flute call, like the sound of air blowing against the edge of a hole.

Oropendola birds.

Those incredible singers and basket weavers. They were red-winged black birds with bright yellow tail feathers, perched in a colony, at times swarming near the tree base.

Now it made sense, and I could barely contain my excitement. When Red Goth had snapped the Sea Creature picture, an oropendola landed on our boat railing. And when the shaman later told us his story, he mentioned a swarm of birds always surrounded the Hipupiara nest and ate some of the eggs.

I'd bet the farm those birds in his story were oropendolas.

They follow the Hipupiara.

Breathless, I turned to Carlos and pointed. "Let's go closer over there. I think we might be onto something."

Vlad radioed his men, and they soon joined us from the other side. Before we dropped anchor and waded toward shore, he traded his rifle for a pistol.

"How many guns do you have?" Carlos carried a machete which Vlad eyed with suspicion.

"As many needed to protect my cargo," he answered through gritted teeth.

"Follow the birds." I pointed upward. "They'll lead us to the nest."

"What do birds have to do with the Hipupiara?" Vlad's voice dripped in doubt.

I took a deep breath. "Maybe nothing. Just a theory."

He gave an impatient grunt. "I'm tired of theories."

"Pace has a gift with animals," Sage said. "Trust him."

I winked at her, silently thanking her for the compliment. But now I really felt the pressure.

We walked into the jungle. Heavy with humidity, and smelling of dirt and moisture, it practically buzzed with primeval energy and reminded me of entering the rainforest with Yeisson before the snake attacked us. *Please no more pit vipers.*

The rattle and racket of a million unseen insects surrounded us, resembling the sound of spraying water from a shower head. Thick and waxy leaves stood like barricades at every step. Carlos led the way and sliced a path with his machete. The swinging plants and limbs slapped me in the face.

The ground squished soft and swampy, and mud oozed around our shoes. Shafts of sunlight streamed between branches and vines. We passed an iguana sunbathing on a limb, camouflaged, looking wholly unimpressed by our visit.

Pressing farther, we trekked over gnarly roots and through pointy boughs, exploring thick curtains of vegetation as the jungle squeezed its arms around us.

Eventually, the oropendola birds again sounded their unique call, so elegant and breathy. Their hanging tree baskets were ahead. We were getting closer. I felt like Indiana Jones searching for the lost ark, both nervous and excited.

In time, we had circled around and directly faced the Amazon. We walked through a wet marsh, and then, between us and the river lay a hollowed-out patch, ten feet across, an oval-shaped mound clumped with vegetation and grass.

A large nest.

It had to be *the* nest. I think all of us saw it at the same moment and inhaled a collective gasp of air.

And inside lay nine large eggs, partially covered in sticks and leaves.

41

I could hardly believe my eyes.

Teal-colored eggs, football-shaped and enormous, two feet long and a foot and a half wide. The biggest eggs I'd ever seen. Placed in a spiral pattern around the nest, the clutch of eggs hinted at the Hipupiara's nurturing maternal nature.

My chest heaved. Only a few humans had ever gazed upon them. A historic moment. The effort to get there was worth it, even with risking our lives, since the healing power of the eggs could impact multitudes.

I wasn't greedy. Just one egg was all we needed. I didn't care about fame or fortune, only Yeisson's recovery. Once we had an egg I'd prepare it on Carlos's propane boat stove, and by the time we arrived in Leticia, we'd take the drink straight to Yeisson's room. Then trust for a miracle. I'd give all the leftovers to the doctors for research.

Vlad stared at the mound of eggs like a man who had found gold. A slight shiver ran up my back. Would he keep his end of the bargain, or take the eggs and leave us stranded? We offered little resistance. They carried guns; all we had was a machete.

He addressed his men in Russian, and the two lumbered toward the nest, hoisting military-sized canvas bags. It didn't take an animal expert to realize their risk.

"Wait!" I spoke just above a whisper. "We shouldn't rush. It's dangerous around nests of large creatures."

Stopping his men, Vlad glared at me and spoke with forced restraint. "Look around. Listen. Hear anything? See anything? If the Hipupiara were here, we'd definitely know about it."

I wanted to smack the sarcastic grin off his face. "The shaman told us about two men who ventured carelessly into the nest. At the expense of their lives. It attacked from the water. We need to watch and wait a few more minutes."

He ignored my words and focused on the nest. "When something's this good, I like taking my chances."

"But by risking other men's lives?"

Anger flashed in his eyes toward me, but then he turned and spoke something to his men. They nodded.

"See?" He gave a half-smile. "I asked if they wanted to go inside the nest, and they both agreed. I'm not risking their lives. They're choosing. So if I were you, I'd keep my little mouth shut and stop questioning another man's courage."

"But what will they do if the creature attacks?"

Vlad raised his shirt and revealed the pistol. “That’s what guns are for, son. We’ll show momma monster we’re not afraid.”

“Don’t you dare shoot her,” I said. “She’s a one-of-a-kind creature. And you can’t blame her for protecting the nest.”

“So what do you want us to do?” he asked. “Sit for a cup of tea and politely ask her for some eggs? You’ve got a friend who’s dying. We don’t have time to crusade for animal rights.”

“But we need to do this on her terms,” Sage interrupted. “If our actions threaten her, it’s all over. Approach gently and patiently.”

“The creature isn’t even here.” Vlad raised his voice loudly to prove his point. “Helloooo! We’re here! Where are you, Hipupiara?” His voice echoed across the jungle.

I grimaced. “Shhh! What are you doing?”

“We’re doing this my way, partner.” He pointed to his chest. “And if you don’t like it, maybe you won’t end up with any eggs.”

“You can’t go back on your word,” Carlos said, approaching Vlad. “We’ve done everything you’ve asked.”

“Sometimes situations dictate changes.” Vlad lifted his glance toward Carlos without moving his head. “So if you want your precious egg, shut the hell up.” He barked at his men, who again walked toward the nest, pulling out their guns.

“No sudden movements,” I said to them, though they couldn’t understand. “Nice and slow.”

"And as quiet as possible," Sage added, in a lowered voice.

Vlad's men weren't slow or quiet, and they recklessly trampled toward the nest. And though both the jungle and river stood eerily quiet, without hint of a looming creature, something didn't feel right. We needed to wait, watch, think. Mommas never leave their nests unprotected.

Sage wrapped her arm around mine and watched nervously as they bounded into the hollow nest. One of them holstered his gun and lifted an egg, so big it required two hands. Judging from his effort, I guessed it weighed about five pounds. He knocked on the shell with his knuckles, showing us its tough exterior. And to my alarm, he then playfully tossed the egg to his unsuspecting partner, who barely caught it against his chest while holding a gun in his hand.

Idiots. What were they thinking?

We listened and observed closely. Still no movement anywhere outside the nest. The quiet only emboldened the men, and they tossed their canvas bags noisily on the nest floor and filled them with eggs.

It took them several minutes, and after they had finished, one bag contained five eggs and the other four. Heavy, large loads even for grown men.

As one straightened and looped the bag over his shoulder, he took a step backward. His shoe crunched on a broken egg shell, one probably cracked by a hungry oropendola. The Russian didn't notice, but the peculiar splitting sound resonated throughout the quiet marsh, like fingernails on a chalkboard.

And behind them, the water stirred.

No, it couldn't be.

At first a few ripples, then a constant bubbling, and finally a massive thrush of sound as if the Amazon River turned upside-down, the displacement of water equal to a nuclear submarine emerging.

The men stood paralyzed.

Out of the water slowly rose the most horrifying and beautiful creature I'd ever seen or imagined. Breaking the surface, dark and glossy eyes rested on top of a broad, V-shaped head, the tip of a mighty iceberg.

I gasped, my throat unable to scream. If the rest of its body matched the size of its cranium, the Hipupiara's immensity would be unmatched in the animal world.

Next, from underneath the water burst its top jaw, an extension of the skull, with the bottom jaw unhinged and opened, designed for crushing bone and wide enough to devour a horse, making a sound resembling a cold wind escaping from a cave. A ferocious killing machine.

The creature bared dozens of serrated teeth, closely packed, long and sharp razors capable of incomprehensible fury and damage. It had a thick and muscular neck, able to coil and strike like a death adder but with the unfair reach of a prehistoric diplodicus.

Part gargantuan alligator, part T-Rex, part dragon.

The Hipupiara's arched back erupted from the river, armored with keratin blades, its scaled and spotted skin the blue-grey color of a tank. More of its body emerged, and I marveled at the revelation.

Its length, from head to tip of tail, spanned half a football field. The tail composed most of its length, counterbalancing the long neck and heavy head, and it swayed loosely above the river's surface like a lash at the end of a bullwhip.

The men dropped the bags and lifted their guns, but it was too late.

With a lightning-fast snap, the Hipupiara thrashed its tail around one man's torso, the brute force of mass and speed killing him upon impact. With a backward heave it cast the limp body far into the river.

A split-second later, the second Russian experienced the same penalty, a gruesome but quick death.

Sage screamed and Carlos crumpled to his knees but Vlad remained planted, his eyes cold as flint.

The breath escaped my lungs and my legs trembled. It seemed like a horrible dream, a nightmare, something one could never erase from the mind's eye.

Why didn't they heed our warnings? The Hipupiara couldn't be blamed for following its natural instincts. Out in the wild facing the tempest of untamed nature, there were different rules: kill or be killed.

The creature gradually submerged its body underwater, a mountain covered by a flood, until only its narrowed eyes remained visible.

Our move.

The satchels of eggs lay in the nest, and directly above us floated the haunting call of a lone oropendola bird, its melody wafting in the air like a funeral dirge.

42

"My God." Carlos stared at the submerged creature. "The Hipupiara is real."

"Why didn't those men listen?" Sage said, more to herself. Then she faced Vlad, her face reddened. "Why didn't *you* listen?"

He focused ahead without answering, like he was pondering his next move.

The canvas bags of eggs lay so close, thirty feet away. *Thirty feet away*. Their discovery would shock the world. Rewrite science books. Empower conspiracy theorists. But all I could think of was the bodies of two men laying at the bottom of Guyerma's Well.

Men who didn't have to die.

Beside me, Carlos mumbled a prayer and Sage wept. My stomach churned with nausea. The blame was mine. We wouldn't have been there if it wasn't for me, and the men wouldn't have died. Like always, I'd made a mess of things. Why didn't I warn them better? I could've protested, argued more; they would still be alive. But instead, we watched them die. Watching death has a traumatic, lasting effect; and it stains the minds of witnesses.

But Vlad seemed unfazed, and he crept toward the nest, raising his gun. What was he doing? Surely he realized a simple pistol couldn't puncture the Hipupiara's armored skin. But maybe it gave him an aura of protection. False protection. With each step he drew closer, and for a few moments nothing happened.

But halfway there, the water around the sea creature's eyes bubbled and stirred, like liquid boiling.

Vlad stopped abruptly, remaining still for a long minute, perhaps fighting an internal battle. He finally backed away, dismay on his face.

Approaching the nest was a death sentence. But how did the shaman survive? What was his secret? Maybe the Hipupiara was smarter than anyone fathomed. Maybe she recognized and devoured greed but rewarded a pure heart.

Or maybe only a shaman could enter the nest, somehow serving as a mysterious intermediary between the natural and supernatural worlds. I didn't have a clue. But one thing was certain: the difference between life and death rested somewhere deep in the heart of that wild creature, the one watching us with assassin eyes.

Whatever the answer, our immediate problem was Vlad. We needed a plan. It was increasingly evident our lives were expendable to him, and eventually his obsession would send us all into the nest. Somehow we had to overpower him. It wouldn't be easy. Since he brandished a gun, we'd have to distract him.

I glanced at the machete Carlos held. Our only weapon.

"What a shame." Vlad shook his head and glared at the nest.

Sage wiped tears from her eyes. "They seemed like faithful men."

"I'm talking about the eggs," he said in a mocking tone. "Men can be replaced."

"You're a real jerk, you know that?" My voice shook.

"I'm focused, that's all." He stepped toward me. "That's why I need you to think, real hard. How did the shaman get those eggs?"

Even if I did know, why tell him? Maybe I could lie and invent some crazy detail. But if he followed the falsehood, and died, I'd have more blood on my hands. I couldn't watch another man perish, no matter how much I hated him.

"He didn't give details." I refused to look at him as I spoke. "He only said he approached carefully."

"And this was after the death of his two men?"

"Yeah."

"Maybe I'm not the only one with a cold heart, huh?" Vlad glanced at each of us. "Looks like we have at least four more opportunities to get this right."

My worst fear was coming true; he'd sacrifice us all.

"No," Sage said, her voice lower than usual. "We're not a part of your suicide plan."

"It's not worth risking any more lives," Carlos agreed. "We've seen the Hipupiara, isn't that enough?"

"Enough? *Enough*?" Vlad's eyes widened. "It's precisely why we can't leave. We stand on the edge of greatness, the opportunity of a lifetime. I'm not leaving without those eggs."

"Is the fame and fortune really worth your life?" I asked.

Vlad gave a wicked smile. "Great achievements require great risks."

"This is where we say farewell, Vlad." Carlos turned and motioned us to follow him. "We're going back to Leticia. What you choose to do is your business. But I beg you, back away."

Vlad's expression turned the color of ice. "I thought we were partners."

"Consider the partnership over." Carlos walked toward the boat.

Sage and I followed.

From behind, Vlad cocked his gun.

When we turned, the barrel pointed at us. "I'm afraid you can't leave," he said. "And drop the damn machete."

I needed to divert him; he couldn't take our lone weapon.

"What are you, mental?" I asked.

"No, I'm a pragmatist." A devilish grin spread across his face. "You said not to risk my life. That's good advice. So I've decided to use beauty over brawn."

"What do you mean?" Carlos asked.

He glowered at Sage. "I'm sending the girl."

A chill over my spine. Heart hammering in my chest, my legs felt as heavy as the surrounding Kapok trees, like someone had swung a Louisville Slugger into my gut. Vlad was a madman blinded to anything or anyone else around him. And his spindly tentacles reached toward Sage.

My Sage.

"What?" I screamed. "Sending a girl to do something you're scared to do?"

He playfully waved his gun. "Working smarter, not harder."

Rage rose from within, and everything in me wanted to unleash vitriol into that coward of a man. "How dare you, you son of b — "

Sage interrupted. "Shoot me if you want, but I'm not going into the nest. Even if I get the eggs, you'll probably kill us anyway."

"True, I see your point." Vlad calmly nodded, then pointed the gun at Carlos. "But if you don't start marching toward those eggs, gramps here will get some lead in his brain. Does pretty girl want that to happen?"

Was there no limit to how low he would go? Sage's eyes filled with tears again and she hung her head, defeated.

"Don't hurt him…" Her voice cracked. "I'll go."

"No, Sage." Carlos stared ahead. "I'm not afraid of his gun."

"Shut up, old man." Vlad stepped closer, his finger toying with the trigger. "Another outburst and it'll be the final words you ever say."

Things had spiraled out of control, and I only had one play left.

"I'll go. Don't bother them." I took a step toward the nest, momentarily distracting Vlad from Carlos. "With my knowledge of animals, I can do this."

Vlad straightened, obviously intrigued by the proposal. "Now that's what I love, willing volunteers." He looked at me, then back at Sage. "But despite you wanting to be a hero, I'm still going with the girl."

His words were a knife between my ribs, slowly twisting. The blood drained from my face. "What… why?"

"Because every good tale has the sacrifice of a beautiful woman. And I'm a sucker for a good story." Vlad's thin lips curled. "But who knows? Maybe the creature will let her pass. Then *she'll* be the hero."

"No, listen to me." I grew more desperate. "I'll go and bring back the eggs. You keep them all. You take the credit. And plus, Sage is the only one who knows how to make the egg potion. If she dies, we'll never know."

A boldfaced lie.

But Vlad pondered it before answering. “I think you’re bluffing, kid. And I don’t like bluffers. If you keep lying, I’ll drop your sweetheart right here. She won’t make it to the nest.”

Looking into his eyes was like staring into dark holes, abysses cut off from all light. I hated him. The real monster wasn’t in the river but standing on the shore. Fire coursed through my veins, and red fury clouded my head. If Vlad turned away for one brief second, I’d lunge at him, attack him, beat him until he couldn’t move, cave in his face with my fists.

But he was careful. He kept a safe distance and watched us, pointing the gun and motioning Sage toward the nest.

She turned to me, and without a word, removed her necklace and placed it in my palm, closing my fist around it. Both of her hands squeezed mine.

I tried objecting, but she touched a finger to my lips and shook her head. She stared for an extended moment, boring into me, her gaze seeming to ask, *What could have been?*

And for the first time I realized I loved her, as outrageous as it seemed. She was the love of my life, though she didn’t know it.

Or maybe she did.

And I was about to lose her.

Why couldn’t we have stayed in the safe hospital waiting room? Why did I push for this? Like the two men, her death would be on my hands.

She kissed my cheek and lingered for a few sweet seconds, her lips laced with gentleness and a disturbing feel of finality.

"That's enough!" Vlad's face burned like cold iron as he stepped toward her and flaunted his weapon. "Get moving!" Then he looked at Carlos. "And I said drop the machete. *Now.*"

Carlos released it from his grip and lifted his hands.

Her chin trembling, Sage turned and faced the nest. Slowly walking toward it, she folded her arms over her stomach.

Black despair washed over me.

Ahead of her, the submerged Hipupiara watched with pale green eyes, large and unblinking, and focused its narrow vertical pupils, glaring at its next victim, the water dripping from the sloping folds of its scaly head.

43

The way the sunlight draped her, Sage glowed like a cherub, an angel sent into the gates of hell.

And the closer she walked toward the nest, the more my body shuddered. A helpless sense of defeat overtook me. Despite my efforts, I couldn't protect her from Vlad, or the creature. Each step took her farther away.

Ten feet, fifteen. Would I never look into her beautiful face again?

I squeezed her necklace and fell on my knees, not knowing whether to watch or close my eyes. The thought of her possibly dying made me want to vomit.

Sage shook noticeably, and I imagined the frightening thoughts running through her mind. She needed help.

Think, Pace, think.

It would be a miracle if the Hipupiara didn't attack. Was there some way of operating on the creature's terms, whatever they may be? There were no answers, only empty guesses. But at the very least Sage needed comfort. She shouldn't feel alone.

"You're going to make it, Sage." I lifted my voice, careful not to yell. "Just take it slow."

"I don't want to die," she responded, her voice soft and vulnerable.

"You'll be fine. Believe it. Tell yourself that over and over."

She stepped within half-distance of the nest. "Can the creature see me if I don't move?"

"I'm not sure." I stared at the Hipupiara's pupils; long and vertical and watching Sage's every step. With those eyes, I'd guess its vision was sharper than an eagle's, but I didn't want to tell her.

"Remember, no jerky movements," I said. "Gentle with your approach."

"Dear God." Sage repeated the words, quivering.

"Take a deep breath." I had been kneeling, but stood nervously.

"She's a protective momma," she said. "How can anyone blame her for lashing out?"

"But she won't hurt you. You two share a female bond." I was grasping for words, though they didn't make much sense. *Keep her talking, Pace.* "Women understand signals. Men don't, remember?"

She remained focused. "How will I know if she's about to attack?"

I swallowed. With little known of the creature's patterned

behavior, I thought of it as the world's biggest alligator. "If she hisses or opens her mouth, then stop. And slowly back away. You must gain her trust."

"But what if that doesn't work? What if she still comes at me?"

"Then run like hell and don't look behind. Run in a straight line, not a zig-zag."

Sage took several more tentative steps, until she stood five feet from the nest's edge.

As if on cue, the Hipupiara swished its mighty tail, warily circling it above the water, and slapped its head up and down on the surface.

My heart stopped. Not a good sign from a wild animal.

"What's happening?" She stopped, her voice terrified. "What does it mean, Pace?"

"It's a sign of aggression," I said, breathlessly. "Back off, real slow."

I could barely watch, expecting the creature's pounce at any moment. Sage's every move mattered.

But Vlad straightened his pistol toward her. "Don't back away, young lady. Your job's not done."

His words fueled the red hot lava already coursing inside me, and I wanted to rage on him like an erupting volcano. But I couldn't. Screaming and fighting would place Sage's life in more danger. Clenching my fists, I shook with fury.

Sage froze, and the Hipupiara continued its loud warnings, splashing and swirling the water. A chilling display of power and intimidation.

But while Vlad watched eagerly, Carlos used the distraction as an opportunity to walk toward him, empty-handed.

Vlad, startled when he noticed Carlos's sudden combativeness, turned and pointed the gun.

"What are you doing? I told you to stay back."

Carlos displayed empty palms. "I'm unarmed."

What was he thinking? And why leave the machete on the ground? With a gun, Vlad still had the advantage. If we tried rushing him, he'd mow us down before we'd get five feet.

"Stop. Now." Vlad's arm twitched with agitation. "I *will* shoot you. Not another step."

Carlos slowed but didn't stop. "Let the girl back away."

I braced for the gun shot.

"You're not in any position to give orders," Vlad said.

"You're right." Carlos continued his gradual approach, only ten feet from him. "But you wouldn't shoot a man cold-blooded."

"I've done it before, and I'll do it again."

"I don't believe you will." Carlos took a deep breath. "Because you know we're good, honest people. We'll let you have all the eggs. But you're not risking Sage's life for them. You'll have to shoot me first."

I finally understood what he was doing — diverting Vlad's attention. And it worked. Without Vlad focused on Sage, she had already taken a few steps away from the nest.

Adrenaline raced through my body; Carlos's bravery inspired me. *Pace, this is your hour.* I walked toward him as a sign of solidarity, prepared to take a bullet for Sage.

Vlad stepped back uneasily, biding time. "Both of you, this is your last warning."

"If you shoot that gun," Carlos said, "the Hipupiara will kill us all. You'll spook it."

Vlad retreated more, closer to the nest, perhaps realizing the truth in Carlos's words. Any sudden, loud movement could bring the creature's wrath.

But then his jaw set, and his red-laced eyeballs bulged from his skull. "Screw it. Let the games begin."

He aimed and shot at the ground between me and Carlos, missing by inches.

I jumped, ears ringing from the loud gunshot. Was he crazy? Did he have a death wish?

The water swirled around the Hipupiara.

"My next shot won't miss," Vlad said, oblivious to the movement behind him, his back toward the river.

Unbelievably, the creature slowly rose out of the water, whisper quiet, the hulking body swallowing the horizon. It hunched its long, serpentine spine like a jungle cat stalking prey.

I gazed in fear and awe. Two large back bumps rose as mini-mountains, and spotty patterns across its armor-plated skin glistened like ancient war paint.

With flaring nostrils and stiffened tail, the Hipupiara cocked its head directly at Vlad, its lizard face one of nightmares and plagues and pestilence. The world's mightiest meat-eater, fully revealed.

I backed away, but Carlos held his ground. He stared at the rising creature behind Vlad, who remained unaware of the mortal danger.

"Please listen." Carlos gasped and pointed over Vlad's shoulder. "The creature. Don't turn around. Walk calmly toward me."

"Yeah, right." Vlad aimed the barrel with murder in his eyes. "I take pleasure in punishing liars."

Then came a hissing breath, like steam escaping from a giant grate. It crescendoed into the rumbling and rattling of a deep growl, one which shook the ground.

Vlad turned around too late.

The Hipupiara attacked in vicious anger, not with its tail, but with its fang-filled mouth opened wide. A deafening roar rattled my bones, and the creature launched across the foliage like a torpedo, with bounding strides of muscle and terror.

It moved in a breathtaking burst of primal savagery and

charged forward with hurricane-force wind as it pummeled the trees lining the riverbank.

Vlad shrieked, having no reaction time before the creature seized him with cavernous jaws.

He somehow managed several gun shots, spraying bullets in wild directions, hopelessly trying to defend himself.

But the Hipupiara's teeth sank through his body, slicing it in half, a torrent of blood alongside the crunching of bone and cartilage.

It shook Vlad's body like a rag doll, its spiked incisors tearing at mangled flesh, ripping his torso like a buzz saw and splaying intestines and organs across the jungle floor.

For a brief moment, the creature stopped and leered at us, deciding our fate, mouth dripping chunks of gore. I stood still, afraid to breathe; a moment of life or death.

And just as quickly, the Hipupiara receded into the river, returning to its underwater lair, still munching on its prey. An unfathomable sight.

The rest of us had been gruesomely warned, again. As the creature submerged, Vlad's white hat bobbed on the surface.

I turned away, hand to my mouth, heart beating wildly.

And then I saw Sage.

Time slowed and the world lost its color.

She lay on the ground, motionless, blood pouring from her

chest.

One of Vlad's stray bullets had hit her.

44

Sage's scarlet shirt matched the color of her blood, its metallic smell hanging in the still air.

Carlos lowered his ear to her mouth and listened for breathing, then checked her wrist for a pulse.

"She's barely hanging on." His face knotted with concern. "We don't have much time."

Thank God she's not dead.

"Where was she hit?" I could barely muster the breath to speak, my heart about to burst from my chest.

"Grab the machete." Carlos pointed to the area where we had stood. "It's on the ground over there."

After searching through the foliage, I handed it to him. He used it to cut away the top portion of Sage's shirt, around her left shoulder, and examined the wound.

"The bullet hit just below the collarbone." He took a long breath. "It probably caused a collapsed lung, and maybe hit an artery."

An artery would bleed out in minutes. Believing for the best, and numb to everything around me, I squeezed her hand. “You're going to make it... you're a fighter.”

Carlos's eyes widened. “We need something to control the bleeding.”

I took off my shirt. “Use this.”

Carlos applied direct pressure to the wound. “She's in shock due to blood loss.”

Touching Sage's arm, her skin felt cold. And could she hear us? Was she scared? I whispered repeatedly in her ear, as much for me as for her: *It's going to be okay. Hold on.*

“We have to get back to the boat.” Carlos's voice shook. “There are first-aid supplies there. But we must leave now if there's any chance for her. The hospital is two hours away.”

Two hours? How could she survive the next few minutes? Her blood covered our arms and hands, and I felt like the one bleeding. Lord knows, I would have switched places with her, if possible.

“How will she survive long enough to get there?”

Carlos shook his head but didn't speak. If a miracle didn't happen, Sage would die long before we arrived in Leticia, and I'd never forgive myself. The terrifying thought of possibly losing both her and Yeisson on the same day seemed inconceivable.

I remembered the first time meeting Sage, beside Silver Lake, her chocolate eyes melting my insides. And to be kneeling beside her by the shores of the mighty Amazon, her eyelids closed, wondering if I'd ever see them open again… Vlad, that coward, did this to her. But at least justice had been served. He deserved his fate. Hatred streamed through my veins.

And a tinge of guilt. I cursed myself for being so cold-hearted; truth was, I wouldn't wish his gruesome death on anyone, and replaying the awful scene sent shockwaves across my body.

Sage's blood saturated the bandage. The bleeding had to be stopped, but there weren't enough supplies, not even a blanket for her shivering body.

She was slipping away. How could we keep her alive? I uttered a silent prayer, begging heaven for mercy. It came out disjointed and emotional and fueled by a mixture of groans and sobs. But God must have heard it, because in an instant I knew what to do.

The Hipupiara's egg offered the only hope. Somehow, someway, I needed one, though the clutch of eggs was guarded by the planet's most fearsome creature.

Carlos would never let me attempt it, not in a million years. And for good reason. Approaching the nest was a death wish, one that had already killed three men before our eyes. Only a fool would try again.

But I made up my mind. If I died for Sage, at least I wouldn't have to watch her suffer. But how could I convince Carlos?

He stood above her, his hands shaking. "You grab her legs and I'll hold her back. We need to leave…now."

We lifted her body and lumbered through the jungle, toward the boat, a roundabout journey of fifty yards. Her listless, bloodied body made my heart drop. For a while, we bowed our heads in silence.

"Be gentle," he said. "There's a risk of causing internal damage."

I looked him in the eyes as we carried her. "One of those eggs is her only hope."

A shadow fell over his face. "Get that idea out of your mind, Pace. Greed for the eggs causes people to die."

"But it's not greed. It's necessity."

"My necessity is getting both of you to Leticia. Alive."

"But look at her." My chin quivered. "She won't make it back alive."

"You don't know that."

"I do know that. And so do you. She's going to die on the boat."

"We must keep the faith, son."

"But doesn't faith require action? I'm going to the nest. I have to at least try."

Carlos flinched. "Stop. Right here. Lay her down for a minute."

We gently lowered her and shook our tired arms. Then he

stepped toward me and grabbed my shoulders. "I can't lose both of you in one day. It's not happening. Going back into the nest is crazy talk. What makes you think your fate will be any different? And we're wasting our time and energy considering it. Do you understand me, Pace?"

I nodded without answering; like me, he felt responsibility for Sage's injury. Carlos gripped my shoulders, not in anger but for emphasis. "You need to tell me you understand. This is serious. The creature will kill you. And if you die, it does none of us any good. Do you understand?"

"Yes." I lowered my head. Maybe I understood, but it didn't mean I agreed. Why walk away from Sage's sole chance of survival?

"Let's move." He wiped his fingers beneath his eyes.

We lifted Sage and again trudged toward the boat, shuffling along the rough terrain, twisting around and under thickets and hedges, broken stumps and jagged limbs. We stumbled ahead and labored to carry her, the jungle's sharp fingers scratching against my exposed skin.

The fading afternoon sun tipped the giant tree canopies with gold but cast long shadows along the jungle floor. Except for leaves rustling, the rainforest stood eerily quiet. Or maybe I had closed everything else out. Focused on Sage, my mind hovered in a place between asleep and awake, fighting the fog in my head.

Finally arriving at the boat, Carlos opened a first-aid kit and applied clean bandages to her.

He pointed toward the back of the vessel. “Grab a blanket from inside the cabinet.”

I opened the lid and rummaged through the items, finding a soft fleece. Behind me, Carlos yelled.

“Sage!” He hunched over her, fear on his face. “Breathe, dear, breathe!”

She had taken a turn for the worst, her life hanging by a thread. He lifted her chin and blew air into her mouth several times, until her chest rose again. I had never witnessed real CPR before, and it looked horrifying.

I turned my head. *This might be the end.*

I couldn’t bear it any longer, watching her life drain away. It was time. With Carlos attending to Sage, he couldn’t stop me. Maybe one day he’d forgive me for disrespecting his wishes. It didn’t matter; Sage’s life was more important. If only there was another way.

A burst of courage unleashed inside of me. “If I’m not back in ten minutes, leave without me.”

Without waiting for his response, I jumped off the boat and sprinted toward the nest, water splashing in my wake.

Carlos yelled behind me with desperation in his voice.

I ignored him.

45

Fifteen feet from the nest, I clasped Sage's necklace around my neck. It offered my only comfort, like carrying a piece of her with me.

In normal circumstances, my legs would have frozen in place, too terrified of moving any closer. But her desperate condition pushed me forward. The goal: securing an egg and preparing the drink.

I felt more foolish than courageous, like someone stumbling blindfolded on a mine field. Why would my feeble attempt turn out any different than Vlad and his men?

I wondered how my family would react to my death. Would they look at my short life as a disappointment? Remember me as a slacker? Or maybe my passing would bring my parents back together, bonding in their grief. It's odd what you think of when facing the end.

The Amazon trip had changed me. I saw life with a new perspective and never again wanted to piddle away opportunities.

Helping others had ignited something inside of me, a deeper purpose. But my family would never know about the new Pace. A few weeks earlier, I wouldn't have imagined putting my life on the line for someone else. Yet facing the nest, I couldn't imagine *not* doing it.

My final regret was Carlos. He had every right to be angry with me for ignoring his warnings and probably regretted ever helping us. He got caught in the middle. And tragically, if both Sage and I died, people would unfairly hold him responsible.

So… don't die Pace.

I stepped toward the nest. If the Hipupiara attacked, at least it would be over quickly. Only a few seconds of pain. But there had to be a way of survival. The shaman *and* his father *and* grandfather survived the nest, for years. But how?

The shaman's story replayed in my head. As I recalled, the shaman's grandfather traveled alone on his first trip, but the second time he brought two men with him. The Hipupiara killed those two men, and their blood splattered on the grandfather. Such a gory detail. Why did he share it?

Wait…

It became clearer. The shaman had spoken of a *reverent process* and said the words, 'Blood repels death.' On the first trip, the shaman's grandfather fell and gashed his arm beside the nest. On the second, the men's blood sprayed his body.

That was the connection. *Both times he approached the nest covered in blood.*

Why hadn't I seen it before? Blood offered the only protection from the mysterious creature. And Sage's spilled blood was still fresh on me.

My heart raced. I smeared her blood across my face and chest, not taking any chances, though the absurdity hit me of approaching a feared carnivore with blood covering my body. Either it was genius or the dumbest move of all time.

With each step closer, the river swirled. At first a few ripples, then a strong agitation.

Another step, two.

The Hipupiara's eyes broke the surface, and though my breath hitched, I didn't back away.

Another step, and another.

Following my actions, the creature's head rose from the water, then its back, followed by a long, curled tail. The closer my approach, the more its entire massive body emerged, until, completely exposed, it moved onto the shore.

My mouth dropped and black despair flooded my brain.

The Hipupiara's thickened, age-old hide lumbered toward the nest, legs wide as mammoth tree trunks, though it slid more than crawled. Giving a sweep of its coiled tail, the water from the steel-spined body poured on the ground like heavy rainfall.

A living, breathing nightmare.

We both moved toward the nest, set on a slow-motion collision course. I walked; the Hipupiara slithered.

Everything in me wanted to stop, but my heart overpowered the fears. My mind was set. Fully committed, prepared to meet death. No time to waste.

In moments, only a short distance separated us, with my feet inside the nest and the creature's gargantuan head and neck stretched toward me, inches away.

How many others had ever stood this close to the Hipupiara and stared into its face?

And what a face. Cunning and intelligent, even probing, yet strong as weathered rock. A rough-hewn mountain with skin of melded stone, as if forged by fire. A face of death.

The monster jaw resembled a steel post, and the hot air from its enlarged nostrils blew back my hair. Saliva frothed from a mouth which sprayed poisonous breath. Teeth rose like swords and claws like spears.

The Hipupiara's eyes remained fixed on me, like it pondered what to do, sniffing the air, studying.

I stood deathly still, though my chest heaved uncontrollably.

And then without warning, the creature snapped its tail with thunderbolt force and bent over me with opened claw and death in those reptile pupils, hot breath misting on my skin.

A low rumble started from inside its belly and rolled up its throat in a menacing growl, before erupting into a tree-shaking roar so loud my ears rang and heart skipped.

Covering my ears and squinting my eyes, I braced for the inevitable.

But to my shock, the Hipupiara slid away and hurtled backward toward the river, lowering its body in the water until only its eyes could be seen.

Unbelievable.

The blood. It somehow gave access. Safe passage. I came to save Sage, but her blood had saved me.

In any other situation, I would have celebrated survival. But my thoughts focused primarily on Sage and Yeisson. Were they still alive? Were their injuries beyond help?

I moved calmly toward the bags of eggs, the ones Vlad's men had packed. How many should I take? Each bag contained several, and my plan was to leave some in the nest. It didn't seem right taking them all.

Opening one of the bags, I carefully rolled its five eggs back into the nest. Taking another from the second bag, I placed it beside the others, leaving three in my bag. More than enough. Sage and Yeisson could easily share one egg, and that left a couple of backups.

I stepped from the nest, walking backwards, afraid of turning too soon.

The Hipupiara continued watching.

As I moved a further distance away, its head gradually submerged into the black depths, disappearing without a trace, a scary memory I wasn't quite sure was real or a dream.

Running toward the boat, I could see Carlos hunched over and attending to Sage.

"I've got the eggs!" I yelled. "Is she alive?"

I dreaded the answer.

"Pace! You're okay!" Carlos stood, his face frozen. "She's still fighting."

I breathed in relief. We had hope. Splashing through the water, I held the bag over my head. "Let's get out of here!"

"How did you get the eggs? And why is blood all over your face?"

"I'll explain it later." I climbed inside. "How is she?"

"In and out of consciousness. But I've controlled the bleeding."

Sage lay on a cushioned bench, wrapped in a blanket and secured with a seatbelt. I knelt and held her hand, then kissed her cold forehead.

"I'll make the drink while you drive," I said.

"I heard the Hipupiara roar." Carlos's eyes teared. "Pace, I thought you had died. It was terrible."

My heart wrenched; my actions put him through hell.

"Believe me, I should have died. I'm sorry for leaving you like that."

Carlos looked relieved, but emotionally drained. He slid behind the steering wheel. "Now get that drink made. Pots are in the bottom cabinet."

Searching the supplies, I found a stirring spoon and a large pot. The propane stove on board was a stroke of good fortune, and I switched it on.

"Hold on tight." Carlos turned and spoke over his shoulder. "I'm flooring it all the way. Might get bumpy."

The engine's grumble offered a welcome sound, and as he hit the gas, the powerful surge flung me backwards. I glanced a final time at Guyerma's Well and shuddered. No sight of the Hipupiara, but Vlad's empty boat bobbed in our wake.

I focused attention back on the supplies. *Don't screw this up, Pace.* Making the drink correctly was the ultimate priority or all my actions proved worthless.

Where to begin? Water. Lots of it was needed for boiling. Thankfully, we packed a cooler filled with ice and water, and I emptied several bottles into the waiting pot.

Carlos gunned the boat and pushed it hard and fast across the Amazon. Supplies slid and the water pot sloshed. The bumpy ride made preparing the drink extremely difficult, and I held the pot's handle with one hand to keep it from sliding off.

Ten parts water to one part yolk; that's how the shaman explained the drink ratio. Time to add the egg.

It was tricky grasping an egg from the bag with one hand while holding the pot with the other. But I managed to cradle it in the nook of my arm; a thick, pink-speckled egg the size of an infant.

The boat jerked and pitched. We went airborne for a moment and crashed down again on the surface, lunging forward. With only one hand, I couldn't grip the egg securely and watched in horror as it slipped from my grasp.

It fell to the floor with a sickening crack, and chunky yolk slopped around my feet.

I cursed at myself, furious for being so careless. A wasted Hipupiara egg. How many lives could it have helped? Another accident would be a catastrophe.

Nervously, my hand reached again into the bag, pulling out a second egg, drawing it close to my chest. No more drops.

Holding it above the pot of water and cracking it carefully on the rim, I emptied the yolk into the container. I stirred it and waited for the liquid to boil. But after guesstimating amounts, the potion needed more water, so I carried the pot to the cooler and poured several more water bottles into it. Ten parts to one, or at least my best attempt.

"What happened?" Carlos's voice boomed from behind. He stared at the broken egg on the floor, then at me.

"Dropped one," I yelled over the engine. "But I made another. Pray that it works."

My hands shook as I waited for the liquid to boil. The stress of the last several hours had taken a toll, and I was exhausted. But no time for rest. Sage and Yeisson needed me.

After a few minutes, the liquid bubbled and popped, smelling faintly of butterscotch. Removing it from the heat, I stirred until the consistency resembled an orange smoothie, then poured it into a cup and placed it inside the ice cooler. Almost ready to drink.

But if unconscious, how could Sage swallow? Carlos must have been thinking the same thing.

"Before you give it to her, make sure she's awake," he said. "Otherwise, she'll choke on it. And give her very little."

Good advice. I'd have to do the same with Yeisson at the hospital.

Several minutes later, I tested the drink's temperature with my finger. Cool enough to sip. Staring at the frothy mixture, I hoped it was made correctly. Sage needed the drink's peculiar magic.

I knelt and nudged her. No response. My lips moved in

prayer, silently mouthing the faith "finger prayer" she taught me.

Nothing. Desperation.

I whispered in her ear. "Wake up, Sage." A pause. "I love you."

A tiny movement in her face. And to my surprise, her eyes slowly blinked open. She gazed at me.

Thank God.

"I've got a drink for you. Can you try and swallow it?"

She nodded weakly. Lifting the cup to her lips, I poured in a small amount. She swallowed. Then a couple more larger sips. She closed her eyes, unresponsive, lost again in darkness.

It was a miracle she woke at all.

I raised my gaze toward the sky and noticed the golden sun fading toward the horizon. Next stop, the Leticia hospital.

There was nothing more I could do.

46

Miraculously, Sage survived the boat ride. Maybe it was only my imagination, but she didn't feel quite as cold.

We arrived at the Leticia hospital and admitted her to the critical care unit. They rolled her gurney away, and she slipped from sight as the double doors closed behind, the second time a bloodied and dying friend had passed through that entryway.

God, the doctors better know what they're doing.

Yeisson. How did his surgery go? He needed the drink, too.

I carried a sports bottle of the Hipupiara drink in my freshly scrubbed hands. We had cleaned ourselves up and washed away the blood residue in the hospital restroom. I wore one of Carlos's shirts, and though it swallowed me, at least it made me presentable in public.

Carlos talked to the hospital receptionist regarding details about Yeisson. I couldn't understand their Spanish, but something seemed wrong.

He ran his fingers through his thick hair and turned to me.

"She can't find Yeisson's room information. Maybe he's still in surgery."

What was the problem? How long did it take to find patient info, especially in a small hospital?

"It's been six hours since we brought him," I said to Carlos.

"Don't worry, she'll find him. They probably haven't updated the system yet."

I stared out a window. "I wonder how the missions team is doing? They'll be shocked to learn all that's happened. Lola's gonna freak out."

"In a minute I'll call Jose and tell him everything," Carlos said. "Sage's family needs to be contacted immediately."

My heart broke for her loved ones, receiving such terrible news so far away. Guilt rolled over me. Her injury shouldn't have happened. I put her in danger.

As the receptionist talked on the phone, Carlos must have read my mind. He led me a few paces from the desk, his face shining kind and warm.

"Son, it's not your fault. Don't carry that burden on your shoulders."

"I couldn't prevent Yeisson's injury, but if Sage dies…" The words stuck in my throat. "It was my decision to search for those eggs."

"Pace, we *all* made the decision to get into the boat."

Swallowing hard, I placed my hands in my pockets, body stiffening. "I'm sorry for putting you through this. And I know I worried you when I ran to the nest by myself."

"I thought I'd lost you." Carlos placed a hand on my shoulder. "You aged me twenty years on the spot. But in the end, somehow it worked out."

He paused. "By the way, how *did* you get those eggs?"

"Blood. It somehow protects from the creature. I rubbed it all over me once I realized that's how the shaman survived."

Wonder filled Carlos's face. "Blood is the last thing I'd ever imagine."

He glanced at the receptionist, still on the phone, then back at me. "Pace, we saw things today we'll never forget. Terrible things. And amazing things. But I learned something. You're a courageous young man. You were willing to sacrifice your life."

I shrugged. "Anyone else would have done the same."

"That's where I disagree. You're something special."

Not counting my parents, when was the last time someone called me 'special'? I'd been called a screw-up and a host of other similar words numerous times. But never special.

In the distance, Dr. Walt walked inside the hospital entry doors. Maybe he'd have more answers than the receptionist. He waved, then motioned us to the waiting room chairs. The look on his face unsettled me.

After we told him about Sage, he sat on the seat edge in shock, his posture tense. “I'm afraid I've got more bad news.”

He spoke softly. “They operated on Yeisson for most of the afternoon. The venom spread and caused his organs to shut down. They tried everything.”

He took a deep breath. “I'm sorry to tell you this. But he didn't make it.”

Dr. Walt's words stole my breath away.

Maybe I misheard him, it couldn't be possible, and for a few moments my brain stopped processing information. *No…*

Yeisson was too young, too full of life. And talk about cruel timing. I held the Hipupiara drink in my hands, ready for him to drink.

A hole ripped open in my chest. I sat in stunned silence and stared at the floor, the only noise being the receptionist's nails typing on the computer keyboard.

Carlos wrapped his arm around me, reminding me it was okay to grieve, and it felt like someone threw open the basement door of my heart and water gushed out.

I sobbed.

It was the deepest cry of my life, one drained of hope, an internal rawness like tiny razor blades slicing muscle and sinew. The strength left my legs, and sinking to my knees in a heap, the grief crashed upon me as an avalanche, burying my body on the cold, tiled floor.

ONE DAY LATER

It was dark outside in the early morning hours, and I sat beside Sage's bed and held her limp hand.

She hadn't awakened since the surgery the night before, and though the nurses said the procedure went well, I couldn't relax until she awoke. A large gauze bandaged her shoulder and a thin tube ran into her arm. Medical equipment blipped and blerped around her.

I studied her face. No makeup, her hair frizzy and unkempt, her lips dry. But still the most beautiful girl in the world. And until those gorgeous eyes opened again, I wasn't going anywhere.

The day before had been the darkest of my life: working through Yeisson's funeral details while Sage's life hung in the balance. I hadn't left her side, except for a short shower.

Carlos encouraged me to catch some sleep at the hotel, but I resisted. Instead, I stole a few small naps beside Sage, waking each time the nurses banged into the room to run tests. Looking into the bathroom mirror, I noticed dark circles had formed under my eyes.

And then at six thirty in the morning, Sage squeezed my hand. I must have been asleep, because outside the hospital window the sun had risen.

I sat up in the chair, my back tight, and leaned closer.

Then Sage's eyes slowly blinked open.

I could barely breathe from the excitement. *Thank you, good God up in heaven.*

Those brown eyes of hers held special power over me, like a spring rain melting away winter. They glistened the color of wet soil, the color of life, deep as a bottomless well. And with one glance, her light shined into my deep despair.

"My sweet Sage," I whispered.

She smiled faintly.

As the day progressed, Sage grew stronger. She didn't talk much due to grogginess, but her improvement lifted a dark cloud off my shoulders. In time, the nurses inclined her bed into a sitting position, and she drifted into another peaceful sleep.

As she slept, Carlos visited with both food and good news. Our team would arrive back in Leticia soon and Sage's mom would land later in the evening. We talked for a while before he left, and then another couple hours passed.

Sage woke for lunch and was more coherent.

"So, what happened to me?" Her voice sounded raspy but her

eyes were soft. “I'm fuzzy on the details.”

I grabbed her hands and leaned close. “You were shot. By Vlad, before he died.”

She stared away for a moment, like trying to remember. Then she focused on me again. “The nest.”

“So you remember?”

She nodded. “Bits and pieces. But how did I survive?”

I lifted the sports bottle off the floor containing a thick, yellowish drink. The Hipupiara drink.

Her eyebrows raised. “The eggs. But how?”

I patted her hands. “It doesn't matter right now. But the drink saved your life. And some quick first aid by Carlos.”

Adjusting in the bed, she winced. “How is Yeisson?”

I dreaded the question, because I didn't know how to tell her. Would the bad news cause a setback in her recovery? Turns out, it didn't matter, because thinking about him filled my eyes with tears and I shook my head, speechless.

Sage didn't need my words. Tears trickled down her cheeks.

A knock on the door. A thirty-something woman with short black hair stepped inside, wearing a doctor's lab coat. She looked like a local from Leticia, but she spoke great English.

“I'm Dr. Barbosa.” Stepping toward the bed, she examined Sage's shoulder dressing. “I performed your surgery last night. How's my fighter doing?”

Sage smiled. "I'm sore and tired. But other than that, I'm ready to go home."

Dr. Barbosa laughed. "Not so fast. Your body's been through a lot. But I have to say, you've amazed everyone in the hospital. There's no reason you should have survived. Not with the extent of your injury and the distance you traveled. You're a living miracle."

"I guess you can say she dodged a bullet," I said.

It was a bad attempt at a joke.

The doctor turned to me. "You've got a point. Are you a family member? A friend?"

Before I answered, Sage interrupted. "Boyfriend."

Boyfriend? My jaw hit the floor. Some fireworks exploded somewhere in my chest.

The doctor tapped Sage's forearm. "You've got good taste, dear."

I showed Dr. Barbosa the sports bottle. It was time to unveil the drink to the wider world, the magic potion for which I risked my life.

"Doc, this is the main reason she survived. It's a mixture from a village we visited. I've seen this drink heal the entire village, and I gave some to Sage before we got here. It saved her life."

I didn't mention it came from the Hipupiara nest. She'd think I was crazy. Lifting it close for inspection, she stared at the contents and sloshed it around with no idea of the power and potential in her hands.

"Hmm... interesting. I'll have the lab run tests and see what we can find."

"I'm curious myself," I said.

She checked Sage's vitals and studied the equipment readings before turning to leave the room. "By the way, Sage, you've got a lot of people out in the lobby. You're quite popular."

The team had arrived. Sweet music to my ears.

"We traveled with a medical missions group," I said. "They just came back from a village upriver."

"That's wonderful." Dr. Barbosa pushed open the door. "But I'd advise few visitors right now. Though Sage has enjoyed a remarkable recovery, she needs her rest."

And with a wave she left, carrying the drink.

I glared at Sage mischievously. "You called me your *boyfriend*."

A flirtatious grin spread across her face. "That's what you are, right? A boy, who is a friend. A boyfriend."

"Right." I nodded and winked.

She pointed toward the hallway. "Go out there and say hello to everyone. I know you're dying to see them. I'm gonna rest a bit more."

I headed toward the door. "By the way, your mom's landing tonight."

Sage's face lit up. "Everything's always better when momma's around. I know she's worried sick."

"She'll be happy to hear you're doing well. And we'll make her feel right at home. Sweet dreams, Sage."

Closing her door, I walked down the hallway into an overflowing waiting room filled with team members. When they saw me, a huge cheer erupted, and they gathered around for hugs.

Slowly, things were returning to normal, and for once normal felt good.

A new normal.

47

Colorful mylar balloons bobbed on the ceiling, featuring a shiny assortment of hearts and smiley faces.

The missions team crammed into the room and swallowed me with handshakes, hugs, and kisses on the cheek. It was a wonderful reunion, and I could feel bits of my heart patching back together again.

And then the crowd split, and Lola faced me.

"Bring it in, dear." She flung her arms wide. "You had this old lady all worried. My pacing wore holes in the floor of that boat."

I laughed. "At least it was good exercise."

She took a step back and held my hands. "You certainly have a gift for finding trouble, don't you?"

I shrugged. "Maybe it's trouble finding *me*."

"Carlos told me how your bravery saved Sage's life."

I bowed my head. "Too bad it didn't save Yeisson's."

"It was his time, Pace." Lola blinked her eyes as they filled with tears. "But I'm sure gonna miss him. Known that boy since he was a baby."

"If only I could've gotten back sooner."

She grabbed my shoulders. "Stop it! You're not Superman. That kind of thinking will drive you crazy." She punched my arm lightly. "Now when can I visit our girl?"

"She's resting right now. The doctor is limiting visitors."

It was wasted breath. I knew Lola's response before she said it.

"I'm not just any visitor." She placed her hands on her hips. "And I don't care what any doctor says. I'm going back there and seeing Sage, whether they like it or not."

Gotta love her. Everyone needs a Lola in their life.

I waved in surrender. "I'm sure they'll give a special Lola exception."

Her face relaxed. "The poor girl doesn't have her mother here yet. So her Amazon momma is gonna step in."

"I'll walk you back in a few minutes."

"I'm proud of you." She paused, her gaze serious. "You got off to a rough start, but you've proven what a true team member should be."

Before I could respond, Jose interrupted and wrapped his arms around me. "I'm glad you're okay, Pace. You did so much for Yeisson, and I'll never forget it."

"Your impact was greater than anyone's," I said to him as my tears flowed freely. "You were a father to him."

"But you were a big brother," he said. "And Carlos told me about the Hipupiara encounter. I've never believed the stories before. But I do now. You all made me a believer."

"It was unlike anything I've ever seen." I shook my head. "Terrifying."

And from behind, another voice. "Good to see you, man."

James. He gave a bro handshake, then brought it in for a shoulder hug. "Sorry for all you've been through."

"How are you?" I asked, happy to see him.

He didn't waste any time getting to the point. "I kissed Sarah last night. But don't tell Lola."

"These lips are sealed." The thought of James and Red Goth kissing. No surprise there.

"Yeah, she's an amazing girl. She talks about things I've never thought of before." He glanced at her, then back at me. "Anything happening with you and Sage?"

I spoke in a sarcastic tone. "Well, in between us getting Yeisson to the hospital, being attacked by pirates, and then her getting shot and almost dying, I haven't had a chance to make my move yet."

"Yeah, that's crazy. I'm thankful she's doing better."

Across the room, Banks and C-Lo sat close together, their legs touching. I nodded in their direction. "Hey, what about them?

Are they together?"

"Oh, man. They're the trip's worst kept secret. Been snoggin' for days."

"Snoggin'? As in…"

"As in kissing, making out. Get your mind out of the gutter, dude."

C-Lo spoke from the other side. Hopefully she didn't know we were talking about her. "Pace, tell us about the Sea Creature, " she said.

All eyes turned toward me. I was at a loss for words. How could I give a PG version of the terrors we witnessed, watching those men die and Sage being shot, along with the sights and sounds of the Hipupiara?

But I tried — disastrously.

My voice shook as I told the story, and at the part where Vlad's men died, my words stammered as the gruesome mental images played vividly.

Stopping, I rubbed my forehead and struggled to catch my breath. It was too soon.

"Give me a while," I mumbled, embarrassed about having a public meltdown.

Carlos lifted his voice and addressed the team. "We experienced some unspeakable things. And we saw the creature, up-close and personal."

I exhaled, thankful he stepped in.

“Believe me,” he said, “it’s very real and big and dangerous. Pace needs more time before talking about it. Me, too. The right words are hard to find.”

“That reminds me,” Lola addressed the team, “we need our final Word of the Day. Everyone gather ‘round.”

Thank God she changed the subject. The team scooted their chairs until everyone sat in a clump, with Carlos joining us.

Banks raised his hand. “How about letting us suggest some words?”

Lola clapped her hands. “Oh, that’s a great idea. I’m glad you embrace team-building. What word do you have?”

He smiled. “I’m thinking *Underarm Dingle Dangle*.”

Laughter broke the room’s tension.

“Excuse me?” Lola crinkled her eyebrows. “What is that?”

“It’s the flappy skin under the bicep.” He wiggled his arm for a demonstration. “See?”

Lola cocked her head. “Okay, I get it. Ya’ll want to make fun of my Words of the Day.”

“No,” C-Lo said, “we’re continuing its cherished history. Imitation is the best form of flattery, right?”

“If you say so, dear.” Lola crossed her arms. “Do you have a Word of the Day, too?”

C-Lo pursed her lips. “I’m thinking *Dingleberries*.”

We snickered and lowered our heads.

"Dingleberries?" Lola repeated. "I'm afraid to ask what they are."

C-Lo leaned back in her chair. "Yeah, google that one. But don't search for the images."

Then James spoke. "I love the word, *Bobiggity*. It's a term of affection."

"Bobiggity." Lola looked confused. "Is that like gettin' wiggy with it?"

"You mean jiggy with it?" he asked.

Another outburst of giggles. C-Lo half-laughed and half-hiccuped.

"Bobiggity is best used in a greeting," James said. "Like saying, '*What's up, Bobiggity!*'"

By the look on Lola's face, she realized things had gotten out of control, but she seemed to enjoy it.

"My favorite word is *Slapperdoodle*," Red Goth said quietly. "It means a pleasant discovery. For instance, 'I found a $20 bill in a pocket. God gave me a *slapperdoodle*.'"

"Oh, I understand." Lola tried her best. "Like saying, 'My dingleberry is a real slapperdoodle.'"

"No!" We yelled, rolling out of our chairs.

I laughed until my ribs hurt. The humor served as great medicine and a relief from the recent stress.

Glancing at Banks and C-Lo, I decided to mess with them. "I've got one. How about the term, *Snog Juice*'?"

"Snog juice?" Lola asked.

"It's the excess drool during kissing sessions," I said.

Everyone chuckled while Banks laughed nervously and C-Lo flashed a wry grin.

"My favorite word is *Hooptie*," Big Country said while adjusting his hat. "It's how we describe old farm trucks, the rusted kind with windows that won't lower and where the blinker works only when manually moved up and down. Daddy drives a hooptie '82 pickup. And the ceiling cloth sags like a pair of old butt cheeks."

"Does it have any dingleberries?" C-Lo asked.

"Alright, children." Lola waved her hands and signaled our time was over. "While your words are... educational, they fail to meet my lofty standards. No offense." She cleared her throat. "So, the official Word of the Day is one of my favorites: *Nascent*."

"Nascent?" Banks repeated. "Sounds like a sinus infection."

"No," Lola said, "it means displaying signs of future potential. You all are amazing and have *nascent* powers to impact the world for generations to come."

We pondered it silently, then Big Country shouted, "You Da Mom!"

And then all of us yelled together, "You Da Mom!"

Lola blushed. "Thank you, all of my little bobiggities. That means more than you know."

Carlos stood and pointed to her. "To the best missions leader I've ever met."

We all stood with him and clapped.

"Sucking up won't do you any good now. The trip's over." She smiled and motioned us to sit. "Now, some directions for our last night here: keep your stuff nicely packed because you're leaving bright and early at seven a.m. Breakfast at six thirty. We're catching a plane back to Miami, then onward to good ol' North Carolina."

The trip, over. It went by so fast, and the Amazon taught me more than I ever dreamed. But I wasn't ready to go. Not with Sage on the mend and Yeisson's upcoming funeral.

"So you know," Carlos told the team, "I've arranged for Pace and Lola to remain a few extra days. It's important for them to stay here, with all the details surrounding Yeisson and Sage."

Everyone nodded. It was news to me — welcome news.

I smiled at Carlos, and he winked. Of all the people there, only he understood my need for a couple more days of healing.

"Time to hit the sack, everybody." Lola stood. "You've got a big day tomorrow. Carlos will lead you back to the hotel while I visit with Sage."

Time for goodbyes. It was a bittersweet moment, like a graduation after-party, scanning the faces of a hodgepodge group that had become friends. Our bond was deep, and it felt like it would last a long time. We gave tender farewells with a flurry of hugs and teary eyes.

James approached me before leaving. “Guess what? My luggage finally arrived at the hotel. Can you believe it? Delivered on the last night.”

“I’m gonna miss your t-shirts.”

“I thought so.” He handed me a folded shirt. “That’s why you’re getting a parting gift. An unworn t-shirt. I expect you to wear it regularly back home.”

Unfolding it, I read the words printed on the front:

I ACCIDENTALLY DID IT ON PURPOSE

Somehow, it summarized the trip perfectly.

48

3 DAYS LATER

It was late morning, sunny with a cloudless sky, as we huddled under the shade of a graveyard tree.

The air wafted with fragrant flowers and freshly turned soil. It was a quiet and intimate affair and only a small group gathered: Jose, Lola, Carlos and Lorena, me and Sage — her first trip out of the hospital.

In front of us rested Yeisson's open casket, hoisted by silver poles and hovering over a deep hole. Carlos and Lorena had generously paid for all the expenses, burying Yeisson in an extra space in their own cemetery lot.

Because my suitcase only had t-shirts and shorts, I had to go into town the day before and buy khakis and a button-down. Unfortunately, my teal shirt stood out horribly since everyone else dressed in black. Oh, well. It was only the second funeral I'd ever attended, other than my grandmother's.

Sage rocked a black lace dress, one her mom bought for her, and it hugged her hourglass figure. Though her shoulder was lightly bandaged, her countenance radiated. And for the first time, I noticed her arm cast removed. Strike up another victory for the Hipupiara drink.

I walked toward the casket, one made of poplar wood with a mahogany finish – better constructed than Yeisson's village hut – and I peered over the edge.

Buried in his favorite yellow soccer shirt, Yeisson had a soccer ball nestled beside him. I stared at his unmoving face, thinking those eyes would bust open and he'd flash that mischievous smile. But inside the silk velvet interior, his thin body laid still for eternity. Death. It wasn't fair someone could be taken so young. Burying old people was one thing, but a vibrant child?

Grief ripped at my insides. I wanted to scream at heaven, *Why?* But no answer would have satisfied.

Jose shared several Yeisson stories that made us laugh and cry, and at times, Lola blew her nose so loudly we all jumped. He spoke from the book of Genesis, when God told Abraham to leave both his country and loved ones and travel to a new land. I remembered Pastor Vin at Defender Church speaking about the same guy.

Jose tied the story into heaven, how death is leaving our present situation and going to the promised land of God's presence. I'd never thought of it that way before, and the idea of an afterlife gave me great peace. At least Yeisson was safe there.

I pulled his knife from my pocket, the one Jose found dropped by the Kapok tree. Holding it stirred a wave of nostalgia, and my chest tightened. How many sticks had Yeisson whittled with it, and how many snakes had he hunted and skinned? The small knife was his most treasured possession.

Leaning over the casket edge, I placed it in his hands and then backed away, my lips trembling. He got his wish; his knife would be buried. A forever reminder of our friendship.

A few moments later, the cemetery worker closed the casket lid with a heavy thud, and I gazed at the pile of dirt that would soon cover Yeisson. If only I could've told him goodbye before his accident. His sudden death left me feeling incomplete, unable to feel closure.

Jose choked up as he uttered the final prayer, and when he lost it, so did I. Tears flowed down my cheeks, and Sage grabbed my hand and intertwined our fingers. As we both sobbed, Lola honked away beside us.

After the last amen, everyone slowly left except for me and Sage. And suddenly, a realization: the moment I stepped away from the casket would start Act Two of my life. If anyone needed an Act Two, it was me.

But it also made me nervous. Standing by the graveside felt

like a type of burial for me, and oddly, a resurrection.

The worker released a crank handle and lowered Yeisson's casket into the ground at a slow, steady speed.

Laid to rest and surrounded by love.

Goodbye, Yeisson.

EVENING

Muted music came from a nearby stilted house, and the sun quickly sank into the horizon and spilled an orange path on the water like a carpet of gold.

Sage and I sat on a blanket in front of the Amazon River, not far from the hospital courtyard, with a picnic basket at our feet. After two weeks of eating only exotic Amazon food, we packed peanut butter and jelly sandwiches, chips, and sodas. Yep, I was all about the comfort food.

It was our last night in Leticia, and Sage seemed stronger with every passing hour. And more stunning, too. She smelled like spring and glowed like summer, wearing a v-neck tribal print top with elbow length sleeves and black leggings. She barely used any makeup, not that she needed any, and her complexion was as smooth as caramel.

We slipped off our shoes and sat barefoot with our legs touching. The picnic was the first time we'd been alone in a while, especially since her mom had arrived. For the past couple of days, I'd given them needed space. But I missed my time with Sage, and in only a few hours, we'd board a plane and head home. Our adventure would be over.

My stomach churned. What would happen to us once we returned? She made me feel alive, bringing out my best, and an undeniable chemistry existed between us. We'd always be friends, but would the relationship fade over time?

I wanted to share my feelings with her, how we could be more than just friends. But what if it backfired? Things might turn awkward and screw up our friendship. Hopefully she felt something, at least somewhere down deep.

But her signals were hard to read. Dang.

So I abided by her Friend Zone rules. Breaking them would require her initiative, not mine.

Opening the picnic basket, I passed her some food. "So how you feeling?"

She touched her shoulder. "I'm still sore, but overall I feel great. The doctors expect a full recovery."

"I know your mom's relieved."

"Yeah, but she's exhausted. That's why she's turning in early tonight after packing."

"Lola's doing the same thing." I took a bite from my sandwich. "She spent all afternoon doing laundry at the hotel."

"My mom loves that place. Carlos and Lorena have really taken care of her."

"They're like family."

She opened her soda can and took a sip, then her face turned serious. "Carlos told me everything you did at the nest. You put your life on the line for me."

I hadn't yet shared the whole story with Sage. "I'd do it all over again."

"Thank you," she said softly, placing her hand over mine.

"I'm thankful for those eggs," I said. "There was one left over, and I gave it to Jose. He's delivering it to the shaman."

"That's a tremendous gift for the village."

"It's safe in the shaman's hands because he knows what he's doing. And he uses them unselfishly."

Sage smoothed our blanket. "So what about the Hipupiara? What happens to it?"

"She'll continue living and thriving in the river, as long as we don't draw attention to her nest location. Otherwise, she'll be hunted and killed. People destroy what they can't explain."

"I bet one day you'll go back to the nest. You're too fascinated with it."

I tossed a piece of sandwich crust into the river. "We'll see what happens. I do feel a responsibility to protect her and the nest. It's an amazing discovery. When we get back home, I'm talking to one of my old professors about it. I trust him, and maybe he'll know what to do next."

"So you *do* see yourself coming back here?" She rubbed her leg against mine, but I couldn't tell if it was on purpose.

"I'd consider moving here. Helping villages, loving kids, studying animals."

She smiled. "And shampooing lice?"

"I had a great teacher. And after facing the Hipupiara, I'll take on lice any day."

Sage sipped again from her soda. "Oh, almost forgot. I hid some dessert for you." With a playful smirk, she reached into the picnic basket and pulled out a ziploc bag.

Two doggie biscuits.

"I found them at a store," she said, "and I couldn't resist."

"You're so mean." My face turned red.

"I thought you liked them." Her eyes sparkled. "The first time we met, you ate one. Remember?"

"Not my most glorious moment."

"I disagree." Her tone changed. "Right after, you said I was pretty." She lifted her gaze. "Do you still think I'm pretty?"

I squinted, like trying to solve a puzzle. "Is that a trick

question?"

Maybe it was time for sticking a toe slightly out of the Friend Zone. Well, forget slightly. I decided to splash in with a cannonball.

"Sage, you're the most beautiful girl I've ever met."

"You're always so sweet to me." She looked away with a blushing smile and stared at the flowing Amazon current.

A few silent moments.

What was she thinking? Had I said too much? I didn't want the night to end. Truth is, another jungle awaited back home, filled with so many unknowns. What would happen with my parents? And how was Cameron holding up? What about school and my future? I had no clue. But one thing I knew for sure: all that crazy stuff could be faced with Sage by my side. Of course, telling her that would probably freak her out and scare her away.

The music played in the background from the nearby house.

An idea.

"Sounds like a love song." I stood and offered her my hand. "Can I have this dance?"

"I'd be honored."

Taking her unbandaged arm, I helped Sage to her feet and nestled my hands around her waist. She leaned her cheek on my shoulder and we danced under the Amazon stars, our bodies moving together as one. As I held her tight, a grin spread across my face. I was finally getting my slow dance.

When the song ended, Sage stepped back with an expression I hadn't seen from her before.

"What?" I asked.

She bit her lip and twisted her hair. "Can I kiss you?"

Time stopped. Did I hear her right? "Excuse me?"

She came closer, inches from my face. "You heard me. Can I kiss you?"

The look in her eyes. *Just friends* don't look at each other like that.

"What about the Friend Zone?" I asked.

"Oh, we left that for good."

My heart beat like a kick drum as she stood on her tiptoes.

Then she kissed me.

Her smooth and perfect lips spoke volumes without saying a word. It wasn't a peck, and it wasn't polite. It was passion. Her hair fell into my face, and all of our emotions and pent-up feelings erupted out in that perfect moment, spilling and overflowing, a thunderous waterfall, stars and stripes and fireworks and marching bands and church choirs all at once. I dreamed of a lifetime of more kisses like that one.

She pulled back and stared at me, her hands around the back of my head. "Thank you for saving my life."

"No," I whispered. "Thank you for saving mine."

Our lips met together again, this time deeper and fuller, more comfortable. It was beautiful, the kind that took my breath away, like the time in high school football when a blindside tackle knocked my wind out and I saw twinkling stars and a sparkly montage of bursting crystal thingees while trying to suck in my next desperate gulp of air.

Yeah, beautiful like that.

ABOUT THE AUTHOR

As a child, Brian Forrester loved to draw, and he dreamed of becoming a Disney cartoonist. As he grew older, a love of reading led to a passion for writing. Then came plays, short stories, and even church sermons. All these years later, he owns a marketing agency and helps business owners with both their art and their words. In his spare time, he writes novels. Brian lives in Williamsburg, Virginia with his wife, Jessica, and their five children: McKenzie, Luke, Jake, Kate, and Sam… and also Cali, their happy-go-lucky Golden Retriever.

You can contact Brian at baforrester@gmail.com and visit his website at www.baforrester.com

Made in United States
North Haven, CT
19 August 2022